ANNWYN'S BLOOD

ANNWYN'S BLOOD

THE PALADIN OF SHADOW CHRONICLES

BOOK ONE

by

Michael Eging

and

Steve Arnold

Taylor & Wells

Chardon, Ohio, USA

Taylor & Wells Publishing
11525 Taylor Wells Rd.
Chardon, OH, USA 44024
www.taylor-wells.com

Second Print Edition

Cover art created by Ina Wong

Printed in the United States of America

Library of Congress Number: 0988709961

ISBN 978-0-09887099-7-3

'Tis now the very witching time of night,

When churchyards yawn and hell itself breathes out

Contagion to this world: now I could drink hot blood

And do such bitter business as the day

Would quake to look on.

—William Shakespeare, Hamlet, III, 2

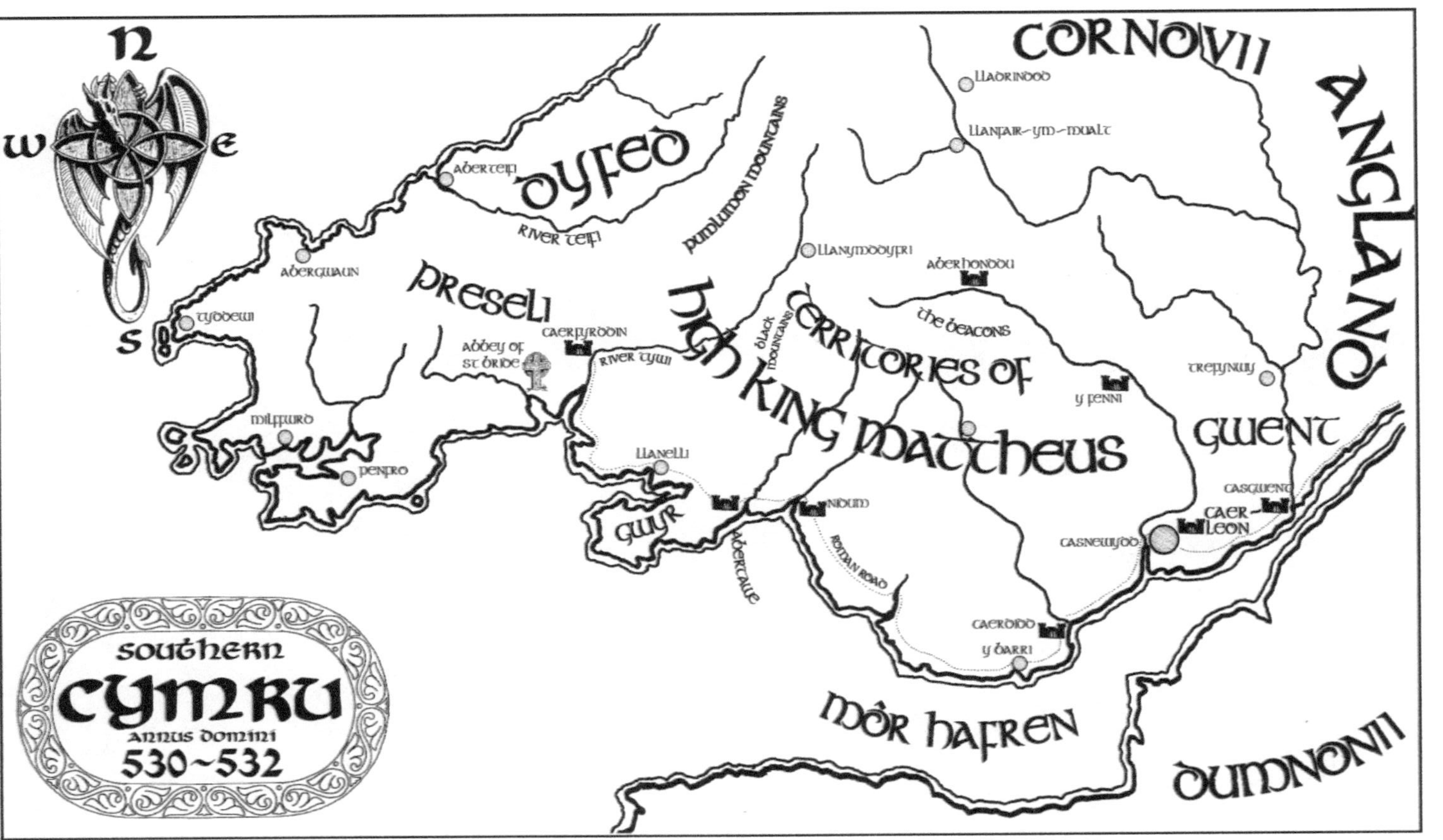

CORNOVII
ANGLAND
DUMNONII
GUENT
CAER LEON
CASGUENT
CASNEWYDD
CAERDYDD
y barri
MÔR HAFREN
ROMAN ROAD
NIDUM
ABERTAWE
LLANELLI
GWYR
CAERFYRDDIN
RIVER TYWI
abbey of st bride
PENFRO
MILFFWRD
TYDDEWI
ABERGWAUN
ABERTEIFI
RIVER TEIFI
DYFED
PRESELI
PUMLUMON MOUNTAINS
black mountains
the beacons
ABERHONDDU
LLANYMDDYFRI
y penni
TREFYNWY
LLANFAIR-YM-MUALLT
LLADRINDOD
TERRITORIES OF
HIGH KING MATTHEUS
N
E
S
W
SOUTHERN
CYMRU
ANNUS DOMINI
530~532

⨳

BLOOD'S CHALICE

THE ROMAN BASILICA at Canterbury rose from the green meadow like an ancient rimed galley, rows of window arches gaping like stony rowlocks over swells of creeping moss and lichen. All around, white robes of rushing novices fluttered past as so much sea-foam. Fearfully intent on their duties, the young would-be clerics rushed through the rutted streets past knots of senior priests engrossed in discussion of the Church's daily affairs in Albion.

Dylan, a scarecrow of a lad topped, appropriately, with tousled, straw-colored hair, sat on the rough wagon seat next to his father. He held his breath in awe of the edifice, this granite symbol of the Holy Communion between God and man. For a country boy, any structure larger than a thatched hut was an extravagance; and this was far beyond that. Yet the building was peaceful and sublime amid the chaotic human activity surging at its foundation stones.

His father, of solid peasant stock, muttered something about the lad watching what he was doing, but Dylan's attention would not be broken—not even by his own flesh and blood. His stomach fluttered as he realized he truly walked the path he had chosen for himself, the path to God and salvation.

Nearby, an old peasant pointed to a hut near the basilica's jutting transept. Dylan's father nodded.

"Git up," he said, switching their bony nag with a willow branch.

Dylan felt his chest lighten as the cathedral loomed higher a higher, a distant dream finally emerging into reality; a sanctuary from the farm labors and the humiliating egg-hawking in the Saxon cattle town of Londinium.

No, such was not the life for Dylan. Since childhood, he had craved a life in the presence of holy things, reading sacred illuminated Latin script—maybe even Greek characters—and blessing the poor unfortunates of the world through divinely revealed wisdom. A fitting life for a shepherd's son, indeed: to walk in the footsteps of David, who begot Solomon.

The wagon groaned to a halt and Dylan's father dismounted with a grunt. The boy followed, craning his neck past the tattered cloak fluttering about his father's shoulders.

Other boys milled around the hut as they approached. A cleric emerged from the doorway.

"Boys, boys, settle down," he pleaded, waving his arms. "If you're to be servants of the Lord, then please act as such." He looked up at Dylan's father and moaned. "Another one?"

"Ye can rap this one across the backside, if he gets out of hand." He shoved Dylan closer to the priest. "But if ya get tired of him, don't ye think of sendin' him back, hear? He's lazy, this one."

The cleric pulled Dylan up straight by the collar. The lad joined the tumble of other youths entering the Church, too excited to hear his father's final mumbling as he turned the rattling wagon toward home.

His fingers were cramping. Dylan looked around at the other novices scratching their inky Latin letters across freshly scraped hide. A...L...V...

Enough writing already, he thought. *I know how to write the letters. I want to read!*

He had seen a room with books, dozens of them, in all forms—a treasure beyond compare. On those shelves, he was sure, were hidden moldy and ancient scrolls and codices from long-forgotten philosophers discoursing on structures of government; ancient scholars postulating on arcane mathematics; and theologians debating the very nature of God and His kingdom. Above all else, Dylan wanted to read those books.

A palm banged loudly on the table next to his inkpot, sloshing black liquid onto the stained wood. Dylan shot bolt upright and resumed furiously inking the letters.

"How do you expect to copy texts, if no one can read your writing?" Brother Timothy asked coolly as he turned to inspect another student's handiwork.

One day, Dylan replied within the confines of his own mind, *when I'm a bishop and you're still teaching handwriting, I'll have you pen my letters for me!*

A . . . L . . . V . . . His fingers continued to ache as he scrawled along the vellum.

The austere Bishop Leo of Canterbury passed away when Dylan had been at the cathedral school for a year and a half. Villagers from the surrounding towns gathered to mourn the loss of a holy man, beloved by all the souls of his diocese, and to pay homage to the new prelate installed by the King in Exeter. Ceremonial pomp in the form of colorful banners and well-borne personages preceded Bishop John to his new diocese, bringing a festive and exotic mood to the novices.

When the new bishop, bedecked in colorful garments, arrived at the cathedral, he toasted himself from a sloshing wine skin on the front steps of the edifice. The priests knelt before his corpulent, grape-stained holiness, kissing his enameled ring and praising Heaven's Hosts for the appointment of their bishop. With a flourish of the emptied wine skin, the bishop retired to his chambers for a nap—he would need to be well rested for the feast to be held that evening in his honor.

"Who is the king to replace Leo with this man?" huffed Cedric, the young lowlander who shared Dylan's tiny quarters. He was a solidly built fellow of farming stock with a sly bit of mischief in his brown eyes.

Dylan rolled over on his cot and punched his lumpy pillow. "The king, anointed as David, has the right to appoint a successor."

"Oh, I know all about the king's authority to oversee and protect the sheep in his flock and all that rot. I've sat with you through all Brother Barnabus' classes on Constantine and ecclesiastical law. But it didn't used to be that way. Brother Barnabus told me once that only the Church could appoint their officials. I couldn't follow when he tried to explain how that had been lost.

"But still, why does the king elevate a sot to holy dignity? Here at Canterbury, of all places? Does the king's authority somehow make it right? What if—" and his voice dropped to a whisper, "—what if God doesn't agree with his choice?"

"Don't you think God would guide the King to make the right choice?"

Cedric was silent.

Dylan fidgeted, uncomfortable with both Cedric's doubts and his own less-than-reassuring response. "Maybe there's no right answer for that question. But I do know the sacraments yet hold their power, even if administered by a sin-touched hand. If not, maybe the other bishops of the realm would step in."

"And risk being deposed? Not likely."

"Well, we've only just seen him. He might not be as bad as we think. What if he is a Noah or a Jonah who just needs the hand of God to mould him into some great instrument of good? I hear tell that Londinium and Ninevah may be akin in spirit nowadays."

Cedric shook his head. "Not from what I've heard of him. I swear, sometimes you listen but don't really hear."

"Hear what?" Dylan asked.

"I'll show you." Cedric pulled a piece of yellowed vellum from beneath his covers. "Look at this and tell me what you think."

Dylan read the neatly penned script and shrugged. He felt a sense of pride that this time his lips had barely moved as his eyes absorbed the words. "So what?"

"That's all you have to say? I found that in a book I was copying about the reign of Arthur Pendragon. It's a fragment from some of Merlin's prophecies. You know—Merlin, the king's advisor."

"I know who Merlin was. But he spoke with demons," Dylan whispered, genuflecting as an added precaution.

"And angels, so some say."

Dylan read the lines again:

And then the day shall come,
the savage blight the land,
whispering of the dead,
and in his wisdom
Albion's rex shall choose
his own man to watch the graal.

"Is that all?" Dylan asked.

"That's all I could get without being found out. There's more." Cedric took the scrap, folded it, and tucked it back beneath his covers.

"About what?"

"Are you going to believe me then?" Cedric asked.

"Depends." Dylan pointed to the verse. "You haven't told me what this means yet."

"I can't remember it all, but there's more."

A bell chime clattered through the open window. Not knowing what else to say, Dylan bolted for the door with Cedric right on his heels. The new bishop's feast had begun and neither novice wanted to miss the festivities.

They spoke nothing about the prophecy to anyone else, nor did they let escape a word that evening when they spirited the entire book from the library copy room to hide within their shabby bedding.

⤫⤫⤫

The book was attributed to a monk named Jonathan, who had lived on the isle of Tusker Rock—a barren chunk of stone jutting from the sea off Albion's southern coast. The chronicle of Arthur was sewn into the binding of St. Eusebius, just after that holy saint's account of Constantine's vision of Christ and the blessed victory at Milvian Bridge over the heathen Roman forces. Jonathan claimed to have known Merlin Emrys and to have written the prophecy of the graal from the mystic's own lips.

Dylan found himself drawn into a fragmented vision of the past as he poured over the words of a man often painted as a foul sorcerer and devilish trickster. According to the account, the graal was carried to Southern Gaul after the crucifixion of the Lord by Joseph of Arimathea, an intimate of Christ. Years later, Percival, a particularly holy knight, transported the cup to Britain by order of Arthur himself. The intrepid warrior fought his way through barbarians, winged monsters, and seductive women, proving himself worthy of the quest. In time, he brought the graal to Arthur's court, where it was secured in the keeping of the archbishop, the most holy cleric in Albion.

Eventually, Cedric's passage drifted into faded texts of ambiguous imagery and mystical superstition, much of which puzzled Dylan. To keep from losing the story, he filled in those parts of the prophecy with associations he could understand.

"Here, look, Cedric. He speaks of one to recover the blood of the world."

His roommate leaned over and read the passage softly.

"'Then comes he with the heart of a man, with blood fouled from the Pit.' Is he speaking of the Antichrist that St. John saw in the Revelation?"

"I'm not sure. He goes on about the world's pain and unlocking a seal to release the souls of the damned. According to this, the graal is in Anglia. Most likely it would be here—and the prophecy you found sounds like the archbishop's appointment at the hands of the king triggers the end of time." Dylan thought for a moment. "Is it possible that the kingdom of Exeter is the great whore that blights the land?"

Cedric raised an eyebrow. "What if you're reading it wrong? I mean, wasn't Babylon the center of iniquity?"

Dylan screwed up his face. "Well," he said, "if we take the scriptures figuratively and then apply the writings of Merlin, it *might* all fit. But the graal is the most important thing. Think of it, Cedric, the graal hidden here, within reach of a man like John. Why, the entire earth could be swallowed up by a curse because of his wicked ways!"

Cedric smiled, "I hear talk that he and a few of the priests have been infected by, shall we say, the disease of the Greeks?"

"Oh, sweet Jesu," Dylan moaned. "Brother Jeremiah said that wasn't true."

"They say the loins of a man need—"

"God could not leave the graal to one such as he. Only a man near sainthood should be consecrated as the bishop entrusted to guard such a sacred relic."

"Unfortunately, this man wasn't chosen of God, but of the king. Seriously though, what if it's all a hoax? What if Merlin made the whole thing up to keep people from finding the real graal that was hidden elsewhere? You know, a false trail."

"Maybe. But if he made it up, why are the texts here in Canterbury? Look at what Merlin said about the king appointing a man like John." Dylan pointed at the passage. "These texts must have been gathered here for a reason."

The bell rang for assembly in the cathedral, spurring the two novices to squirrel away their research before rushing from the cell.

The barren hill squatted outside the tall city gates. Heat rose from the arid landscape like wriggling phantoms in the dust. A crowd of people, dirty and agitated, pressed up the narrow, twisting path, following closely the knot of soldiers in plumed leather and iron. Some in the crowd wailed above the tromping of martial feet; others plodded in silence, dumbfounded; and a few jeered the torn and tattered man who stumbled in the center of the troopers.

Dylan found himself climbing up the slopes with the crowd. He strained on his toes to see over the others. Through the dust, he barely made out the outline of a thick pole being dragged along, the wood dark and rough.

Someone laughed and babbled in a tongue Dylan could not understand. A dirty, scruffy man cursed the soldiers in coarse Latin. Dylan blinked as the dust stung his eyes and fostered an irritating thirst deep in his throat. He coughed and smeared sweat across his brow with the back of his hand.

The mob crested the hill in a confused gaggle. Dylan heard the sounds of a hammer, *smack, smack, smacking* against a nail. A woman shrieked as the soldiers lifted the cross, the man pinned upon it by nails in his bloody wrists and mangled feet. Dylan struggled against sweaty bodies to get a closer look, horror tightening his lungs against his pounding heart as he realized where he was. The crowd grew tighter around him and stopped his progress to the Cross.

The man stretched on the tree moved his lips, speaking so softly Dylan could not hear the words. Then he slumped down and hung heavily against the raw iron. One of the soldiers, who had gamed for the man's robes, grabbed a spear and thrust it up underneath his rib cage. Water and blood gushed out. An older man, stooped with age, shouldered his way through the crowd and lifted a cup to catch the flow before it fell to the dust. Dylan could not see the cup clearly, but he knew it had to be the graal. Lightning streaked across the sky and clouds blackened the sun. The people began dispersing. A blast of thunder shook the ground. Dylan closed his eyes.

Gone. The dream was gone and Cedric lay nearby, his breath softly rasping in and out, in and out. A chill quivered up Dylan's sweaty spine. God had revealed the death of the Son to him. To *him,* a simple novice of no consequence. He pulled his knees up to his chin, closing his eyes and mouthing a hasty prayer. What did God want of him? Surely this was a sign from the heavens that the sacred cup was near at hand. Dylan looked at Cedric, and, afraid his friend would think him mad, said nothing of the dream.

A few mornings later, Dylan slid into the back of the chapel and joined the rest of the clerics in prayer; silently hoping no one would hear him kneel. He whisked the remnant of sleep away from the corners of his eyes and peeked around his fingers. The bishop's back faced him, as did the backsides of the other ecclesiastics. He breathed a prayer in his heart only after he had blended his voice into the solemn, monotone oblations, masking his tardiness in the Latin praises.

"Thy nativity, O Christ our God, hath shown forth upon the world in the light of wisdom. For it is those that worshipped the stars who were taught, by a star, to adore Thee, the Sun of Righteousness, and to know Thee, the morning star on high. O Lord, glory unto Thee! Glory unto Thee forever!"

Another late night in the library had come and gone, and his sight remained blurred from long hours reading beneath the flickering light of a single candle. He had scanned page after yellowed page for snatches of information about the holy symbol; it fascinated him far more than the moldering relics of St. Abelard, which the bishop received a few days before from Treves. Or so the Gothic merchant had billed them when the coin was exchanged. The Holy Graal, Dylan thought as his mouth automatically formed the words of the liturgy, held the precious blood of Christ, the very fluid that had coursed through God's veins while He lived in the flesh.

Bishop John of Canterbury knew nothing of the significance of his office, of this Dylan was sure. Nepotism was no measure for filling a position of this importance. The novice was convinced that all were in ignorance and John's installation was the result. Dylan genuflected and the bishop turned, offering his blessings to the assembled clerics with his palms turned heavenward. The prelate then extended his beefy arms, a signal for the altar boys to rush forward to remove his vestments. He mopped his brow after being lightened of his burdensome clothing and, in his casual way, dismissed his flock while admonishing them to mirror Christ in their lives. Then he retired to his chambers, where all assembled knew he would drink himself into a blissful stupor.

Someone slapped Dylan on the back and chuckled. "So, Brother Dylan, late again this morning?" Dylan turned to throw a retort, but

Cedric raised his hands and warded it off. "I don't think anybody else saw you. Honest."

Dylan smiled and he drew Cedric into a corner.

"You're sure? The bishop didn't notice?"

"Pretty sure," Cedric answered, and then lowered his voice. "If he did, you'd catch hell for sure."

Dylan gasped, startled at Cedric's language. "Not in here, this is God's own house."

Cedric shrugged. "I don't think that God would mind. How else should I describe what happens to those who meet with the bishop's disapproval?"

"Who knows the mind of God? Or that of our bishop?"

Cedric laughed. "Well, I do know that the most righteous Archbishop John of Canterbury will be publicly interring the knucklebone of St. Abelard beneath the altar. They say that the foundation has not been moved in almost five hundred years."

"Five hundred years?" Dylan queried. "It was opened before?"

"That's what the bishop said, but you missed it. What of it?"

"Opening up the altar," Dylan mumbled. "The only reason someone would open up it so long ago would have been for the king to place the graal here! Now John is going to crack it open and put some old sheep's bones inside."

"Brother Dillard says they're pigs' knuckles and that there are more pig knuckles being worshiped across the whole of Christendom than pieces of the True Cross." Cedric glanced back at the altar, a rough-hewn pile of stones held together by crude, crumbling mortar. "But why do you think it might be under there?"

"It seems proper. Where else could it be hidden? Think about it—it couldn't be in Cornwall or anywhere near Camelot or Glastonbury Tor. That's the first place fortune hunters would look for it. If someone hid the prophecy of Merlin here, that means no one outside these walls is supposed to know the graal's location. It's here. It must be. Archbishop John became the guardian of the flock and of Christ's blood, and he doesn't even know it!" Dylan paused, his face aglow with excitement. "When will they open the altar?" "The bishop said they'd pull it aside this afternoon then place the reliquary in tomorrow. After the ceremony, the altar will be sealed again as a shrine where the afflicted can come to beg solace from Saint Abelard."

"Of course," Dylan snickered. "And then the bishop will be able to afford the new robe and vestments from newly levied tolls, as befitting a man of his station. Look, we must find out if the graal truly lies here."

"Why?" Cedric asked. "This is a responsibility way beyond us."

"What if it falls into the bishop's hands? He could unleash a cataclysm beyond imagination and not even realize what he bumbled into. Only the righteous can care for the graal."

"Truly? Are you worthy enough to even contemplate seeing it, let alone touching it? And what do we do if we do find it? Do we run?"

Dylan put his arm on Cedric's shoulder, "If it truly is here then we must do more than view it; we must protect it from the likes of John."

Dark shadows hugged the slender pillars, branching out across the nave of the basilica and up into the shadowed rafters. Moonlight filtered through the thick, milky windows, silver shafts illuminating spots of wall and floor. Avoiding these pools of light, Dylan and Cedric darted toward the altar. Dripping tallow candles flickered

13

around the hole in the floor to prevent anyone seeking nocturnal devotions from falling into the pit and breaking their contrite necks.

A figure huddled near the opening, bent over at the base of the knotty, splintered crucifix set up in the apse. Dylan stopped and signaled for Cedric to do the same. He pointed at the worshiping priest. Cedric shrugged, unsure how to distract him. Dylan snatched Cedric by the robe, pulling him forward with a clatter.

"Brother, brother," he huffed, breaking the silence surrounding the worshiper's devotions.

The cleric turned, startled, blinking sleep from his eyes. It was Brother Theodosius, the bishop's gardener—who was also a culinary master who had journeyed from Monte Cassino in Italy to cook for Albion's royalty.

Before the man could wake completely, Dylan blurted out, "The bishop needs you to collect and prepare fresh herbs and vegetables for his table. The king may be riding this very minute from Exeter to attend the internment of the reliquary tomorrow!"

"The king! Why, the bishop told me he wasn't coming! Oh my, I asked him just before Vespers. Why I—I've many things to do then. Are you sure this is the word from the bishop himself?"

"Straight from his own lips. The messenger just barely arrived with the news. I think he's still draining a cup to wash down the road dust." Dylan nudged Cedric.

"Yes, yes, that's right," Cedric chimed in. "He said the king needed a special favor of the saint, something to do with the fall harvest."

"Well, of course, the harvests *have* been bad," Theodosius muttered, half to himself. "Oh, there's so much to do before morning." He nimbly genuflected and tottered to his feet. "God forgive me this interruption. But I must go." He hurried from the chapel, mumbling about calling down to the village for fresh onions.

Dylan breathed a sigh of relief when the last of Theodosius' footfalls faded into the dark of night.

"God forgive us for sending a man to work this whole night," he said, eyeing the nearby crucifix. He was very grateful that they weren't standing in the altar's place at that moment.

Cedric shrugged. "No one knows the mind of God." Then he added, "Maybe not even wise old Merlin. The graal better be here, or we'll have hell to pay for this little prank."

Could Merlin have not known the mind of God? Certainly God revealed His will to men—the scriptures provided ample examples of cryptic prophecy. Had Dylan not received a dream to confirm his own mission? The graal was at Canterbury, the young novice knew this with all his soul. And if subterfuge was the only way to keep the sacred relic from falling into that sot John's hands, then so be it.

Cedric pulled back the thick, oily tarp covering the hole and wrinkled his nose at the odor that wafted up. Dylan took a sputtering torch from a niche on the cathedral wall and thrust it into the blackness. A weak breath of air brushed his cheek as he leaned over the hole for a better look. The pit was deeper than either of the novices was tall. Cedric slid down and landed with a heavy thud. Dylan glanced over his shoulder, worried someone might have heard; but no sound arose in response. He tossed the torch down.

Cedric caught it deftly and waited for Dylan to skid down next to him. Together, they looked around. Close-fitting tiles covered the bottom of the hole, and one wall looked to be a bricked-up arch.

"So what do we have here?" Dylan asked. Cedric felt along the wall's bricks and mortar, then along the arch. "The arch seems to be better built. See here how this is crumbling?" He scraped the edge of an irregularly shaped brick in the wall with the iron crucifix around his neck. "The arch is old Roman, but this wall is not. It's not much more than mud."

Dylan nodded. "We should be able to get through in no time."

"Let's hope so," Cedric whispered. He looked pointedly at Dylan. "I hope you're right about this."

"I'm sure," Dylan replied. "After all, what if John does know the graal is here? Or what if someone breaks through this by mistake?

That's a big chance to take, leaving it here. I know we're doing the right thing." He pulled a flat length of iron from under his habit and started chinking away at the mortar.

"Where'd you get that?" Cedric asked.

"What? This? Oh, I brought it just in case there was digging to do," Dylan lied. He'd actually brought the metal bar in case they ran into someone like Brother Theodosius—fortunately, the cleric had left on his own.

Bricks soon began breaking loose as the metal bit into the crumbling mortar.

"There! There, see?" Dylan panted. He thrust his hand into the gap and pulled hard. A few more bricks tumbled out, breaking into pieces on the ground. He thought fleetingly of Camelot and wondered if its spires had been built of the same crude brick as this. If so, Arthur truly would have built his kingdom of crumbling clay.

Cedric gave his torch to Dylan then poked his head through the opening. "Sure is dark in there." He heaved on another block and wriggled his shoulders in. "I think . . . I . . . can . . . fit," the young man gasped, his body twisting and wriggling until he slipped into the other side. "This is not a fit place. No, not fit at all for a living body."

Dylan heard Cedric grumble as he sloshed through puddled water. Once his friend was out of the way, Dylan squirmed through himself.

The sputtering flame of their torch revealed crude drawings near the ceiling, one of a fish and another of a Greek cross, both outlined in faded crimson. Latin letters were scratched underneath. Dylan lofted the torch closer and read them in an awed whisper.

"'The sanctuary of God, meeting place of the saints in this the third year of Septimus Severus.'"

Cedric whistled softly. "They must have worshiped here while pagan Roman bureaucrats labored in the basilica above."

The tiled tunnel floor extended straight ahead, a groove worn in the center from centuries of water trickling along its surface.

"Shall we get this over with?" Cedric said, looking nervously down the little stream. "Who knows what sort of old bones or other disgusting things we'll run across? I hope none of them try to grab and keep us here."

Dylan shuddered at the thought of moldering remains tucked away in some damp crevice. Once dead, they're no harm to the living, he reminded himself. Yes, no harm to the living. Christian dead certainly do not harm Christian living! The novice thrust the torch ahead of them and sloshed into the water, his eyes darting back and forth into the flickering, moving shadows.

Rats, he told himself. *Rats must be the worst of the creatures in the subterranean gloom. Just plain old ordinary rats.*

Both Dylan and Cedric shuddered. Eyes watched them, eyes that pierced the entombed darkness as the novices stumbled deeper into the catacombs.

A roughly carved niche appeared in the wall; inside lay a man's skeleton, clad in armor of greened bronze, his rotted arms folded across his chest and his finger bones clenching a corroded sword. They ran past it down the tunnel, stumbling over each other to get away from this manifestation of death, which neither had ever truly faced before.

Cedric stopped and leaned against the cold stone, panting like a frightened puppy. Next to him, Dylan dropped to his knees.

"Sh-sh-surely G-God didn't intend for us to disturb their rest," Cedric forced out between gulps of air. Dylan pulled his robes up tight to his shoulders and shook his head.

"Who can truly tell the mind of God?" he responded.

Cedric kicked water at him. "You always sound like you know what you're doing. Then you say something like that. It's such a stupid answer! Are we *supposed* to be here or not? If not, then we should go! What if we disturb something else, something that we're not supposed to? Will you just shrug and say, 'Who knows the mind of God?'"

Dylan reached into his habit, pulling out a small crucifix. That had always been their stock answer. But it wouldn't do here, not this time. He placed the holy symbol to his lips and whispered, "Please God, help us to do Thy will." Then he looked his friend in the eyes and said, "I need to tell you about a dream I had . . ."

The words tumbled from Dylan's lips, filling the fetid gloom. Cedric listened in rapt disbelief, shaking his head.

"Honestly? Why didn't you tell me sooner? I told you of Merlin's prophecy as soon as I read it!" Cedric threw his hands in the air and kicked the stream once more. "Did you think I'd tell someone?"

"No, it's not that. I—I just thought I shouldn't tell because the vision was sacred."

"Sacred? You can't share something sacred with me?" Cedric stood and slogged back up the passage to the edge of the torchlight.

"Look," said Dylan, his face flushed and his ears tingling. "I'm sorry. You're right. I should have told you everything right away."

Cedric threw a handful of pebbles into the stream, his face grim. He didn't reply.

"I truly am sorry, Cedric," Dylan continued. "It's just, I've never had a friend like you before. I thought you'd laugh at me or tell me I made the whole story up just to be right."

"I'm here, aren't I?"

"I know," Dylan said. "Sorry."

Without another word, Cedric trudged past him down the tunnel. Dylan fell in behind him, feeling the silence more than any raised voice.

Unadorned by elaborate arch or decorative stonework, the tunnel continued on a few hundred paces beyond the warrior's remains. Dylan led the way through the unfinished opening at the end, stepping carefully through loose stones and mud into a narrow cavern. He held his breath, his heart pounding in the back of his throat, and grabbed Cedric's hand to pull him along. Forgotten in the excitement were anger and shame. Remembered were the thrill of discovery and a shared friendship.

At the far end of the cavern stood a crude altar of flat, gray river rocks stacked on top of each other without mortar. Upon the altar sat a gold-chased box, encrusted with the grime of the ages and raised from its surface in precious metals a snarling dragon with ruby eyes whose tail curled around the container's corners—the symbol of the Pendragon. Other holy signs, painted in reds and blacks on the walls, faded in and out of the torchlight: crosses, a flowering vine, a shepherd staff, and still other characters unfamiliar and strange in design. Both young men fell to their knees in the muck, genuflecting fervently and bowing their heads to offer up hurried prayers.

A slight smile turned Cedric's trembling lips. "I believe, I do believe," he whispered.

They rose and approached the altar, eyes lowered in reverence.

Dylan handed the torch to Cedric and carefully rubbed the dust from the surface of the box with his sleeve. An etching was revealed, of a knight with long lance charging a creature with a woman's head and a lion's body. He recalled the sphinx from an old text, a beast that tricked men with puzzles and feasted on them after they gave the wrong answers. The dragon's ruby eyes flashed as Dylan reached out to pull the lid off the box. He froze—the light seemed more than just reflected torchlight. But he had come too far, he reasoned, and too much was at stake. He moved closer.

As his hands touched the etching of the knight and sphinx, tingles crawled up his hands, into his arms, up his neck, and across his scalp. He pulled his hand away with a start. Gritting his teeth, he determined to continue in the belief that God wanted him to do this for a purpose and would shield him from whatever came next. With a slight tug, he lifted the lid away, and Cedric raised the torch over the open box.

A smooth-fired clay cup stood nestled in a mildewed silk lining, full to the brim with a deep crimson fluid. Dylan grew dizzy as he felt his soul drawn into the liquid to far deeper depths than the physical cup could possibly contain.

"Dare we?" Cedric asked.

"I don't know." Dylan's voice broke. He slowly reached out with a fingertip to touch the graal, but stopped short. "Do you think we're worthy to even look upon this?"

"You're the one who had the dream, not me," Cedric answered.

Dylan gently curled his fingers around the graal and lifted it from the box.

It was a simple cup, the glaze on its surface fading and cracked like the intricate pattern of a spider's web. The liquid within danced without moving, sparkling flecks of light effervescently rising like burning ashes from a hot fire.

"Do you really think it contains the life-blood of Christ and the salvation of the world?" Dylan asked, but he already knew deep inside the answer to his question.

Cedric said nothing as he leaned in for a better look, his eyes wide. Neither of them was aware of how long they stood admiring their find, basking in the presence of the holiest relic in Christendom, their souls communing with the warm feelings of the Spirit, their faith fulfilled.

Angels—are these truly angels singing in my ears? Dylan mused. *Or is my heart pounding so loud that I believe the Heavenly Hosts are—*

A sound in the tunnel shattered their reverence into shards. Startled, Dylan looked up and gasped. The entrance was filled with the bloated, ghastly Archbishop of Canterbury, who stepped daintily into the chamber. In one hand, the prelate held a guttering torch and, in the other, the long, curled, gold-leafed staff that signified his office. His vestments draped down in the mud, wet and stained. Cedric's face drained to a blanched white. Dylan's hand shook, but he quickly steadied himself to keep the precious fluids in the graal from spilling to the dirt.

The Archbishop's mouth twisted into a toothy grimace and a meaty tongue slid across his wicked white teeth.

"My sons. Oh, my sons. What have we found here?" he inquired as he stepped forward, his voice slick and oily. "Oh, what is this?"

Dylan shrank back, wishing he could sink into the stone and earth, stealing the graal away with him.

"He can't take the cup," he whispered to Cedric. "He just can't."

Dylan's foot caught on a rock as he stepped back, tripping him and twisting his ankle with a wrenching crack. Cedric reached out to steady the graal as it tipped, but too late. The liquid splashed to the ground.

The earth pitched, rocks shattered, and the chamber groaned. The Lord's blood had been spilt as on Golgotha.

The Archbishop laughed mirthlessly, the sound of it intertwining in cruel ecstasy with the earth's pain. Dylan and Cedric crawled to a corner, tightly holding the cup between them. As John shook with the earth, his body changed and blurred. The familiar lines of his form melted like tallow, clouding away into purple, white, and gold folds of fat. A slender, elegant gray form, dressed in the deepest black, stepped out of the writhing mass. It cast away the staff and held the torch triumphantly aloft.

"The time is now and the deed is done! Take what is thine,

O Death, the battle has nigh been won!" cried the figure, his face turned upward, lean features masked in living shadows.

The ground soaked by the Blood quivered and sank away, billowing white steam and swirling grey vapors. The creature stood at the edge of the newly-sunken pit and smiled.

"My Lord shall be truly pleased to have such a prize as the blood of the chalice; yes, pleased indeed! It shall brighten his dark and dismal day. Let the fools above do as they wish with your precious religion and moldering relics."

With that, the creature leaped lightly into the pit, vanishing from view. On the box, the glimmer in the dragon's eye faded to a dull red.

Later that night, a priest found the rotted corpse of the Archbishop in one of the many closets of his bedchamber, the heavy smell of incense covering the putrid stench of his rotting flesh. Dylan and Cedric were gone, adding fuel to the scandalous stories that sprang up around the once sleepy community of Canterbury.

———∞———

Chapter One

THE FIRST CITY

MATTHEUS, HIGH KING of all Gwent, Unifier of the Southern realms of Cymru, and Ally to Cynric, the Saxon king of Wessex, sat glumly within his tent. Outside its flimsy canvas walls, the massive stonework of a crumbling Roman amphitheater rose into the air, more than four times the height of a man, to catch the first light of the dawn. Outside the amphitheater lay Caerleon, the *Isca Silurum* of the Romans—now Mattheus' First City. It was his capital, his home, and the eastern boundary of his lands near the banks of the Wysg River.

The arena itself served as the drilling field of Mattheus' Home Guard—fifty of his trusted veterans, staunch warriors who had been bloodied and battle-hardened in the wars that had swept Mattheus to power and now kept him there. Being a king in Cymru was no easy task, for there were many who already held the title, and even more ambitious cutthroats who wanted it. Even now Mattheus' soldiers sharpened their swords and fletched their arrows against the hour when they would march.

But this time, the threat was different. This time, there was no precocious pretender advancing on the outlying marches. This time, the enemy was aggravatingly unknown.

Mattheus heaved a sigh from deep within his barrel chest and ran his fingers through his beard. It, like his hair, was trimmed short in Roman cavalry style, shot with gray that hinted to his age. Still, he was no decrepit old wraith like some of his contemporaries. His large, sinewy arms belied strength equal to that of any of his younger champions. Numerous scars mapped out decades of combat. Years of hard living had etched his face in a fine tracery of wrinkles that had deepened in the five weeks since hearing of the massacre at Merthyr Tydfyl. The trials of life had not beaten him; rather, he burned to meet their challenges. He tapped his fingers on the tabletop.

A map of the Celtic lands lay spread across the table before him. Mattheus' holdings were outlined in bold red ink in the center, separate from the independently held lands on the east, north, and west. A fleeting thought ran through his head to offer thanks in the chapel on Sunday that the waters of the Môr Hafren lapped against his southern verge; for if God had seen fit to place more land there, Mattheus knew it would be in the hands of another rival.

Small wooden markers indicated the positions of the men scouring the surrounding lands for a trace of his lost daughter, Marianna. On the first day of spring, she had embarked on her annual pilgrimage north to lay flowers on the grave of Princess Tudful, martyred nearly a century before in one of the bloody battles that had brought Mattheus' family to power. For six generations, the eldest daughter of the royal family had made this pilgrimage without incident. Events had unfolded differently this time.

On her return journey to Caerleon, marauders had ambushed Marianna's train, and all her guards and retainers had been brutally slain. Now there was no trace of his daughter. Five weeks he had waited for a ransom demand, all the while trying to piece together whose blood-soaked hands were behind the deed.

But no ransom demand had followed the kidnapping. No communications. No threats. There had been nothing at all.

Mattheus maintained over two dozen men in the field—stalwart and trusted men like Ahern and Guerdon, two of his lieutenants from his youthful conquering days. He also counted on allies from other lands, like the renowned Merrovaine of Exeter, who had come to Caerleon bearing messages of support from King Cynric. The knight had put aside his return home to offer his services in the search. Finally, besides these, there were smatterings of younger men eager for adventure. Mattheus had paired them with the more experienced warriors in the hope that their brashness would be offset by their companions' tried and proven skill.

A shadow flitted across the tent's canvas wall, and a moment later the flaps parted as another man entered the king's tent. He was younger than Mattheus, not much over twenty, and wearing ornate gold-and-silver-chased parade armor that contrasted starkly with the King's much more serviceable mail hauberk. He carried himself as if he believed, even here, that scores of admiring ladies from the finest of families watched him, twittering his name in each other's ears. The young dandy paused to smooth back a lock of dark, oiled hair before taking one of the stools by the table. He sat down heavily, removed a flimsy, soft-soled boot, and regarded the King with a pout as he massaged his toes.

"Honestly, my lord, why must we spend so much time drilling? March, march, march. Dear Lord, I'm a cavalryman. I ride to battle! Surely the men are ready by now. When can we begin?"

"We've begun," Mattheus answered, a belligerent edge in his voice. "Preparation is key to victory in the field. And that's why we spend so much time drilling. We are not undisciplined barbarians."

The younger man was Aldonzo of Septimania, a Visigoth prince who was betrothed to Marianna—and little more than a glory-seeking child, in Mattheus' opinion. He had long grown tired of Aldonzo's incessant prattle and, given a chance, would send the boy packing back to Gaul. However, Marianna's mother, the Lady Allana (God rest her soul) had arranged the betrothal, and he didn't want to reverse one of her last wishes.

Still, it rankled him that when the search parties were selected, Aldonzo had been conspicuously absent. He suspected the boy would rather ride to Marianna's rescue at the head of a victorious army than slog through the mud with the rest of the scouts. Now that all the search parties had set out, all he ever asked was, 'when can we leave?'

Their pattern of conversation had grown all too familiar in the past month.

"Any news from the search parties?" Aldonzo asked, true to form.

Why didn't you go with them to see for yourself? Mattheus thought. But he let the barb die unspoken on his tongue and reached behind him for a damp wineskin hanging from the tent pole.

"Drink?" he asked.

Aldonzo shook his head, lazy curls bobbing about his face.

Mattheus took a long pull from the skin, but cut himself short. It would be foolish, getting fuddle-headed over this minor irritant. He capped the skin and dropped it on the table.

"Broderick and Fowler believe they've found something in the north," he grumbled. "Torrey's lead has come to nothing and he's turning back. All the others have given up." He stopped for a moment, reflecting on the futility of their efforts. "Except for Merrovaine and the boy from Birkenshire. They're following a lead westward."

"That old wives' tale?" Aldonzo replied with a foolish grin. "Honestly, my lord, the Black Knight? How can Merrovaine take that seriously? He's been listening to that Birkenshire boy. By St. Michael, it sounds like something of his doing."

"How? It's the best lead we have! Fable or not, the trail is there or Merrovaine wouldn't pursue it."

"I beg your forgiveness, my lord, but I feel all they will return with is a story meant to frighten children. I've no doubt the real kidnappers left the whole foolish tale as a false lead to throw us off. In fact, I'll wager they're having a good laugh about it at this very moment! Now, it seems to me that Dyfed is the one—"

Mattheus rose to his feet and donned his cloak. He stepped past Aldonzo to the tent flap. *This constant worrying is getting to me,* he thought as he turned back to the boy.

"If Dyfed truly is the problem we'll know soon enough," Mattheus said. "Then you can wet your cavalry blade."

He thrust the tent flap aside and stepped into the brisk morning air. Yes, the dandy would wet his blade simply because it was strapped to his leg.

Fog lay over the land in a thick grey blanket, making shadows of all but the nearest soldiers. Aldonzo followed the King out of the tent and paused as both of them noticed a commotion to the right. Before either of them could make out the cause a guardsman materialized from the mist, slipping on the slick grass as he skidded to a halt before them.

"My lord, a message from Merrovaine!"

Before the soldier could utter another word Mattheus pushed past him, his cloak swirling around him like the wings of a great, predatory bird. He strode to the center of the arena, where he found a horseman surrounded by several foot soldiers. The man wore the colors of the Royal Messengers and had clearly ridden hard from the villa on the other side of Caerleon. Mattheus shouldered through the gathering crowd and stopped by the rider's knee.

"News?" he barked.

The courier reached into his tunic. "Yes, sire. Come in last night, it did. Brought in by one of those pigeons of his." He extracted a tiny bone scroll case and handed it over.

Mattheus broke the seal and removed the sliver of paper. He squinted at the tiny characters then looked to Aldonzo. "You know Latin better than I. Read it."

The Visigoth took the note and examined it closely. "Your Highness . . . rumors of fort off coast . . . attacked by ravens?" His eyebrows rose in surprise. "Separated—no sign of Erik or trail . . . seems hopeless . . . will continue . . . Humble servant, M."

Mattheus stood quietly as the men around him broke into a babble of voices. He ignored them, took the message from Aldonzo, crumpled it into a tiny wad, and looked up at the rider. "How many birds has he sent back?"

"Uh—twelve, sire."

"All of them, then."

"Yes, I believe so."

Aldonzo spoke up quietly. "We won't be hearing from him again, then. Until he returns."

Mattheus shook his head. He looked around, noticed a stableman, and jabbed a finger at him. "You! Prepare two horses. I leave within the hour. Reeves!"

A burly officer stepped forward. "Yes, sire?"

"You're in charge here," the King bellowed. "See to it the men are ready to move on short notice."

"Yes, sire. Will we be marching soon?" the officer asked.

"I'm not sure. But have them ready in any case. Aldonzo, gather your gear."

"Me?" The younger man was taken by surprise.

"Yes. You're coming with me."

"Ah . . . of course, sire! May I ask where?"

"The villa, of course! We've some planning to do!"

Aldonzo's idle finger traced over the lion's menacing fang, following its contours up the side of the intricate doorjamb. The workmanship intrigued him. That and little else in the dreary whitewashed chamber that served as the King's planning room. He breathed heavily with boredom and turned back to the group gathered around the massive oak table in the center of the chamber. The tabletop was a jumble of maps, scrolls, and missives from all over Britain.

"But, my lord," Chamberlain Hugh said, "the very idea is absolutely preposterous! There are no strongholds on any of the small islands off the western coast." His owlish eyes blinked rapidly from agitation.

Mattheus appeared equally disturbed. "There must be! Merrovaine indicated as much in his message! Besides, how would we know? How can you be so sure? Half these maps are older than me!" He swatted at the faded parchments in irritation.

Aldonzo and Mattheus had arrived at the villa at mid-morning, but gathering all the advisors together had taken until early afternoon. Aldonzo had paced up and down the villa grounds, impatiently snapping at everyone within reach until Mattheus had banished him to an upper room to await the start of the meeting. He looked wistfully out the window at the bleak countryside beyond. Not at all like the mostly sunny coast of southern Gaul.

Mattheus and his advisors argued back and forth over the veracity of Merrovaine's message, hoping to uncover some clue that would point the way to Marianna. That she was still alive had been taken for granted, as she was worth a considerable fortune in ransom. All the counselors argued and sniped at each other, for Merrovaine's message represented the first substantial lead they'd had in days—and the significance of his note grew greater with each man who returned empty-handed.

"There can be no argument," Kendrick, the Saxon emissary, interjected smoothly, "that Merrovaine's word is above reproach. I've known the man for over twenty years and his integrity is indisputable. However, I think we should keep in mind that he speaks of rumors; he does not say that he actually saw this place."

Chancellor Orin, grey and withered, slapped a blue-veined hand on the table, rattling a nearby inkpot. "Still, I agree with Hugh! These 'island realms' are few and far between."

"But they do exist!" Mattheus growled. "I've seen such myself on a clear day, rising out of the ocean mists, as have all of you."

"Well, yes, there are some examples, my lord," Orin continued. "But to the best of my knowledge, there are none to the west of us."

"Why not?" asked Aldonzo. "It would seem a perfect location from a strategic point of view. Easily defended, with ample privacy."

Master Cartographer Weylin, a short, stocky, middle-aged man with flecks of grey in his beard, clasped his hands together and gave the prince a wizened glance. "In a case like this, practical considerations outweigh the military advantages. There are simply no islands in the western Môr Hafren that are large enough."

Aldonzo regarded the chartist coolly. He'd never liked the man;

it was said that he spent a lot of time primping in mirrors, though Aldonzo couldn't see what he had to be so vain about. Not much for looks, and judging by this last statement, not much for sense either.

"I don't understand," he said with a hint of sarcasm. "How big does an island have to be to put a fort on it?"

"It's not that simple, my prince," Orin answered. "There must be enough land around the fort to support it."

"Yes, but exactly what do you mean? Are you referring to cropland? Why not just extort peasants on a nearby shore?"

"Well, you see . . . how can I put this?" Orin continued. "No one would build a fortress on a small island because of the difficulty of maintaining control over a holding of any respectable size from such an isolated position. Everything would have to be done by ferry, you see. The extra time and effort to accomplish even the simplest of tasks would be too great. That is if one was trying to rule a piece of land large enough to provide adequate food and labor—"

"And the cost!" Trevor, the Steward, broke in. "Imagine transporting lumber and workers across the open sea, day after day, month after month for years! And then to ferry across all the food and supplies to the workforce, let alone feed the inhabitants once the construction was done! It would be astronomical! Such things may have been possible in Rome, but not here. Not now."

Aldonzo's face crinkled around his eyes with a doubtful expression.

"Why not build a bridge?"

Orin snorted. "Here? The first stiff gale and strong tide would wash the entire effort away."

Aldonzo cleared his throat carefully. There was a fleeting thought, an image he had seen, that challenged Orin's answer, but he couldn't grasp it; another took its place. "With all due respect, Chancellor, I'm sure a man as well-traveled as yourself has seen Emperor Constantine's Bridge at Cologne? Still standing after nearly three hundred years?"

Mattheus had been standing thoughtfully throughout the exchange. "Aldonzo, please stop baiting my counselors. And as Trevor said, this is not Rome. Building a bridge of that magnitude would tax a kingdom, let alone a robber waylaying pilgrims on the road." He turned back to the table. "So what all of you are saying is that there are no places like Merrovaine described?"

"Logical examination would seem to rule it out, my lord," Orin affirmed, bristling from Aldonzo's challenge.

"Then we have nothing. Nothing!" Mattheus slammed his fist on the table. "Five weeks we've searched and still nothing to show for it! Five weeks and my daughter remains in the hands of God knows who, and we can't find a single thing!" His voice rose to a shout. "What do we do now?" He stopped, head bowed, hands flat on the table as if to keep them from striking something. "Where else can we go from here?" he whispered. "This is the only lead we have."

Aldonzo looked at the King worriedly. "But, my lord," he began cautiously, "what of Broderick? Surely he—"

"Nothing." Mattheus' voice held a grim note of finality. "He cast about for more clues but found nothing. His trail has ended. I just received word a short time ago." He balled his fists in frustration. "Merrovaine is our last hope. Are there any alternatives?"

The assembled aides whispered among themselves, and then Hugh stood. "I'm sorry, my lord, but we can think of none. We can only assume that the rumors Merrovaine heard were just that—rumors."

"Then she is gone? Just like that? Vanished like the morning tide?"

And the elusive image in Aldonzo's mind suddenly leapt into view. "Wait a moment!" he blurted out.

All eyes swiveled to him, and suddenly his idea didn't seem so credible. "Uh . . . actually, I'm not sure, but . . ."

"Stop dithering, Aldonzo, what is it?" Mattheus demanded.

"Well . . ." The murderous look in the King's eyes urged him on. "What if the fort weren't always on an island?"

Mattheus' aides were too well-bred to laugh at him outright, but they came close. Kendrick rolled his eyes to the ceiling and Hugh

threw his hands into the air. The others just gawked in disbelief. All except Weylin, who choked dramatically.

"Really, my lord," Hugh snapped. "Such rubbish. I suppose next he will tell us that the kidnapper is a terrible giant that lives amid the clouds and blows chunks of frost from his nostrils!"

Mattheus' face sagged with the weight of his disappointment. "Aldonzo, why do you do this?"

"But I know of a place, my lord. You won't believe me, and to tell the truth, I didn't believe it myself when I first heard of it, but in Gaul—or rather, off the coast of Gaul—and not that far across the sea from Britain—"

"Get to the point, Aldonzo!" the King bellowed.

"Er, yes, my lord. There is this island, a mountain—rather, a mound of solid granite that thrusts up out of the beach a half-mile from the shore. When the tide is high it is an island. But when the tide is out you can walk across the sand to reach it. If you can avoid the quicksand, that is." The others were still looking at him doubtfully.

"Some call it St. Michael's Mount. My point is, maybe this place Merrovaine speaks of is on such an island, a tongue of rock that is joined to the shore by a bridge of land, accessible only at low tide."

Still there was silence. Then without warning Kendrick jumped to his feet, startling the others. "Off the coast of Brittany! Monte Tombe is its name. It bears an abbey built by the archbishop of Avranches. I, too, have heard of it!" He slapped a palm against his temple.

"Yes, that's it. Have you seen it?" Aldonzo asked.

"Well, not with my own eyes, But Greek sailors speak of it," the noble replied.

"There, gentlemen, you see?" Mattheus looked a little more hopeful. "Wouldn't that be more practical for the construction of a fort?"

"Well, yes, I suppose it would," Hugh conceded. "It would eliminate the need for a ferry at the very least. As a matter of fact, there would be little difference between that and a very long drawbridge, in a practical sense."

Most of the others sat in stunned silence as the import sank into their minds. In the year that Aldonzo lived at court he'd garnered a reputation for vanity, glory-seeking, and recklessness; in a word, a typical, spoilt royal brat. He had not presented the image of a thinking man. Such a flash of insight from him left them one and all, for once, speechless.

Mattheus simply smiled. Allana had known what she had been doing after all. "Chancellor Orin, would you happen to recall any place like that?"

"Ahem . . . I'm afraid, my lord, that my knowledge is not that detailed," Orin said.

"I see," Mattheus said. "Weylin, do we have a better map of the area? A seaman's chart, with soundings on it?"

"Nothing here will suffice, but I could find one, my lord. If you will excuse me." The mapmaker tapped his fingers on the table as if considering something.

"Please," the king agreed urgently.

Weylin trotted out the door in pursuit of his task and the others broke into an excited discussion.

"I say, Aldonzo, have you actually seen this Monte Tombe?"

"No, wait! How do you drive a wagon across quicksand?"

"Fool! Build a causeway!"

"Do you suppose there are any places like that in the west?"'

"We can only hope and wait for Weylin to return with a map."

"Actually, I did see Monte Tombe from a distance," Aldonzo interjected excitedly. "Brittany is hostile to the Goths, and to be honest the northern Franks aren't on very good terms with my people, so I couldn't get—"

"But what would you do if there was an emergency and the tide was in?"

"Have you ever seen a boat?"

"What if it storms?"

"Well, you wouldn't be that far from shore, and besides—"

"Think of the strategic advantages!"

"Exactly!"

"Only one approach."

"Pull up the drawbridge and no one could touch you!"

"And when the tide comes in, hah!"

"But one approach means only one exit. What if they lay siege and block the bridge so help can't get through?"

"I say again, there are these things called 'boats.'"

"Of course there are, fool! Resupply could be blocked by warships. Or Scoti raiders. How would you get through that?"

"In the dark, by God! Run the bloody gauntlet at night!"

"How daring!"

"How foolhardy! That near the shore there'd be shallows and rocks. You'd run aground!"

"You've always got something negative to say, don't you?"

"I'm only examining the feasibility of such a thing!"

"Gentlemen, please!" Mattheus held up his hands for silence. "Weylin is back."

They cleared a space on the table for the vellum sheet the mapmaker unrolled before them.

The chartist shook his head. "I fear we've nothing conclusive, my lord. As you can see, our information is sketchy at best. This chart was copied from Roman originals, but it seems to be focused on roads rather than the small intricacies of the coast. In any event, it doesn't show sufficient detail to either verify or deny the existence of a place such as we are looking for."

"I see. Do we have the original?" the King asked.

"We did at one time, but it was drawn on parchment and didn't survive the damp weather," Weylin said. "Even if it did, though, I doubt a minor geographical feature like this 'island' would attract the attention of a cartographer on its own."

Silence fell over the group and once again Mattheus turned away in disappointment. He stood very still, looking like a great tawny statue in the late afternoon sunlight.

"Hellfire," he muttered under his breath. Then, more firmly, "Hellfire and brimstone! Is there any way we can find out? Quickly?"

Orin rose and put a hand on his liege's shoulder. "Those are hostile lands, sire. We could march in with a search party, but it would draw attention and only cause more trouble."

"You're right, of course." He squared his shoulders. "That's why we will send only a single ship."

"A ship? How do you mean, sire?" Orin asked.

"We'll send a ship up the coast," Mattheus said. "Not a warship, which would be too obvious. Yes, it would be much too obvious. Instead, we shall dispatch a merchantman, a small, fast one, plying its trade, but manned with troops. You see?"

"Yes. Yes, my lord." Orin's voice firmed with conviction. "I think it could be done."

The discussions continued as the sun fell from the sky and the stars emerged. Plans were laid well into the night, one by one, as they hammered out the final details. Then the lords of the kingdom struggled from their chairs to bed in the dark of the night.

All, that is, save Mattheus. He remained alert, pacing the grounds until dawn, driving his fist into his palm in a mixture of frustration, relief, and anticipation. His paths were blocked at every turn, and his options were rapidly vanishing from sight. But, thanks to Merrovaine, he had a new plan to grasp at, and it would not be long now. He hoped fervently that his shipboard spies would find his daughter.

Chapter Two

A CALL

I N THE VERDANT DEPTHS of the thick forests blanketing the slopes of the Cambrian Mountains, off the numerous pathways that crisscross the Backbone of Cymru, there stood a striking reminder of a faith long since vanished from the world. Rising like stolid giants from the mists, a great circle of standing stones took silent council among themselves, turning their backs to the forgetful men that laid out drunken tales of their significance. They stood alone, but not entirely so—for adjacent to their secluded domain nestled a small and unassuming cottage, the home to an equally small and unassuming man.

He was the last vestige of the People of the Stones, a people driven out long ago by the advent of more recent dwellers that brought with them blood and iron. The simple folk living nearby knew him simply as a healer and a wood wizard, a man of religious and magical persuasions; best left alone unless assistance was sorely needed.

He did not discourage this perception; in fact, he subtly promoted it, for otherwise he would have been overwhelmed by simple folk with relatively trivial requests for love philters, curses, and occasional blessings for sick cattle. A more important calling occupied his thoughts, and he would have been hard-pressed to find time for anything more than simple or gravely needed requests.

As always, he rose early that day, finished his morning oblations, and was about to step outside to check on the sheep when the sound of Merdydd crashing through the woods assaulted the still morn. He stopped with one hand on the door and grimaced. Would that boy never learn? His apprentice was willing enough, but at times his exuberance overbore proper respect for the Ways.

Without warning, the door was snatched from his hand. Merdydd's tall figure filled the doorway; a hunting bow strapped across his back, dark hair tumbling in disarray to his broad shoulders, and his homespun shirt damp with sweat.

The old man was about to deliver a sharp reprimand for the interruption when Merdydd stopped gasping long enough to cry, "Master Thelwyn, come quickly! Fychan is sick!"

Thelwyn's apprentice spun around and bolted for the far side of the clearing where two of the local folk waited, with a third laid out on a bier between them.

Thelwyn swept across the grass on Merdydd's heels like a wraith. The two farmers each took a step back as the pair approached, wary eyes watching the old man's every movement.

"What's wrong with him?" Thelwyn demanded.

"Feverish, master." Merdydd huffed. "He moans and screams, and knows not where he is, nor who is with him."

"How long has he been like this?"

"Three days," Merdydd calculated.

Thelwyn knelt down and, with a healer's expert eye, began to examine the prone figure. He found no obvious signs of injury or disease, nothing to hint at the cause of Fychan's affliction. Then Thelwyn noticed the strange mark on the man's left palm—a black smudge, almost as if it were merely charcoal from a carelessly handled brand. He reached out to touch it, and Fychan lunged at him, eyes glazed and open, mouth full of yellow teeth. His swollen tongue lashed at Thelwyn, hissing with an adder's head and teeth. Thelwyn scrambled backwards, as Fychan's transformed tongue struck again, tearing his garments and leaving a poison stain.

"Beware, de Daanan, lest you find the bite more than you can resist," foamed from Fychan's lips. "For you will be found."

Fychan lurched again at Thelwyn, the adder tongue coiled to sink teeth into his flesh, when he suddenly crumpled to the ground, hissing out a sigh, and went limp. Merdydd stood over him, fists clenched.

Thelwyn shot back to his feet. "Get him inside! Quickly. There's not much time."

Merdydd lifted the possessed man and ran with him into the house. Thelwyn followed, leaving the two farmers shaking and holding to one another while they prayed.

Once inside the small dwelling Thelwyn rushed straight to the narrow stairs leading to the cellar.

"Remove his clothes and lay him on the bed over there. Watch him. Watch that serpent. There. Make him as comfortable as you can," he commanded Merdydd. "Stoke the fire and put a kettle on to boil. I'll be back in a moment. Hurry now, or *my* sting will be worse than his bite."

The old druid disappeared down the cellar steps. He returned a few moments later with an armload of woolen blankets that he draped over Fychan's limp body and a fistful of leaves that he crumbled into the kettle. He bent over the fire and stirred up the concoction as he whispered unintelligible words; small motes of light danced in the air over the kettle and a peculiar, sweetly odor filled the room.

For several minutes, he stood nearly motionless over the pot, until the brew was ready. When it bubbled to a finish, he carried the boiling tonic to the bed, cooled it with a dash of rainwater, and dribbled it between Fychan's pale lips. The unconscious farmer spat and then coughed, but Thelwyn stroked his throat until he swallowed most of it. Thelwyn pried open his mouth with firm fingers. Fychan's throat was raw and red, but the beast within was gone.

Finally Thelwyn sat back and sighed.

One of the farmers timidly cleared his throat from the doorway. Thelwyn hadn't noticed that, overcoming their initial fear, they pressed into the opening for a better look.

"How is he? Will he live?"

Thelwyn shook his head. "Too soon to tell. Come back in the morning. If he lives through the night he should recover. It's a good thing you didn't wait any longer to bring him here." He rose and crossed the room to the window. "You'd better go now," he said with his back to them. "You've done all you can."

Without another word, the two farmers hurried out of the house, glad to have handed off their charge and brushing at their clothes and limbs to make sure none of the disease remained on their own persons.

Thelwyn shrugged his shirt from his body as the venom stain blackened the fabric. He threw the shirt on the fire, the flames sputtering and smoking as they consumed the poison, and sorted through his things for a clean garment.

There was a long silence in the room. Finally Merdydd spoke. "I've seen many things since I came to you. But this, master—please tell me this isn't real."

Thelwyn regarded his young apprentice carefully. "Here," he said at length, "I'll explain it for you." He walked back to the bed, withdrew Fychan's hand from under the covers, and displayed the mark he'd found earlier. "Do you know what this is?"

Merdydd shrugged. "Some kind of burn?"

Thelwyn shook his head. "It is a mark of evil. This man suffers no physical affliction. It is a sickness of the soul."

"Can we save him?"

"Perhaps. Only time will tell. It's very likely he won't live, but there is hope. Whoever put this mark on him left him alive for a reason, or perhaps as a warning. Maybe he went somewhere he shouldn't have. I cannot tell. Have confidence, apprentice. We are not powerless in this test. Now, put your mind at ease. I need you to prepare my pack. I'll be going on a long journey."

"How soon?"

"Now, I'm afraid. You'll have to attend the sheep, as well as our guest, until his friends return on the morrow. I don't know when I'll return." Thelwyn fell silent. Whispers had reached him even in these far-off lands, whispers that disturbed both his days and his nights. Rumors were one thing, but now proof lay upon his own cot. The old evil had risen again, and the thought of it frightened him.

Chapter Three

One Dark Knight

S IR ERIK OF BIRKENSHIRE dropped the lance from the heaving chest of the peasant, letting the cold iron tip rest against his sunken gut. The poor man's pallid face quivered as he stammered his reply.

"The . . . the castle is . . . is . . . is over the hill to the east, great lord!" The peasant pointed a bony finger to a low ridge in the distance that stood between them and the coast. He seemed as if he were going to choke on the words and crumple to the ground in a heap like a discarded string puppet.

Erik cursed under his breath.

The sun already sank low in the West, casting long shadows across the meadows. Above them another storm appeared to be rolling in on the quickening wind.

"Hard by the sea, you say? Speak quickly now!" Erik demanded, prodding the man again with the lance. The peasant staggered, raising his hands before him.

"Yes, yes, by the sea!"

"Cur! If you've lied, I'll return to cut out your damned heart!" Erik whisked the man aside with the lance as he spurred his mount forward. He could smell the *shite* and dirt that clung to the peasant's clothes.

"N-n-no, lord! I've not lied, I swear! Just beyond the hills it lies!" The pathetic creature scrambled back toward the squalid hut huddled beside the road.

Erik spat after him. The mean folk of this place disgusted him. Obviously, he thought, not all smelly, spineless fish lived beneath the sea. He booted his horse into a canter in the direction the peasant had pointed, through the rolling hills.

The young knight recalled one very like the peasant who wore the garments of royalty, though none too well. After Marianna's abduction off the north road, King Mattheus had been in a frenzied state, but his frustration had paled compared to that of Aldonzo, the prim dandy courting the princess' affections. When the disturbing news reached court that the bodies of her attendants had been found in their own blood, he nearly pulled his finely crimped hair from its perfumed roots, roaring oaths heavenward that he would sally forth in glorious retribution, riding through the streets of Caerleon to the king's villa with her abductor's head slung across his saddlebow. Alas, Aldonzo's courage proved as fleeting as the scent of perfume on a swineherd—elusive and quickly lost when it came time to feed slops to the pigs.

Feats of valor had only been a dream for Erik, a stirring desire fueled by the fireside tales of the old warriors on long winter nights; tales of glorious battles and of knightly quests to dangerous exotic lands. Enthusiastic to serve the king, he was spurred on even more upon seeing Mattheus' displeasure when his future son-in-law complained of a head cold and excused himself as plans were finalized and assignments given.

Erik of Birkenshire had been amazed to find himself paired with the near-legendary Merrovaine of Exeter; in a thrice, they'd set off to hunt down the rogues and free Marianna. At first the clues had been difficult to find, but in time they became more distinct, as if the princess' attackers became careless and boorish.

Progress remained excruciatingly slow, however, for even as they followed their quarry they were obliged to conceal their movements into the lands of other lords who would have liked nothing more than to cause King Mattheus mischief. They lost many hours avoiding patrols and unburdening their purses to silence wagging tongues. As if that wasn't enough, nature herself conspired against them, for the land was often mountainous and difficult to cross in the maddeningly soggy weather.

Merrovaine had speculated in those early days that one of these other lords was somehow involved, but that theory was put to rest when the trail left Dyfed on the verges of the Cambrian mountains and turned southwest into sparsely populated, unclaimed lands. From that point onward their trek was marked not only with snapped twigs and disturbed undergrowth but with rumor and hearsay as well. Locals they chanced upon spoke of a great dark lord, a master of occult magic called the 'Black Knight', who lived to the south and whose men were spied roving about the forests in recent weeks. Merrovaine dismissed their superstitious chatter with a shake of his head. He had recounted similar legends from all over the

Continent, yet deep within Erik they struck an eerie chord of familiarity.

Tales of the Black Knight's terrible exploits had terrified Erik as a young child, told to him by kitchen servants or traders who frequented Birkenshire. He had always thought they were stories meant to scare children to bed. The rogue was painted as the lord of a castle, a highwayman, a diabolical adversary to God and men; said to be in unholy concert with the Devil himself. Many a firelit evening his mother's Celtic serving women had woven mystical tales of the wild and uncivilized lands of their birth in the Emerald Isles, full of such creatures as the Black Knight, or worse. Banshees, ghouls, and the open graves of the undead filled the ranks of such a rogue.

But as Erik grew, the Roman ways of his father and of Britain replaced the wild and fantastic creations of his imagination. A Greek by the name of Demetrius taught Erik classical rhetoric and the stoicism of the old Christian monks guided him in the ways of the Scriptures and other sacred literature. By the time he had finished his education he had thought himself, as befitting the scion of a patrician, above these lurid tales of the supernatural.

Yet since losing Merrovaine a week ago, amidst a wildly confusing incident involving a flock of crazed ravens, Erik had begun searching over his shoulder into the shadows more often than he'd care to admit. And under those shadows lay the bloodthirsty legends of his childhood.

Frothy sweat began dotting his horse's flanks as they labored up the darkening hills. Erik patted his steed's solid neck.

"Come on Hadrian. Just a bit further," he urged.

Lightning flashed a jagged streak across the distant sky, closely followed by the resounding boom of thunder. Turbulent clouds broiled and churned to the horizon, the red and orange hues of their bellies diminishing as the sun slipped into the earth. Rain splattered with a tinny thump on his helmet. He laughed at himself for being such a fool to believe the old tales. This—this was real. The knight licked the water from his upper lip. Seeing and touching differentiated the fantastic from reality.

Hadrian slowed his pace as the mucky ground gave way to the slick, broken rock of the hills' crest. Erik didn't push the horse, for it would do no good if Hadrian stumbled and left him with a lame mount this far into strange territory.

The sun had dropped completely out of sight by the time he crested the hills and could look down on the eastern side. A steep slope meandered into the lengthening shadows to the seashore. If Demetrius' geography lessons and his own reckoning of his route were accurate, then the water before him was the Dinbych-y-pysgod, a bay in the Môr Hafren reaching many miles westward from its eastern shore by Gwyr. But he could be wrong; accuracy was often not very important to mapmakers, as Demetrius had often pointed out. Many filled in whole gaps of knowledge from a fabric of imagination and legend.

A scraggly wolf crawled upon a far off rock and began crooning a sorrowful song, dimly heard over the storm, to the deaf hills and the lively waters of the bay. Beyond the wolf, a tall dark shape of fixed angles loomed above an outthrust tongue of rock. Erik tugged on the horse's reins and descended to the foamy beach.

The rain's pattering increased as the storm blossomed into wild ferocity over the land. The knight cantered down the sandy strand, rounded an outcrop of rock, and pulled his horse up short. Here, the shoreline protruded a couple hundred yards further out than elsewhere. Amid the bursts of lightning, the shape he'd glimpsed from the ridge became a fortified manor perched atop a spur of granite in the middle of the extended shore.

It appeared to consist mainly of a curtain wall, built of large logs, that surrounded a strongly built keep that was topped by a single watchtower. A gatehouse in the wall faced the rocky hills backing the beach. Oddly enough, next to the gatehouse was a drawbridge to a causeway that spanned the narrow stretch of sand to the beach that Erik's horse stood upon. Erik wondered at the necessity of an elevated walkway; he could see no tactical advantage to such a construct when there was not even a moat.

Nevertheless, he hoped this was the place he'd searched so long for—the place where the brigands had spirited away their prize.

A small grove of wind-bent trees offered Erik meager shelter against the increasingly hostile elements, the slapping bite of the rain against his face and the sharp billowing wind whistling through the crevices in his helmet. He dismounted and led Hadrian into the trees as a plan formed in his head to enter the keep. He tied the horse to one of the trees and stripped off his weighty equipment, stowing it in the canvas bags strapped to the horse's saddle. Once finished, Erik settled down among the trees to wait, the rain soaking through his cloak, as the hidden stars traced their paths high above the clouds.

Slowly the hours slipped by, until he judged the time to be near midnight. The keep's guards would probably soon be relieved at their posts and at this time they would be the most vulnerable. He took a good length of rope from the saddlebags, knotted a three-pronged scaling hook to its end, slung his spatha over his shoulder, and stuffed his leather gloves into his belt.

In his heart, Erik reckoned some of the untested squires and young knights he trained with might have called his sketchy plan daring. However, over the last few weeks riding with Merrovaine through the wilds, he'd come to realize that heroic acts usually resulted from an overwhelming lack of better options. If this Black Knight fellow proved to be merely a wandering robber lord, as Erik suspected, then by the time he returned to distant Caerleon for help, the robber could be gone. Marianna's life was too precious to king, country and the young knight to leave in the Black Knight's murderous hands any longer. With Merrovaine lost in the deep forest, the plan was decided upon without contest.

He wiped rain from his face as he surveyed the heights of the keep for his next steps, but his mind had already cut a path back through the wilds to an abbey he had seen four or five hours previously down the coast. He reached into his jerkin and pulled out a small ivory crucifix. He closed his eyes, kissed it and mouthed some words for divine help in outrunning the brigands long enough to reach the abbey and dig in behind stout walls.

Driving rain pounded his skin on its mad rush earthward, and for a moment it felt like an invigorating response to a request from the divine. Lightning stormed about the sky like a pagan god's wrath and thunder boomed its gigantic footsteps in the heavenly courts above.

Erik huffed water from his face, clenched his teeth and struck out for the castle.

The strand of beach was thick with clinging sand as he made a dash for the keep. The ground near the hills had seemed solid enough, but he soon found out why the original builder of the keep had seen fit to add the causeway. The beach became softer and more difficult to travel the further out he went toward the fortification. He sank ankle-deep and after many slogging steps nearly couldn't get free.

Fear clutched at his heart as he struggled to pull his foot loose, caught in the open for guards to see. But no faces appeared over the walls and no challenges were called out. Finally, he pulled his foot free and pressed slowly forward. By keeping near to the pylons of the causeway, he reached the spur of rock and clambered up its slope to the base of the wall. The rock sloped steeply upward. He slipped on the slick surface, scraping his hands and knees as he crawled up to and huddled against the huge, smooth logs of the wall.

After a few labored breaths, he stirred to work once more. Soon, any guards on duty above would be replaced by a fresh rotation and his plan would have to wait, risking his exposure if the weather cleared. So, his cold, stiff fingers fumbled at the rope and, with muscle numbing effort, he swung the hook into the air. It struck the battlements with a muted clatter. With a quick pull he tested its perch, and the hook plummeted to the sand.

Erik spat a curse, gathered the rope in for a second try, and lofted the hook back up. This time it caught and held firm. Hand over hand, feet desperately clamping the rope, he climbed up the wall. More than a few times he slipped on the slick cord, swinging precariously, and scrambled to catch himself.

Again the lightning screamed from the torn clouds, the flash illuminating a ferocious face and spreading wings—a carved image set upon the wall to frighten enemies. The climbing hook was wedged beneath the monster's hideous figure; its beaked face surveyed the land below with cold eyes, tears of rain running down its face because the beast was trapped in stone and unable to wreak havoc amongst the helpless folk of the land.

With raw, bleeding fingers, Erik pulled himself over the sharpened spikes of timber comprising the wall. He gave the stone figure a consoling pat as he caught his breath. No guards were visible on the short span of catwalk, and if any were present in the watchtower or gatehouse they were probably huddled around warm hearths with large mugs of steaming drink, sheltered from the downpour. Shaking the drops from his face, Erik reversed the hook on its perch, pulled up the rope, and let it fall into the courtyard. He carefully descended into the swirling mist and cloying darkness.

Though the pouring rain made seeing doubly difficult, the high walls shielded the yard from the whipping wind. The knight slid his cavalry spatha out of its scabbard, the blade's steely ring absorbed by the drumming patter around him. A sharp clatter of steel and wood caught his attention. A flitting shadow faded into the darkness. It *might* have been his imagination, but he knew it wasn't.

He ducked as a blade swished viciously past his head and countered the next attack with a clash of scraping steel. His attacker grunted, surprised by the unexpected parry. The impact reverberated through Erik's stiffened arm.

Erik attacked. His keen blade bit deep, and a moan followed. Before he could strike again, however, rough hands grabbed him from behind, wrestling him to the ground. Damp, foul bodies pressed in close. The sword slipped away as their fists struck again and again, beating his flesh and skull until he felt nothing more.

***

"Wake him!" pierced through the aching fog in his head. Erik tried to respond as someone jerked him upright. Several sharp blows to the face cleared his mind somewhat, and two powerful, ice-cold hands twisted his face upward.

The voice spoke again. "Who sent you?"

"I—I'll not tell the bleeding likes of you," Erik forced out groggily as he struggled to regain his faculties.

One of the hands smashed his face, and blood rolled across his tongue. Erik swayed, but kept his eyes locked steadfastly on the face of his inquisitor. The man was pale, almost sickly grey, and yet his face bore the strong, handsome features of a man in his early thirties. The black armor he wore glistened in the torchlight. His dark, bottomless eyes locked onto Erik's, revealing an intense ferocity fighting the chains of his will. The man knew he was dangerous and restrained himself with powerful effort. Erik had found his legend, the Black Knight, in living flesh.

"Quite an introduction," Erik managed, spitting flecks of blood to the floor as he spoke. "Must be some sport on the wretches living in the hills."

The man raised his bloodied hand for another blow.

"Wait!" cried a woman's voice. A slender form forced its way through the group of brigands that surrounded Erik.

It was Marianna.

"Please, don't hit him again. He's Erik of Birkenshire. From my father's court!" The princess wavered and suddenly buried her face in her hands and wept.

The Black Knight smiled, savoring the pain around him. His roomful of lackeys chuckled as if on cue. The two holding Erik upright twisted his arms painfully.

"A soft lowlander, eh?" the Black Knight sneered. "Come to be a hero—to rescue yon princess, young whelp? Extremely foolish. Take heed in your next life, boy, for this is the fate of the impetuous." He waved a hand to one of his men. "Kill him, Owain."

Erik's instincts responded before he could think; he wrenched an arm free from the brigand holding it, grabbed the wet gloves from his belt, and hurled them to the floor.

"The gauge is cast!" he shouted.

A brigand's hand struck him across the face, staggering him. The Black Knight glanced at the gloves without emotion.

"If you are indeed a knight, as everyone says that you are," Erik hissed through the blood and loosened teeth in his mouth, "then pick them up and accept the challenge to combat!"

The brigands around the room began to mumble to one another, glancing frequently at the Black Knight and Erik, their faces dark.

When the Black Knight replied, his voice was flat.

"The stakes?"

"You should know," Erik said.

Anger suddenly seethed beneath his pale skin. "Insolent dog. The lesson I teach you will do more than destroy your feeble body. It will crush your soul!"

He bent and snatched up the gloves. The bandits roared their approval like a pack of rabid wolves, yammering and jabbering as they grabbed Erik by the front of his tunic and thrust him to his knees, ripping open the woolen fabric. His simple ivory crucifix swung into the light.

The Black Knight groaned and shrank back, the skin around his eyes and mouth yellowing. "Get that off him!"

A brigand snatched the holy symbol off Erik's neck and tossed it into the shadows beyond the torchlight. The Black Knight regained his footing, panting.

"Your paltry God will not—no—can not save you now. Tomorrow at sunset your worthless soul will be forfeit to the Dukes of Hell, and I will slake my thirst with your blood!"

The Black Knight stormed out, shouting orders to his men as he went. A couple of the ruffians laid their dirty hands on Marianna, dragging her away after him. The remaining men cackled with pleasure, grabbing Erik's arms and carrying him out another door.

They traversed a musty hall to a flight of stairs; halfway up he was thrust into a room with a single narrow window looking out onto the sea and the warm golden rays of dawn. The apocalyptic storm had passed with the night.

The brigands clamped rusty manacles around his wrists and, after amusing themselves with some kicks to his stomach and sides, left him. Erik slouched down on the filthy floor in exhaustion and sunk his head between his torn knees. His mind whirled with confused thoughts and adrenaline.

Fitfully, he wondered if he would wake and find himself relieved of the aches and pains, someplace far from this nightmare and the quest. Or, would he wake at all? The thoughts could not keep sleep from stealing upon his weary body, however, and he slipped into a fitful, aching slumber.

"Erik? Erik, wake up." Marianna's voice whispered into his fitful dreams. Erik cracked open his swollen eyes and found her tear-streaked face above him. He sat bolt upright, suddenly alert. She knelt before him, her dark hair pulled back from her slender face and her quivering lips.

"Princess. You're here!"

"Yes, yes. Here, drink this." She pressed a cup to his cracked lips. The water rushed into his throat in a refreshing wave. He gulped it down with painful swallows. When he opened his mouth to form some words of comfort, she placed a cool finger on his bruised lips.

"Say nothing!" she urged. "I had to sneak past the guard to bring you this. Oh, Erik, I'm so sorry. He didn't bring me here for a ransom. He wants a bride, a wife to spend eternity with." Her voice trembled. "You won't believe me, but I'm going to tell you anyway. He's dead. He's dead, and yet he lives. I don't understand how he lives, but he does. Please, don't look at me like that. I'm not mad! He wants me to become like him so that he can have companionship. He's promised not to touch me until I consent, but I don't trust him. I keep thinking he'll do something terrible to make me consent against my will. Sweet Mary, Erik, you of all people must know I don't want him—ever." Fresh tears tracked down her face.

Erik's head throbbed anew as he tried to make sense out of her words, but he managed to get the gist of it. This bastard was trying to scare her into submission with tricks and illusions.

"By St. Michael, what do you mean, he's *dead?*"

"He's alive, but not alive." She shook her head. "He bargained with one of the old gods for the gift of immortality. The Black Knight's half of the pact is . . ." She faltered.

The chain stopped him as he reached out a hand to lift her chin. He tried to wipe the tears from her cheeks but only succeeded in smudging them. "It's all right." His voice sounded brittle "I swear to avenge your honor tonight. I will make him wish he'd not offended my liege and his daughter."

"You need to listen!" Her eyes were wild with fear. "He steals the life-blood from the people surrounding this place to keep the contract."

"Steals it?" he asked.

"He slaughtered my attendants, drank their blood."

"Victorious warriors have been known to drink the blood of the vanquished," Erik answered, yet something in the way she spoke sent shivers up his spine.

"Yes," Marianna looked into his eyes, exposing the depths of her fear. "Yes, they do. But do they lap at it like a dog as it gushes from their torn throats? Tonight, when the sun sets, he'll fight you, Erik. You'll be killed and he'll force me to watch him consume your blood!"

Footsteps fell in the corridor beyond the door.

"Here." She tucked a small bundle into his tunic and fled the room. A moment later the door opened again. An ugly head appeared, the unshaven face glaring. Erik returned his gaze, unconcerned, silently daring the bandit to try something. But the man only spat on the floor and left.

Once the guard had gone, Erik pulled out the object Marianna had slid into his shirt. It was his crucifix, wrapped in her kerchief. Placing the symbol to his lips, Erik whispered, "Please, give me strength, like David of old, dear Lord."

Erik leaned against the wall and closed his eyes, his mind working again and again over what the princess had said and the fear evident in the very fiber of her being. Supernatural powers had always been part of the legends surrounding the Black Knight, and this man had obviously gone to great lengths to convince her that he was one and the same with the tales.

Erik slammed a fist against the wall. No amount of lies would prevent him from cutting the brigand up to break the spell that had been cast upon Marianna.

The sun had barely slipped over the western rim of the earth when the guards came for Erik, hauling him into the dank passages by the yellow light of a guttering torch. They descended a stairwell to a small bedchamber where his armor lay piled in a heap on the floor.

Erik surveyed the room to make sure no one waited hidden behind a tapestry with a knife for his back. The straw mattress on the simple bed was a mess. Small spots of fresh blood dotted the tumbled sheets. He reckoned common robbers didn't have the decency to change them after abusing some poor local girl.

Erik stepped to the table, which bore a small earthen bowl brimming full of clean water. He thrust in his hands and sloshed the cool liquid on his face.

Donning his armor brought confidence coursing back to his weary, aching limbs. Young Birkenshire experienced a warm glow that was not the quiet calm of an experienced veteran, but rather the brashness of a young man who had never yet been bested in combat. Brashness would be tested against the trickster who tormented his captives by playing on their fears of the supernatural and blood. He was determined to put the huckster's head on a pole so Marianna would see the end of the tales.

He hefted his spatha, a long, straight Roman cavalry blade. The sword had been a gift from his father upon coming of age, passed along in their house from the days when the men of the family served as knights in the Roman legions that fortified Albion against the barbarians north of the Wall. As a squire, he'd worked hard to be worthy of the weapon; now it was his, along with an adventure to use it on.

The bishop had consecrated it during Erik's knighting ceremony. As he rubbed the blade with a cloth, he recalled the priest's words when the liturgy was done: "And if nothing else, be brave." Many times since, he'd learned to curse the hollow meanings of the words bravery and honor, as well as the deeds men do to gain them.

The spatha slid tightly into its scabbard. Fully outfitted, Erik pressed the crucifix to his lips, and then looped it around his belt. He tied the princess' kerchief around his arm as a symbol of her favor. When the brigands came to retrieve him, they weren't so bold as before, now facing a warrior prepared for battle.

"Out of my way, you flea-bitten curs!" Erik commanded, pushing one of them aside as he entered the stairwell. They descended in single file to the corridor, where the brigands gathered in a tight cordon around him, directing him to a large double door that squealed defiantly on rusty hinges as hands on the other side pulled the doors wide. Erik stepped through into the clamor of the courtyard beyond.

Smoky torches cast oily shadows onto the craven features of the brigands who ringed the courtyard, giving their faces the cast of death masks—ready for the killing to begin.

At the far end of the courtyard, by the main gate, the Black Knight sat astride a tall ebony charger. The steed's mane shot out in straight black bristles. Its strong neck strained against the reins. Hazy mist billowed from flared nostrils and orange sparks chinked as the beast pawed the flagstones with iron-shod hooves.

The visor of the robber lord's horned helmet hid his face. For an instant, Erik thought there was a flicker of red deep inside, but he shrugged it off, blaming the torchlight. A sword with blackened furniture swung at the Black Knight's side, while on his arm was strapped a shiny black shield bearing a scarlet raven.

"Come, puny Erik," he roared. "Come and pit your arm against your doom!"

"Such insolence for a common murderer!" Erik laughed back humorlessly. "In the name of God and King Mattheus, I'll curb your tongue and avenge this insult to Marianna's honor!"

"Your feeble god won't grant you aid here, nor will your doddering

king be of any help. You'd do better to rely on the prowess of your own arm."

"God will strengthen me. Never fear for *my* safety."

The Black Knight laughed, his mirth as appealing as the festering sores of leprosy. "Good Erik, in death your soul will go screaming to the deepest pits of eternal torment. There you shall experience the exquisite tortures of the Grey God. It's time to face thy wyrd."

Brigands shoved Erik toward his waiting horse. Hadrian was of sturdy cavalry stock, a gift from Erik's father when the knight was but a squire of thirteen summers. He mounted the prancing charger, gripped the reins, and leaned forward as Hadrian strained against the bit.

"We'll see blood tonight," Erik muttered and patted his horse's neck. Erik surveyed the courtyard to gather his bearings and mark the players. A couple of armed brigands dragged a limp Marianna into the courtyard. She slumped between the ruffians, seemingly drugged. Erik swept his eyes past her to the open gate at the Black Knight's back. The brigand chief noticed Erik's attention shift that direction.

"If by chance you should win past me the gate will remain open. I am a man of my word," he said.

Scampering henchmen carried the Black Knight's lance into the yard, a long deadly weapon with a heavy iron-barbed tip. Two other brigands brought the rest of Erik's gear. He slipped his left arm through the straps of the shield as a man pressed the long ash lance into his right hand. No sooner was Erik equipped than the Black Knight's steed reared and charged.

Erik spurred his horse to a gallop, leveling the lance to his adversary's chest. Pounding hooves echoed violently off the court's walls. His lance struck the Black Knight's shield square on the embossed raven, shattering on impact. He leaned into his shield to turn the Black Knight's lance tip as he sped past.

Dropping the remnants of his lance, Erik pulled his sword from its scabbard as he wheeled to face the next attack. The Black Knight's lance struck solidly against his shield, the force of the collision reverberating through his joints and sinew. He swung the spatha to strike, but Hadrian slipped on the flagstones. Erik sliced air as they stumbled.

The Black Knight cruelly pulled his horse's head about for another pass, flecks of blood spattering from the bit.

Erik twisted, shield up, and braced against the stirrups. The crushing impact from the Black Knight's lance tore him from the saddle, bearing him to the ground. He staggered to find his feet.

Through the young warrior's muddled senses the steed's hooves rang off the stones like a smithy's anvils clanging, clanging as rider and mount bore down. The lance punched his shield, hurling him to the ground. Time seemed to swim around him as he struggled to his knees, raising the tattered remnant of the shield once more.

The lance tip shot past, grating with a crunch across his helmet and twisting him to the ground. White sparks flew past his blurry eyes as the metal split and shrieked. Blood flooded his vision; his helmet clattered and rolled away. He knew the Black Knight was toying with him, and rage welled up, pounding against the base of his throat.

As the Black Knight reined his dancing charger in for a final pass, Erik wiped the red from his eyes. His sweaty knuckles flexed on his sword's hilt. The robber raked his spurs cruelly into the horse's flanks, catapulting it into a frenzied gallop. Erik crouched on the balls of his feet.

He barely deflected the lance with the fragmented shield, causing the Black Knight to lean off balance. Then he swung his sword in low, the keen steel slicing through the horse's rear leg, severing the sinews with a snap. The floundering animal crashed to the ground, pitching its rider in a clatter.

Erik stumbled past the writhing animal, sword scraping along the flagstones. The Black Knight lay still. Erik plunged the spatha between the overlapping plates of armor covering his belly. The sword crunched and grated, piercing flesh and bone as it thrust up into the fallen man's abdomen.

Suddenly, the Black Knight's hand grabbed Erik's ankle and sent him sprawling. Before he could regain his feet the Black Knight was on him, gauntleted fingers crushing his throat. Erik fought, but the grip clamped down firm as a hangman's noose, constricting tighter and tighter.

The Black Knight's face pressed close and Erik heard his hungry breath rasping wolfishly, carrying on it the stench of blood and death. The robber's feral red eyes bore into his, stopping Erik's breath in his chest. In the heartbeats that followed, his lungs burned and shrieked for release.

Erik fought to keep his head clear as he fumbled for his dagger, but the pommel was wedged tightly under his collapsed breastplate. He couldn't budge it; the more he tried, the more the pommel buried itself into his ribs. Then the ivory crucifix brushed his gloved fingertips.

With the barest thought, Erik tore the small crucifix loose from his belt and jammed it through the eye-slit of his opponent's helmet and into the soft flesh beneath.

The Black Knight reared back, clawing savagely at his helmet. The helmet's great horns shattered into glistening shards as he bashed them against the ground.

Erik staggered to his feet. Several brigands tried to pull their leader's helmet off, but he drove them away like a furious whirlwind.

The Black Knight howled again, pushed his fingers into his eye-slits, and tore the helmet off with a final chilling scream. The stench of charred flesh pinched Erik's nose. After a moment, The Black Knight pulled the blade from his abdomen and tossed it to Erik. It skipped across the flagstones to his feet.

"Sweet Jesu," Erik groaned.

He picked up the blade and faced his opponent, guts twisted at the sight of the Black Knight's face. His eye socket had been torn into a raw oozing wound and the flesh from his forehead to his cheek had shriveled back from the bone lying beneath. A perverse smile curled his still-handsome lips, exposing a sinister pair of yellowed canine teeth.

The Black Knight plucked the crucifix from his eye, tossing it to the ground, and crushed it beneath his boot. He hauled the black blade from its scabbard, a wicked curved weapon of Eastern origin.

Reality appears to be playing tricks, Erik thought as he warily danced in a predatory circle with his enemy, moving slowly and painfully. His mind whispered that this was nothing more than battle fatigue, even as the Black Knight's movements shimmered and flashed with unreal speed. But his face remained fixed in Erik's vision—face ruined and raw. Yes, that must have been all Erik saw, just a ruined eye.

The young warrior breathed deep to clear his cobweb-filled head, but it was no use; the Black Knight's awful face leered at him, a horrid taunting smile stretched across thin lips. By the Heavens, Erik knew of no explanation for this. He had time to ask for none.

Erik lunged at his opponent, aiming for the throat. The Black Knight turned his blade and cut back. The black steel cut above Erik's ribs and bit flesh. He staggered, sucking air through gritted teeth, but the marauder didn't press his advantage. Instead, he wriggled off a gauntlet, ran his fingers up the bloodied blade, and licked the blood from his hand.

Erik cursed and threw himself into another attack. The spatha blade struck the Black Knight's shoulder solidly, bounced off the darkened plate, and skittered across the ground. The counterattack hammered on Erik's back, sending him sprawling after the loose weapon, but the blade remained out of reach.

Erik rolled over and something jabbed into his back—the broken remains of his lance.

He grabbed a length, bracing himself as the Black Knight yowled like a beast and leapt at him. The stout wooden shaft ground between the plates of his opponent's armor with grim finality. The Black Knight's teeth scraped against Erik's breastplate, foul saliva dribbling on the metal and bubbling up like acid. The lance's tip protruded from his back.

Erik shielded his eyes against a rushing wind that whipped down into the courtyard with hellish fury. Then the wind just stopped.

Erik's body protested as he pushed against the Black Knight's inert carcass and rolled him off. This time he did not rise with a leering grin. He lay still. Some of the brigands moved forward, brandishing weapons, intent on breaking the commitment for freedom. He quickly grabbed his sword and leaped preemptively at them, spilling their blood with relish and driving them away. A cluster of men milled in confusion about Marianna, while others headed for the inside of the keep, probably to loot their leader's wealth.

The young knight from Birkenshire fought to Hadrian's side and mounted. The group contesting over the princess fled from his sword as he spurred to her side, pulled her up into the saddle, and raced for the open gate.

They dashed through the portal onto the wooden causeway. Once on the other end, he turned Hadrian northward and hurtled down the beach. The sound of the crashing ocean roared in concert with Erik's own rushing blood as he made for the safety of the abbey.

Chapter Four

⬯⬯⬯

THE ARCHIVES

ALDONZO, dressed in wildly-colored traveling clothes, clattered into the port town of Loughar at the head of a troop of soldiers and selected members of Mattheus' personal staff. To say that the prince stood out was an understatement, surrounded as he was by martial armor and thick woolen cloaks.

Beyond Loughar, the Môr Hafren glittered like fire in the crimson light of the setting sun. A few miles across the water, the Gwyr peninsula lay along the horizon like a rolling, green mantle, serene and peaceful. The tumultuous noises of town quickly absorbed the hoofbeats of the Aldonzo's escort as the group merged with the crowd of peasants, merchants, and sailors. The soldiers at the head of the expedition shouted themselves hoarse to the throng to clear the way.

After much jostling and swearing, they arrived at a more-or-less comfortable inn that boasted Loughar's most elegant accommodations; not to mention rare wine from southern Gaul and a particularly dry ale from Umbria. Once within, the group disposed of their gear and armor, settling en masse in the inn's common room for much needed refreshment and rest.

There were a few exceptions to the assault on the bar. One was Kien, Master of the Horse, a solid, easygoing man to whom Aldonzo had taken an immediate liking. The discharge of his duties drew him from the table—he proceeded to the bustling docks to hire a crew to man Mattheus' ship.

The other was Weylin, the cartographer. Earlier that day he had surprised Aldonzo when he appeared before the assembling troops outside the gate of the old Roman fort at Caerleon. Scholars of Weylin's renown seldom accompanied expeditions into hostile lands. He had looked disheveled on his tall grey mule, as if he had ridden the entire night to get there from the palace and not slept a wink. Word was that Weylin appeared under a last minute command from the King.

With Weylin came an assortment of maps and written references from which he would prepare a chart for the voyage. Apparently, the previous night had not provided sufficient time to complete the map, and Mattheus wanted to make sure it was ready when the party set sail. Upon arriving at the inn, Weylin requested a separate room and straightaway locked himself inside.

Aldonzo followed the others to the large, rush-floored common room and prepared to avail himself of the fineries of this little backwater town. As the night wore on, his anemic efforts at drinking and merry-making did nothing but illuminate a nagging feeling he had experienced the whole day. Eventually he gave up, excused himself, and stepped out into the cooling night air. Clouds overhead obscured the stars and wind kicked up along the harbor—all signs of a storm blowing in.

He walked the muddy streets aimlessly, trying to put a finger on
the cause of his nervousness. Once he focused his thoughts on it, it
became readily apparent—he didn't want to wait. Frustration ate at
him for sitting still even a single night, now that he had a goal. He was
restless and anxious to do something, anything.

What he wanted the most was get inside Weylin's room to see
what they could expect over the next few days. The old codger had
firmly warned against any interruptions short of the inn burning
down, before he had retreated to his upper chamber and barred the
door.

Then Aldonzo remembered something he'd been told on the trip
to the port, perhaps by Weylin himself. A few miles further down the
road lay the monastery of Llanelli, a place reported to have one of the
most extensive libraries in Britain. The prince stopped and brushed
his crimped locks from his face, his eyes merry with a sudden thought.
If he could not get in to see the maps Weylin slaved over, then maybe
he could see others at the monastery instead. He was so taken with the
idea that he spun on his heel, trotted back to the inn, saddled up his
horse, and rode out on the western road.

Aldonzo followed the young acolyte to a plain door at the end of
the hall. The youth knocked twice, announced Aldonzo, and
departed. The young boy didn't have to look quite so relieved to get
away, in Aldonzo's opinion.

The latch rattled and the door opened to reveal a typical priestly
cell—small and bare. Then his eyes focused on the pale, balding
archivist, squinting eyes glaring from beneath bushy white eyebrows.

70

"What is it, my son?" The tone of voice held none of the cordiality of the greeting.

"Father Guddry? Are you the archivist?"

"Yes, yes I am. What do you want at this hour?"

"Pardon me, Father, I hate to disturb you," Aldonzo said. "And I know it's late, but I was hoping to look at some of your maps, if I may."

"Look at maps? Now?"

"Father, I'll be sailing at dawn to the West, and I was hoping to see some of your maps so that I might get an idea of what is out there."

"Why not just wait until you get there?" the priest asked. "As the Lord said, think not of yourself, but be like the lilies of the field, worrying not about this world's cares."

Aldonzo thought for a moment that he knew why the holy fellows of Llanelli locked up the archivist in a library all day. But he held in a biting retort and instead said, "Well—I was hoping to be a little forewarned. Forewarned is forearmed, you know."

The priest impatiently touched the four points of the cross on his breast and yawned as he gathered his sleeping garments closer about him. "You know prayers come early here? Of course you do. Well, West you say? What maps do you want? Hibernia?"

"No Father. Just the west of Cymru, if you please." Father Guddry shook his head. "Sorry, can't help on that one." He stepped back from the door and it began to close with a creak.

Aldonzo hastily slipped a foot against the door. "Can't help? Why not? I only want to look at some maps. Please, Father."

"I am sorry, but I can't help. I don't care how strong your desire, you cannot see what is not there."

It took a moment for the priest's words to sink in. "You haven't got any maps? You mean you loaned them to someone?"

"No, son, I mean there aren't any. I don't have them in the archives because I've never found any."

"Surely the Romans made some," Aldonzo said.

"Oh, I'm sure of it, lad, but none of them have been left here, or else they have not survived. May I retire now?"

"But there must be some—King Mattheus' mapmaker has some."

"Oh, no he does not," Guddry said with a shake of the head.

"Huh? Are you sure? How—begging your pardon, Father, but how would you know?"

"Because," he said curtly, "when Mattheus appointed Weylin as his new cartographer, Weylin came to us for his his source material. He's had scribes here ever since his first week. If he had a map of the western end of Cymru, the map would have come from here."

Aldonzo narrowed his eyes and glared ever so slightly at the cleric. "Are you sure he couldn't have gotten it from somewhere else?"

"From where?" he replied with a snort. "Londinium? A Saxon town?"

"Not the North, either?" Aldonzo pushed further.

Father Guddry shook his head. "Not on good enough speaking terms with them."

"So there are none, none at all?"

"Now that's what I've been telling you, son. And by the Holy Mother of God, I'd not lie to you, now would I?"

Aldonzo stood in disbelief. "No, no I guess not." He scratched his head. "Well, thank you, Father. I'm sorry for disturbing you."

"That's all right," the priest said, but his eyes spoke differently.

Aldonzo rode slowly back to town, his head bowed, his earlier enthusiasm drained. If Weylin had gotten his maps from this depository, and they claimed to not have any maps of the West, then what sources could the cartographer be drawing from? He puzzled over the question until he found himself back at the weatherworn doors of the inn. He stabled his horse and walked back toward the main building. On the second floor, a lamp burned, flickering in the open window. He supposed it was Weylin's room.

Aldonzo paused, letting out a steamy breath of air through pursed lips. Then he thought he saw a shadow dart out of the window and speed into the sky. He could have sworn he heard flapping wings, too, but scanning the sky, he saw nothing.

He was just too tired from the long day's riding, that was all. Shaking his head, he staggered up to his room and sprawled on the bed. Sleep overcame him in a breath, and he did not dream at all that night.

Chapter Five

THE SIGHT UNSEEN

THE SOUND OF BOOTED HEELS echoed off the misty stone floor, only to die in the enveloping gloom. A tall figure walked steadily in the half-light, straying neither right nor left, focused in direction despite the lack of visible walls. His rustling black cloak swirled and skirted about his ankles, rippling the calm mist that obscured everything beyond his nose. The lead studs on his black jerkin clinked in time to his step.

The man abruptly stopped at an ornate door, almost hidden in the fog. He curled his fingers into a fist and struck the door once, his sweaty palms betraying his unease while his face remained stony and impassive. There was no immediate reply, and he waited in silence. Then the door latch clacked and rattled open and a faint voice cooed from within.

"Enter, Magwyn."

The words slithered to his ears like an adder's deadly hiss. Magwyn shuddered as he entered into the presence of the Grey Prince. Head reverently bowed and hands clasped over his heart, he approached the great black throne that stood on a dais on the far end of the room.

"What is it now, Magwyn?" Each word was barbed.

Magwyn lifted his eyes to those of his lord Arawn, the Grey Lord of the Otherworld and Prince in Annwyn, the Isles of the Dead. The Prince's piercing, steel-colored eyes clamped down on his soul, threatening to twist his frail being in a brutal death grip.

"M'lord, our agents are in place and preparations are nearly complete. The setbacks we suffered should no longer trouble us."

"And there is no Gwydion to take up the sword in defense of the mortals and stay my hand. You have done well this time." Arawn sat back, his thin lips stretched in a mocking smile. He idly toyed with the narrow iron circlet in his wispy gray hair.

"My life is to serve you, m'lord," replied Magwyn with a grateful bow.

"Of course. And your afterlife, as well."

A chill crawled up Magwyn's spine.

"We need to move quickly," Arawn continued. "Beltane is nigh and we must be finished ere dawn. Blaine's stupidity and current condition makes things more difficult, but we cannot afford to fail now, not when we are so close. You do understand this, do you not, Magwyn?"

Magwyn nodded, sweat beading his brow. "Completely, m'lord. I believe the young warrior will prove a capable replacement." He paused and took a deep breath. "It will be as you wish. Will there be anything else?"

"No. Attend to your duties. Leave me."

Magwyn turned on his heel, breathing an imperceptible sigh of relief.

"Wait." The curt command sent a tremor through Magwyn's jaw as he stopped. He twisted back around to face those unyielding eyes, narrowed in suspicion and studying him closely. "What have you not told me?"

Magwyn exhaled very slowly, his own breath chilled. He'd hoped this would not happen.

"M'lord, there is one in the forest . . ."

The look in Arawn's eyes told him everything he needed to know. "But, m'lord, he is of the Old Faith—of the ancient people," Magwyn said quietly, hoping not to incur his master's wrath.

His lord growled, the noise rumbling the floor with its power until it escaped his lips in a mad, rushing howl of incoherent rage. No further words needed to be said. Magwyn bowed.

"Yes, my lord, I shall report when the deed is done."

The prince settled into his throne, pulling shadows closely around him. Magwyn briskly retreated, his heart pounding in his ears when the door snapped closed behind him and he stood once more alone. Alone but for the reverberating of the god's laugh through the thick door. He hurried on his way, the sound burning like a white-hot brand in his mind.

Magwyn navigated long halls for an immeasurable time until he eventually escaped the palace and came to the featureless non-place of Between. Space warped around him. Somewhere in the murky twilight of shifting mist there appeared substantiality, a solidifying of the aether. As Magwyn hurried through the gloom, non-substance swirled around him and slowly revealed the stone walls of a narrow corridor.

No longer illuminated by the eerie glow of the Between, Magwyn was compelled to conjure a burning torch from the dissipating fog.

His pace grew slower, more self-assured, settling into the stride of a man in control of the fates rather than the skulking lackey of a god.

Presently he arrived at a door, not so ornate as the one he had left behind. Magwyn pushed through into a storeroom scattered with dust and cobwebs. Behind him, the door closed, disappearing into the stone. He picked his way among the crates and barrels to another door across the room.

Ascending from the depths of the basements to the fortress proper, Magwyn began encountering the shades and undead that staffed the keep, first a few disheveled rotting guards, then the shambling body-servants, intent on their mindless tasks through monotonous eternities for a demanding master.

The raised dead disturbed him more than the dregs of humanity that were drawn into Blaine's service. They possessed a dull gleam in their glazed eyes that looked like a fleeting remnant of life, anxious for release. At times in the past he had wondered what would happen if their master's power were removed; judging from the chaos that had broken out earlier that evening, Magwyn decided he did not want to be around when that happened.

All stood aside to let him pass. *Good,* he thought, *order is seeping back into the confusion.* He rapped smartly on the door of the master of the castle. There was a muffled acknowledgment, and he entered.

The room was furnished with rich plunder hoarded from the far corners of the world. Brilliant oriental rugs layered the floor, overshadowed by exquisite works of art and sculptures from ancient Syria and Thracia. No one else was visible in the room, but Magwyn knew he was not alone.

He cleared his throat. "M'lord Blaine, I have come from our liege."

A sourceless voice replied, "Yes, castellan, what intelligence do you bring me?"

"I have reassured Lord Arawn that all arrangements are in place, but he urges haste. Tonight is Beltane and we must have her here before dawn."

"Aye. On that count his lordship need not fear. The two of them shall not be difficult to find. But first we must attend to another pressing matter. Wait upon me in the audience chamber in a quarter of an hour."

"But, m'lord, I beg to remind you that there is still much work to be done in the courtyard."

"It can wait, Magwyn. This is far more important."

Magwyn bowed to nothing. "As you wish, m'lord."

⌇

Blaine of Dacia, the rogue and blackguard, lounged on his black iron chair, proudly resplendent in immaculate, shadowy dark armor. Never in life had he possessed such a fine suit; only now, in final death, could he alter his essence beyond the limits of both functionality and expense.

But he did not sit entirely at ease. As a shade, he exerted a great deal of concentration to maintain the shape of a constructed body, and he had only undertaken it so his followers would know he was still in control of the keep. He stood to gain a great deal if his current machinations could be brought to fruition. At the culmination of his plans, he would need every man who could kill.

Blaine shifted in the chair. First there would be a little pleasure before the work.

The door opened and Magwyn entered with Boca, the scraggled cutthroat who commanded Blaine's ruffians, on his heels. The castellan left Boca at the foot of the dais and climbed the steps to Blaine's side.

Boca spoke first. "You summoned me, my lord?"

Blaine nodded once. "You let the boy escape."

"But my lord, we were taken by surprise."

"That is what you are paid for, Boca. To be ready for surprises and to obey orders."

Boca glanced quickly around the room, his meaty fists clenching spasmodically as he groped for the right thing to say. His shoulders slumped. "Yes, m'lord."

"You led him here. You left too many signs on the trail." Blaine's voice was as cold as the wind over a glacier.

"M'lord, surely you don't believe I could do such a thing! I never left a trace, I swear."

"Enough!" Blaine surged to his feet, his shape blurring for a moment as his anger loosened his control over the constructed form. "Do you really think I'm unaware of your midnight messages? I have the mirror you used to contact your accomplice during the night watch. Who was he? What did he pay you? What is the price for your betrayal? Did he promise to save your soul, Boca? Your precious soul?"

Boca clutched at his chest and fell to the floor screaming. He writhed in agony, spittle and blood spurting from his mouth as he bit his tongue. Blaine stepped over him, eyeing him like a raven—his eyes became keen and black with renewed concentration.

"Do you realize what you've done? It's not just me you offended." He knelt, clutched Boca's shoulder, and hissed in his ear. "You've interfered with the plans of the Grey Lord. What do you think he'll do with your useless spirit? Believe me, my misguided friend, he will not be an easy judge to satisfy." Blaine paused, and then his voice took on a softer tone. "But I may yet be able to salvage something from this. I may even be able to save you, in gratitude for your years of faithful service. You're fortunate I no longer hunger for blood in this form."

He stood again and returned to his seat with a snap of his cloak. Propping his chin in his hands, Blaine narrowed his eyes to regard Boca's thrashing, whimpering form. "I can help you, Boca. With the proper incentives, that is." He sat back and threw an arm casually over the back of the chair. "Tell me who you were in contact with. Tell me who betrayed us and I will forgive you your misjudgments."

Slowly Boca's spasms subsided. He laid still, his chest barely moving as his mouth gulped in shallow breaths of air. After a moment he mumbled something, and then fell limp.

"What was that?" Blaine asked, sitting erect.

"I heard it, m'lord," Magwyn answered from where he kneeled at Blaine's elbow. "He said, 'the priest.'"

"The priest?" Blaine repeated. "That's all?" He slumped back.

"That helps," he muttered sarcastically. "Which priest?" He leaned forward again and shrieked, "Boca! That's not enough! Which priest? Which priest was it? Tell me!"

Boca did not move.

Blaine shook his fist at the ceiling. "Gods help us if it was a Christian priest. We'll never find out which among all their wretched droves did this to us."

"If I may, m'lord," Magwyn ventured, "I do not believe it was a Christian priest at all."

"Why not?" Blaine hissed, his form wavering as his control slipped.

"They do not use mirrors to pass their messages."

Blaine's eyes narrowed. "Of course, of course. But that still leaves—wait." He scratched his head, a thoroughly useless gesture in his ghostly form. "But how would he have known, unless . . ."

A satisfied smile spread over his thin lips. "I know who has done this to me, Magwyn, and may Arawn spare his treacherous soul when I am through with him. For a while, anyway." He threw his head back and laughed.

Magwyn did not bother to ask for the name of the unseen enemy, for he had reached the same conclusion. Instead he merely waved a careless hand toward the figure on the floor.

"And what of him?"

Blaine's laughter dwindled to a chuckle. "Yes, what of him? Years of faithful service cannot go unrewarded, eh, Magwyn? Put him in the middens for now." He stood and stepped over Boca as he headed for the door. "At the moment, I have business elsewhere. I must repair the damage he has done." He paused with a hand on the door latch.

"By the way, Magwyn . . . what of the one in the forest?"

Magwyn's face clouded over. "He is to be removed."

Blaine nodded. "I thought as much. When?"

"Soon."

"Better do it now. The last thing we need is another distraction."

"Lord Arawn indicated as much."

"Very well then. I'll take care of it personally." He stepped into the corridor. The guards outside the door hustled into the room to take custody of Boca.

Magwyn waited and followed them back into the empty corridor. Blaine's fabricated form had already dissipated as his shade winged its way northward.

Chapter Six

INTO THE KNIGHT

E'RIK HELD MARIANNA TIGHT as they rode along the twisted path to the rocky beach, the wind blowing stiffly over the cliffs and out to sea. It smelled of an approaching storm bearing more rain. The turbulent gusts of wind provided Erik with some relief, trapped as he was inside his thick garments and armor. He sucked in the crisp air, felt it burn his lungs, and grinned. Fortune remained with the young knight from Birkenshire. But, Fortune was always the most fickle god of the old Romans, and he never paid her much heed.

Yes, Fortune surely smiled, and so would Marianna's father upon her return to court. And how would Mattheus reward the one who delivered his own blood from vicious robbers? The young knight bore a hidden hope.

Erik reined Hadrian to a stop and slid from the saddle.

"Marianna," he whispered as he supported her swaying body, "Princess, are you all right?"

She nodded, her hands covering her face, raven-black hair cascading in a tumble around her ivory shoulders. Deciding to give her a moment to herself, he walked stiffly to the foaming waves and rinsed his face in the stinging surf. He puffed and blew salty water through his bruised mouth, gritting his teeth against the sharp sting.

What did we escape, he wondered. Sharp teeth, a ruined face; it made no sense. Two days before, the princess had spoken of the undead, her face haunted with torment; but her story could have been no more than a tale used to scare her into submission.

The glamour cast by her tale had affected Erik during battle, he was sure of it, and the horror of what he saw was already fading and blurring into a cloud of action and blood. The Black Knight's face remained mostly an outline in his recollection; the only thing he could focus on was the mouthful of teeth, sharp and yellowed, but he began to doubt even seeing them. The rogue could have merely filed them to points to intimidate his enemies in battle.

A tremor worked through Erik's spine at the thought of a file grating across his teeth.

When Erik turned around, Marianna wasn't on the horse. He frantically looked up the beach and breathed in relief. She was walking slowly in the sand, leaving narrow prints behind her, head still down and slender white arms crossed under the curves of her chest. The wet folds of her dress clung in damp linen folds around her ankles. The rest of her features were obscured in the softening starlit shadows.

Erik bent and splashed more water on his face, blowing salty mouthfuls through his aching teeth.

A wild howl breaking from the trees spun him around. An enormous dark shadow was bounding on four feet toward the princess—a great black wolf, probably even the same beast he'd noticed as he rode from the village two days ago. He cursed himself for having let her get so far away. He could not reach her in time to save her.

The wolf rushed through the surf and Marianna turned to face the wild onslaught. But she did not shrink away. She stood up straight, her hand extended as if to a tamed fawn. The wolf slid to a halt, lapped out its long red tongue and licked her fingers. The princess stroked its head with her other hand.

Erik stopped in mid-charge, unsure of what was happening.

"Erik, go away," the princess hissed.

"What?"

"Get on your horse and ride."

"I'll take care of this," he reassured her, raising his sword. "Now move back, very slowly."

"No."

"Marianna, do it!" His voice was firm as he took another step forward, wishing for a good long spear in his hands, rather than just the spatha.

She glared at him.

"You still don't understand, do you?" she asked, raising a finger to her lips.

"You're standing by a wild beast that could tear you to shreds. That I understand. Now move away!"

She waved her hand carelessly at the wolf. Erik breathed in relief that the beast didn't maul her. She was lucky keeping all her fingers, let alone her life. But after a final snort, the wolf trotted back into the trees without uttering another sound.

Erik edged closer, still wary, blade poised. Her smooth face tilted up to his, a faint smile dancing on her full crimson lips. The scent of her tickled his nostrils as he noticed the barest hint of flowers about her. His apprehension ebbed as she ran a finger down his ruined breastplate, a caress as casual as any lover's.

The young knight was intoxicated, a drunkenness he'd experienced once before this past spring when the princess had found means to escape her father's estate in Caerleon to meet him in the nearby woods. Duty and honor then had kept him from draining the cup.

"I'm so sorry, Erik," she whispered, looking up sheepishly.

He slid his arm around her in a gesture of reassurance.

"Let's get to the abbey," Erik said more gruffly than he intended. Catching himself, he added with a grin, "You gave me a start, you know, m'lady."

"Do we have to go now?" she said, gathering her skirt about her smooth thighs and skipping into the sea foam—almost as if she were prancing on top of the waves. With the water rushing wildly about her, she was a dream, far more tempting than the nymphs who'd tried to lure Odysseus over the side of his ship and into their dangerous arms.

"Come, this is folly," he said, walking back to Hadrian. Erik needed to clear his head, to shake off the thoughts and desires that would complicate his task.

"Oh Erik," she laughed, kicking a leg up. Water splashed, sparkling in the starlight. "I've been cooped up in that dirty old fort too long. Can't we have a little fun before I'm re-caged with some wrinkled old nuns? That is your plan, isn't it?"

Grabbing Hadrian's reins, the knight strode back to the edge of the sea.

"You're going to catch cold." He pulled a wool cloak from the saddlebags. "Here, put this around you," he said.

The icy water chilled his feet and sent goose bumps up his back. Erik wrapped the princess in the cloak's folds. She snuggled closer, her arms instantly around his neck. Her flesh pressed firmly against him.

"Now look, we've got to push on." He tried avoiding the scent in her hair.

"I remember," she whispered and rested her head on his chest, "the day you were presented at father's court for knighting. Don't you?"

"Yes."

"I thought to myself, what a brash young man. But Erik," she looked up at him, her eyes piercing deep into his, "I was drawn to you, that day when I first met you." Her lips, her face, the scent in her hair; she was closer than the young knight thought ever possible. "Why did you leave, that day in the woods?" she asked.

He pushed away and began leading his steed down the beach, kicking the toe of his boots at the soggy sand. *She should understand why I fled without it being spoken,* he thought. *Who can fall in love with the king's daughter?*

Certainly not the son of a retired soldier, lately raised from the ranks of the minor nobility. Even though she was betrothed to a fop, the Visigoth's house represented an important alliance on the continent, and Erik knew this. Such a power overshadowed the tales of his own family's distant past; a past barely remembered by members of his house, let alone by the High King. Surely the alliance

Mattheus sought was worth more than an odd mixture of family lore and love.

Erik stopped and pulled a long, deep breath through his teeth.

"Look, Marianna," he said. "We've got to reach the abbey before those brigands sniff out our trail. It's but a few hours away. When we get there, we'll talk. I promise."

He was only buying time before facing the inevitable. He knew if he returned her safely, ensuring a successful alliance between Caerleon and Septimania, his family would benefit. His father had labored too many years, fought in too many battles to have the family once again represented at court, for him to spoil it with youthful lusts. If he took her for himself, his family would be burdened with the disgrace. It would be the ultimate betrayal of his father.

Keep telling yourself this and maybe you'll believe it, his tired mind repeated over and over.

"Princess, look," Erik continued, "everything in the past couple of days has happened too fast. I'm sure there will be plenty of time to straighten things out later. First, let's get as far from here as possible. Agreed?"

Such an opportunity as this would probably never come again, but he didn't for a moment consider himself cavalier enough to take advantage of Marianna's distraught state. He put his hands around the princess' waist to help her into the saddle. The young knight's cheeks burned when she tilted her head back and pressed her cool lips firmly against his. Her mouth tasted sweet, the freshness of spring past, stripping him of resolve and chasing honor's logic from his mind.

They tumbled to the sand.

Marianna's lips flooded his face with soft caresses that were cool against his scrapes and bruises. She had been the reason he wanted to be at court, the reason he had insisted on following the quest. Even if she were to be Aldonzo's one day, she could be his tonight.

He returned her affection with a passion that had been chained since he first laid eyes on her—a consuming passion, a burning wildfire that would soon leave his soul in smoldering ashes.

The armor's buckles frustrated her nimble fingers. She answered his chuckle with a reproachful jab.

"The least you could do is help," she laughed.

"Help?" he grinned, wincing when his lip cracked. Erik's abused body promised to be a reminder of the previous night's ordeal for some time to come. "This was your idea, remember?"

"All mine?" She arched an eyebrow.

They laughed together.

Gone was the sound of the foaming sea washing against the broken beach; gone were the questions of his battle with the Black Knight; gone were the aches. The monastery was close enough, he concluded. They could spare a little time.

Marianna's breath tickled his ear, followed by her moist tongue tracing the lobe with an occasional nibble. Shivers prickled down his spine as she moved down the back of his neck to leave a soft kiss on his shoulder. He took her face in his hands, pulling her mouth to his.

Erik's tongue suddenly swept across something sharp. A foul wisp of breath choked his lungs, but Marianna's fair arms swept him back to that somehow still sweet mouth, all the while drawing his body into the heat radiating from her smooth pale thighs. She could only taste of honey, Erik mused, as they rolled onto his traveling blanket, their hearts racing through the limitations of flesh towards each other.

Erik cried out as cold teeth suddenly tore deep into his neck, his lust ripped away. He struggled to push Marianna away from him, but her fingers clawed his back and her writhing body tightened on him like a winged scavenger swooping down and clenching a hare.

The pain spread as hoary winter frost through Erik's already tired limbs and into his constricting lungs. Sticky blood flowed down his back and into his throat. He forced Marianna's name through the blood that foamed on his lips.

The bitter darkness began stealing his soul.

⧉

"It has begun," said the voice in the void, through the eternal blackness. "The age of ploughshares is over. Now is the time to take up the sword and bleed the land."

Mists swirled about him. Erik's feet were not touching the ground, for there was no ground, and he had no body.

A man took shape from the shadows, a tall grey man in a long black cloak. Atop his head sat a narrow band of spiked iron—a crown. He reached out to what was Erik and the young knight trembled, a trembling deeper than anything he'd experienced in the flesh. This man clenched in his fingers the essence of Erik's eternal soul.

"For more than a millennium I have waited for one such as you, Erik of Birkenshire, one who would taste death with such pleasure and do the bidding of my every word. Here you are, stripped to the barest of threads, ready to be used for what you are."

Visions fluttered into Erik's view, filling his mind with their clamoring and confusion. Life, death, the thousands of years Albion had known bloodshed and war. Celts, Romans, Picts, Gauls, and countless other peoples marched to bleed themselves like fatted cattle over the sacrificial stone that was this war-torn land.

Events reeled around him in a mad jumble and then swept on past. Fire spewed from the earth, and legions of monstrous deformities spilled from the cavernous bowels of the nether worlds, waging war, with a man wielding a wicked squirming two-handed sword at their head. Great numbers fell in his path. Gouts of red-hot insects spewed from flying beasts that swooped down in a buzzing roar, causing the inhabitants of the land to run to crumbling buildings for cover.

As the man fought closer, Erik was stunned to see that man was him. He swept the sword as a scythe, blood flowing in steaming streams from beneath his booted feet. The sky darkened and the earth shook with the savage blowing of brazen horns and the booming of leather drums.

Erik shrank back from the scene, but the grey man held him in place and laughed.

The vision dissipated like a thin morning fog. He stood alone in a familiar landscape, emerging from the rent fabric of dark dreams. After a moment, he raised his hands, examined them, flexed his fingers, and then wiped sleep from his eyes.

Erik looked around and knew where he was, standing in the fair green fields of Birkenshire. The small stream flowing from the highlands gurgled in the distance as it wound its way through his father's bottomland. Erik's lungs hungrily sucked in a deep breath, smelling the fresh scents of the open fields and pasture. He had been dreaming, and he was still home.

He began to walk, relishing the fresh sun, the sky, the trees; everything his senses could consume. As he climbed the knoll overlooking his family's villa, Erik noticed a faint curl of smoke rising and he smiled.

Father must be anticipating guests, he thought—the smell of roasting calf tantalized his nostrils and his stomach mumbled its pleasure in response. It seemed like months since he'd tasted fresh roast meat, smothered in honey, crisp and brown. His mouth watered as he topped the hill.

The villa lay smoldering, black and charred.

Erik hurled himself down the hill to the ruins, his arms pumping. Soot, ash, charred beams—destruction all around. Tears washed his face as he plunged into the ruins, calling for his family.

"Father!" He rubbed a filthy hand across his face to keep sweat from stinging his eyes. The sun rapidly fell over the horizon, yet Erik continued scrounging through the rooms. The remnants of his parent's room lay in the north end of the main corridor, collapsed from its second floor position into a blackened heap of jutting, broken beams and brick. His fingers desperately sifted through the soot, finding only a blackened dagger. He dropped amid the broken beams and walls, covering himself in soot and ash.

Erik didn't move for a long time.

When the moon rose, the young knight looked up at the stars. Sniffling like a child would change nothing. But he wondered where had he been. Had he been close by when this happened? Rolling the blackened sooty dagger around in his fingers, he closed his eyes. A plan of action was needed. He blocked all emotions and stoically plotted the next move, but a crack and clatter broke his concentration. He sat up.

Shadows in the moonlight tramped through the burned-out villa. Erik crouched and held the dagger tight. He could only think they were the same marauders who robbed his family of their lives. There was no place to hide, so the stand had to be made here, on the ruin of his ancestral home.

"There he is!" one of the figures called hoarsely. The voice was a young woman's, familiar.

"Julia?" he called back. "Praise be, it's me, Erik!" He picked through the collapsed rooms, expecting warm arms and welcome embraces from his father and sister.

The welcome home disintegrated into blackened, blistered bone and sinew. Monstrous flesh wrapped around him. Voices screeched accusingly in his ears.

"A roast calf, you thought? It was our very flesh!"

"Where were you when they raped—"

"Burned alive—"

"You know I didn't abandon you, I wouldn't!" he pleaded with them.

His father's face was melted from heat, spewing black spittle in Erik's eyes.

"You're no offspring of mine," he rasped. "To speak of your own kin's burning flesh as a feast! A feast of your own flesh and blood! You bring disgrace upon this house!"

Burned, blackened hands grabbed his arms, wrestling Erik to the ground as his sister cackled in delight. Cruel sharp fingers ripped at his exposed throat. He struggled and fought, but the battle was lost. With each heartbeat, his blood pulsed out to the charred earth beneath him.

Swirling mists again enveloped Erik as his essence winged back to the grey man, who laughed as his hands still strangled Erik's soul.

"Time has passed for you, Erik. You now walk the Valley of Immortals, and with the word of covenant you shall be mine."

"What have you done with my family?" the knight groaned. "What have you done to Marianna?" He was no longer sure what had been an illusion—his days with Merrovaine and rescue of the princess, or his dead family?

But *he* knew all things, this man of shadows. Through the chaos his steely grey eyes pierced Erik. Beyond any doubt, the youth knew that the grey man had an infinite number of answers locked behind those eyes.

"First the covenant, and then all will be revealed. First, covenant to take the blood and become my arm, my eyes, my very being on this earth of man. Swear by the blood of thine own throat, that this will be so. Become mine."

"Who are you?"

"Ah, you know me already," he replied.

"The one banished from the earth by Gywdion, son of Math, during pagan times—before the coming of our savior, Christ," Erik said.

The grey man winced, but his cold gaze remained fixed on him. All around them burst the sounds of war, banners dipping in mists and blood. The din of battle crashed as mighty breakers against Albion's rocky coast, back and forth, a flooding press of bodies and armor. The moaning of the wounded droned subtly beneath the mounting crescendo of warring arms.

"I have given you the power to wrest ultimate control from the chaos shrouded over the world; power to crush all beneath your heel. Pwyll never realized such might as flows through your veins. Swear the covenant to me—swear that which will make all of this complete." His grip tightened and Erik felt the force of that will crowding in on his own.

"Swear to me!"

Erik fell into blackness as his existence slipped away like the embers of a dying fire.

The sound of battle abruptly stopped.

Marianna appeared, crowned, with her raven-black hair bound regally about her face. Her slender frame was clothed in a gown of the finest crimson silk, laced with exquisite gold.

"Erik," she whispered, "Erik, this is what it means to live with the gods. This is true power."

"What? What do you mean?" Erik asked, confused.

A large scepter of finely wrought gold appeared in her delicate hand. A ruby bird topped it, its wings spread open as if to take flight—the same symbol that had been embossed upon the Black Knight's shield.

"This," the princess continued, "this is the power promised to you if you will but take up the covenant, if you will become one with the Honored Dead."

"Marianna . . ."

"Think of it Erik. You could take me now. We can be together for an eternity, not just until my father separates us for the convenience of an alliance. You'd not have to ask for my hand. You'll never be a beggar in your own land."

"Marianna, no." He looked to the dark figure. "What have you done to her?"

"I've taken the covenant, Erik," she pleaded. "You must too! Please."

Her regal features softened into the girlish countenance Erik had fallen in love with. Yet he was repulsed—repulsed by the unveiling of what lay behind the visage.

"No. No, Marianna! There must be another way."

"Erik!" she shrieked. Crimson blood ran from the corner of her mouth, sparkling like a dark southern wine. "I've tasted blood; I'm damned in the covenant without you!" The blood blackened against her ivory flesh.

Agony consumed Erik, for somewhere deep within him the reality lit like a beacon flame—he had just lain with the princess, and their coupling was linked with the grave.

The grey man spoke again. "Take the covenant of blood, become one with life and death!"

A clot of congealing blood choked Erik as he tried to scream. Even as he struggled to clear his throat and mouth, his body tingled from head to toe, each sensation acute and vibrant. He groped through the gritty sand of the beach until his hands found his coarse blanket and the coolness of his discarded armor.

The darkness was still except for Marianna's quiet sobbing. Beyond her, beyond the immediate noises, beyond normal perception, there was more. There was a heartbeat close by, hot and rapid. Wild blood coursed through constricting veins, carrying energy through a creature's body. Each beat, each movement, every breath was as if his own. The wolf had returned.

He spat black clots to the sand while Marianna huddled beneath a tree, her head tucked between her knees, her slender body convulsing. Every brush against the tree, each rustle of fabric, Erik heard them all, all but the beat of her heart.

"Marianna," he rasped. "What—"

"Damn you, Erik," she snapped. "Couldn't you have just agreed? For once, couldn't you think of someone else?"

"What are you talking about?"

The princess faced him coldly, her eyes sparkling with a vicious fever. Her teeth were suddenly yellowed and old, but only for an instant.

"Either way I was going to be taken, no matter what happened. I thought to spare myself of an eternity with that wretched Blaine, or worse. That's why I brought you your crucifix—I couldn't bear this alone. Not for an eternity. Can't you see that, Erik? I took the covenant, and now *you* can partake of limitless life. I swore, Erik—"

She raised her hands as if examining them for the first time, still sticky warm, still red with his blood. Erik noticed with a start a wound on her neck that was now bleeding.

"I swore by the blood flowing from my own wounds!" she cried. "Erik, what have I done? What have I become? I'm so hungry, so terribly hungry and I don't know what to do!"

Erik turned away. So that was it. He had been an unwitting rube, used for some profane ritual for the benefit of this pagan god.

Marianna had been taken to be a consort for this Blaine, this Black Knight, and she had taken matters into her own hands.

Somehow he should have felt honored, in a perverse sort of way; but this girl, a princess of royal blood, had spilled his blood to satisfy her need for companionship in a decision she had made alone. Even now his stomach knotted, twisting with desire, a horrifying rapacious yearning. He wanted to be glutted, to sink his teeth into warm flesh, to drink from beating pools of life.

"It's no longer about just you. It's your father's kingdom. It's me," he whispered. Marianna rose and came to him, her soft footfalls brushing the sand. He didn't look at her—he continued staring at the sea as it lapped lazily against the beach. "You planned this, didn't you?"

"I don't know," she said, close to his ear, the stink of his blood still on her breath. "Not at first. Not until I faced the death. Not until it was clear I would face eternity like . . . this. That was when you came along, and I realized I had an alternative." Her eyes suddenly flashed. "You didn't take the covenant, but the seeds are still sown. There may yet be time for us."

"Seeds?" he spat, grabbing her and wrestling her down. He wrenched her face to his. "Seeds? I didn't ask for this! I came to take you home!"

"Home?" The princess's voice was cold, flat. "I can't go home now, not like this. I should have just let them kill you, Erik, or killed you myself. I was foolish to think we would end up together—that you would accept the covenant to be with me. Damn it, Erik, I thought you loved me!"

His body shook with rage, a wrath black and vile. Sensations careened through confused senses, muddling up his thoughts, dreams and reality blurring into his consciousness.

"Can you feel it? Can you feel it, Erik?" Marianna hissed in his ear. "Power! I've given you the chance for real power, undying power that will keep us whole and together for an eternity. It's more than either of us could ever imagine in a mortal life. Take it, it's yours—take it."

Her sweet voice soothed him to lower his guard and open his mind, seductively leading him to the edge of the precipice. Slowly the fibers of his soul entwined like hands around a drug-laced goblet, a goblet full to the brim. Yet the hunger gnawing his gut told him that somehow it was an empty drink.

"No." Erik forced through pursed lips. "No, not this way."

He breathed harder now, the exertion sapping his strength as he fought the deadly lure.

"No, I won't do this, Marianna. I love you, but not this way!"

When he opened his eyes, the power of the glamour was gone. Erik saw Marianna's still-lovely face had been altered—her pale eyes were shot through with blood and her creamy skin was drawn tight over the bones of her face. She was no longer the frightened maid who had sobbed in his cell.

"I wanted company for the eternities, someone that I could love. Someone I *do* love." She continued, calm and cold. "I want to be young. Remain young. Don't you look at me like that, Erik Aurelianus. I know what you're thinking. You think I had that at court. I could have married Aldonzo." She mouthed the Goth's name with a sneer. "I could have taken a lover—you perhaps. Raised a family with no cares, the best of all worlds, and had the endless ministrations of the best handmaidens to hold off the appearance of age for as long as the treasury would put up with the expense.

"But I want my own life. I wanted my own life forever, and even the best formulas and dyes can only cover the wrinkles, the aching limbs and the drifting wits. When death comes, it steals everything. Then what? Off to the same god that beckons me now regardless. Now I don't need to worry about the long slow decay." She threw up her arms and smiled. "I'm free, and if it costs the lives of a few beggars, who cares?"

His mind was clear, impossibly alert, trying to resolve what all this meant. Eternal youth came at a bloody price. She had become a hunting beast, enslaved to the search of more blood, her elixir of youth. Stabbing pains twisted Erik's guts. He groaned and doubled over, clutching desperately at his stomach. Marianna grabbed his writhing hand firmly in her own. Her fingers were cool and solid, as they pressed tight and without passion.

"This wasn't supposed to happen. Not like this." She turned his face so that his eyes met hers. "I could rip your head off your damnable shoulders for ruining this moment, Erik. Why can't you just accept things and take the covenant?"

"Because he's too damn noble for his own good," said a new voice, a familiar voice.

A nearby rumbled growl marked the return of the grey wolf, the beast but a few yards away. Its hackles were raised and it snarled. Marianna silenced it with a wave of her hand. Then she turned to face a small form shrouded in darkness and shadow.

"Do you still think he loves you enough to follow you in death? Such a romantic notion," it continued. "Can you convince him?"

Erik squinted at the figure, his uncanny vision piercing the veil that surrounded him. "Who are you?" he asked.

The creature turned its misshapen head, a diminutive ghoul from the darkest pits of any nightmare. Its eyes locked onto his from under a ragged hood, malevolent and throbbing with hunger like an inexorable pulse.

The creature spoke. "Know this, Erik of Birkenshire. Know this and fear. Beyond death is the Power. It is in you. You are death and you are life, so take the covenant now." Each word was calculated and precise, but as the creature spoke, the intelligence that dwelt behind the facade of its eyes dwindled until it faded completely.

"What the hell?" Erik asked, crawling to his knees for a better look.

"Just a courier," Marianna replied curtly. "You've heard what he came to say, and now his job's done. The flesh can now be cast aside and the essence returned."

"That's all?"

"Yes!" she snapped. "Now, since you've seen the power of the dead, tell me, will you take the covenant?" Her voice demanded action, but Erik ignored her and looked at the creature again.

"Who are you? Where have you come from?"

The creature shook its head slowly. "Me?" The voice was different, shrill and nervous. Erik could now see puffy grey flesh beneath the black cowl, flesh covered with all manner of pockmarks and swollen lumps. Small beady eyes darted back and forth.

"Yes, you. Who are you?"

"Enough of this!" Marianna's voice rose, but Erik ignored her.

"Speak!" he ordered the creature.

"Me?" the creature said. "I am voice. Yes, voice of dead. I am finished. Send me home."

Before Erik could respond, Marianna leaped on the pathetic thing, her clawed hands and wicked teeth ripping it to shreds. Erik leapt into the confusion, trying to separate them. But there was blood already on her hands and on her breath. He staggered away, his shirt spattered in black blood, and clenched his eyes shut to drive out the hunger.

"Are you finished?" He risked a glance.

She daintily wiped her lips on the creature's shredded clothing. Her eyes were wild. A snarl fouled her curved mouth.

"What has happened here changes nothing," Erik continued. "We still need to reach the abbey. Damn you, Marianna. I don't understand everything, but you're coming with me, or I'll wrestle you down and drive a splinter through your heart like I did that—what was his name? Blaine?"

She winced.

"You're a naive fool, Erik. Do you think you could kill him that easily? To think I wanted to spend an eternity with such a milk-sucking weakling! I can't even stand the sight of your face any longer. Just leave me alone. I can take care of myself."

She stood and straightened her skirts.

No matter what sort of creature she had become, she was still a princess of Caerleon and daughter of his liege lord, and Erik loved her. The disgust in his breast deflated, no longer able to sustain itself in light of his feelings.

Yet, as he struggled with his next course of action, the sickness continued to spread through his veins. To the king, his life or death held no great importance, but his daughter's was of the utmost priority and responsibility. Regardless of the cost to his person— to his soul—the princess had to be returned to Mattheus. The weight of judgment would then fall on the king, and by his own word he would decide what to do with his daughter.

Erik straightened, drew the spatha from its scabbard and pressed the tip of the blade to Marianna's throat. "You're coming with me," he said. "Or do I have to take off your head?"

Even to him his words sounded silly, as if he were repeating the tales related to him by his childhood tutor. Demetrius had shared legends from his Greek homeland about the vrykolakas, or the Higher Dead—all the while teaching him the rational thought of Aristotle, Plato and Augustine. Now the paradox sounded almost humorous. Demetrius would probably have had something profoundly stoic to say about all this, Erik thought.

"You are going to the abbey, where you will remain until I get in touch with your father."

The princess hissed as her slender hand reached over to the wolf, which still lay nearby. Her fingers toyed with the thick fur on the beast's shoulders. Erik was surprised it did not rise up against him. Of all things, it seemed tired. Marianna glanced at the tip of his blade at her throat.

"And if I don't," she asked softly, "do you think you've the strength to impale me on a spit, or cut off my head as a present for my father? I don't see that in you, Erik. No, past the hunger, I don't see that in you." Then, cryptically, she added, "Yet." She continued, almost warmly, "So much change has happened to my body since yesterday. I feel it. I'm more connected to everything. Do you feel it too?"

"You will go with me to the abbey."

The princess raised an eyebrow.

Erik slumped, senses spinning, suddenly caught in the weariness and the glamour cast by the princess. He found himself on the ground. The words came unbidden to his lips as they wormed through his fogged mind. I accept the covenant—I accept . . .

From deep within him, in the place where no logic or reason held ground, instinct rallied. In that place, he found he would rather die than live under this curse.

Erik groaned as he fought the onrushing curtain of blackness by force of will alone, drawn from previously untapped reserves of strength that had been a secret, even to him. He desperately clawed back from the precipice, not knowing what he was doing, or how. But he rebelled against her will with the warrior's instinct to survive. Erik's mind burst and then thrust outward—unshackled, blazing like the sun at high twelve.

Gasping for air, Erik rolled to his knees and came up in an unsteady crouch, ready to face another attack.

But there was no threat. The wolf was gone. The princess slumped limply, her eyes open and very vacant as they regarded the infinite heavens. Erik swayed to his feet and approached her.

She didn't move.

Erik passed a hand before her face, which elicited no response.

The attempted witchery had somehow rebounded back upon her. He took her limp hand in his, and she followed him to his horse without a struggle. His limbs ached as he lifted her onto the saddle and then pulled himself up behind her. The stiffness came not from aches and pains of the living, he thought, but rather the slow creep of rigor mortis. The knight from Birkenshire spurred Hadrian on, eager to outrun the gathering storm.

⸙

The waning moon rose as they reached the Abbey of St. Bride. Its walls stood shrouded in the silvery moonlit mist, obscured from view by heavy-laden, dew-covered branches. As they drew closer, its shape took form, huddled in the shelter of the cliff-ringed cove.

The abbey consisted of a group of buildings clustered around a tiny chapel, the whole surrounded by a low stone wall, hard against the cliffs. The wall had been constructed between rough-hewn giant standing stones that projected upward like thick thumbs—the menhirs of the Tylwyth Teg, who had worshipped here long ago.

Hadrian reluctantly cut a track up the sharp slope from the beach, working through the wind-whipped yew trees to a solid wooden gate bound in black iron. Erik reined the steed to a halt and slid down, alighting softly. Damp moss blanketed the earth, lending to the impression that the abbey was one with its surroundings.

He beat at the gate with a clenched fist, but heard no report from within. After a moment he pulled out a dagger and pounded the hilt against the iron bands with a resonating clang. Satisfied with the resulting sounds of scurrying, Erik sheathed the weapon and waited.

In the back of his mind he sensed the movement of the sun below the earth's rim, or at least believed he did. It would be morning soon, and he was compelled to have the princess secured behind these walls. For all Erik knew, the hordes of hell or the Black Knight's vagabond lackeys could be sniffing out his trail, even nipping at their heels.

105

A scraping sound immediately drew Erik's attention to a small window that opened in the door. The two eyes peering out were wide, straining to take in all they could through the restricted space.

"Who do you be and what do you want here, brother?" a woman's voice asked timidly.

"I'm Erik of Birkenshire, here with a charge from the High King to your abbess. Open this gate in the name of Mattheus of Gwent."

"None can come in, but by the name of God," she whispered.

"Sweet Jesu. Alright, in the name of the Lord God of all Heaven, please allow us refuge."

Erik was exhausted. He tried to think of something else as his head throbbed—he could sense the woman's body behind the door. Her heart beat in rhythm with the ache in his head.

The nun closed the window, and after a few moments the door squealed open, protesting the admission of the diseased creatures—Albion's unholy lepers. Erik staggered through and hoped the wrath of God would not topple the walls down upon them.

The nun ran away.

For a frantic moment he wondered if she had read the hunger in his eyes—in his breaths. Safety for the princess and refuge was all he required. Only the church could provide haven and solace from the strange events that had ensnared them.

The nun returned at a trot across the grass from the chapel. With her was another woman.

Erik's strength ebbed from his limbs, and he collapsed.

Chapter Seven

THE ABBEY

THE DORMITORY within the Abbey of St. Bride lay deep inside the great crack that split the cliff face behind the community grounds. The fissure itself served as a rough hallway reaching a hundred feet into the layered rock, into which the individual cells had been hewn. The entrance towered twenty feet over Abbess Gwendolyn's head, moss-covered and wet with a shimmering trickle that ran from the rock above. She hurried with the group of nuns carrying the young knight into one of the isolated cells.

Her destination, however, was a few doors away.

By the time Gwendolyn reached the room to which Marianna had been taken, a gaggle of nuns had already relieved the princess of her dusty, tattered gown and had begun to bathe her lethargic limbs. The elderly Sister Mavis directed a handful of younger girls in a husky baritone as they sponged the snow skinned girl down, while others brought in clean bedding for the cell's straw pallet.

The abbess pulled grey-haired Mavis aside to a quiet corner. "How does she look?" the abbess asked.

"Not sure, ma'am. She feels rather cold . . . much *too* cold. She is quite senseless, though sometimes she moans and tries to resist."

"Has she awakened at all?"

"No, nary a flicker of her eyelids. It's easier this way though."

Gwendolyn nodded in agreement. "I'm going to see Branwyn and ask him to carry word to Mattheus. I'll take Erina and Meleri with me after matins."

"But abbess, the May festival is tomorrow. You *must* be here for that! How will we finish the arrangements?"

Gwendolyn put a reassuring hand on Mavis' shoulder.

"We should be back before the festival begins. Besides, most of the preparations are already done. I know these things aren't our usual fare, but I have little choice. Mattheus must know his daughter is here."

"I'll do my best," Mavis answered, raising her eyes heavenward and mouthing a silent prayer.

"Don't worry so. Everything will be alright," Gwendolyn smiled.

She glanced at Marianna again. Mattheus remained a good, dear friend, and for his sake she was relieved the princess had been found at last—and alive, at that. But the circumstances of her deliverance disturbed Sister Mavis. Something about the young man who'd brought the princess to them troubled her as well. She shook herself, clearing thoughts of darkness from her mind, and tried to take heart in Marianna's return.

"Abbess, are you alright?"

"Hmm? What? Oh, I'm sorry sister. I forgot . . . forgot myself for a moment. No, thank you, I'm fine." But something nagged the back of her mind. "Sister Mavis."

"Yes, abbess?"

"Take extra precautions around Marianna's room." Gwendolyn rubbed the end of her nose with her finger then said softly, "I want this room sealed when she sleeps. And have someone watch the cell at all times. You understand, don't you?"

Mavis nodded.

"I want no one in or out without our knowing," the abbess continued. "The robbers who took her could be on her trail, and it behooves us to take an extra dose of caution."

"Yes ma'am," Mavis said. "But we've no arms. No weapons."

"And hopefully we won't need any. You'd best get on with your duties. May the Mother of God watch over you."

She turned from the room, mouthing a silent prayer for all their safety. Before she could get all the way across the courtyard, however, an eruption of screams and wails chilled her blood, staining the night air with alarm.

Gwendolyn turned back, bursting through the cell door she had just left, her habit a flurry of disorder. Inside, she found the room in chaos.

Marianna writhed on the bed, howling terribly, drowning out the frantic cries of the nuns trying to hold her down. Sister Mavis loomed above the confusion, calling out orders in the firm and unflappable voice of a field general over the din of battle. Without another thought, Gwendolyn snatched off her cloak, wound it into a crude rope and plunged into the tangled fray.

A few tense moments later, Marianna lay bound to the bed, shrieking like a muffled, captured banshee. Sister Mavis' strong hands took the girl's head and held it still as Gwendolyn took a bowl of herb broth from another sister then forced the brew through Marianna's lips and teeth.

The princess choked and gagged, spitting broth onto the sheets, and then let loose a shriek that rang off the walls in high-pitched peals. She cried out once more, though not as desperately, and slowly trailed off into an injured whine. Finally, she lay motionless. Her eyes slid closed. The sisters breathed out their tension as they saw she was not about to burst into another fit.

Gwendolyn and Mavis exchanged nervous glances.

"She's in worse condition than we first supposed, ma'am," Mavis puffed. Her cheeks glowed red from the exertion.

Gwendolyn nodded and drew a shaky breath. "Indeed." She looked at the princess' contorted face that still showed traces of an inner struggle. "I cannot wait any longer. The sooner Mattheus can get here, the better for all of us. Sister Erina," she motioned to a smallish sister of about twenty. "Gather your things and fetch Sister Meleri."

Erina nodded obediently and slipped out.

"Now Mavis," continued the abbess, "take care until our return. You will have someone watch her through the night?"

"Yes ma'am. Sister Wynne will care for her."

"Very well then. I must be off. God be with you, sisters."

Time passes slowly in the still dark of the night.

Sister Wynne sat on a stool by Marianna's motionless form, musing quietly to herself beneath the single light of a guttering oil lamp. The other sisters had long since retired to their pallets. Soon, she reckoned, the predawn would lighten the sky. Not long ago, the princess' features had finally eased, losing the taut pain that had held her in its grip through most of the night. Her breathing lost its ragged edge and was now as regular and gentle as a newborn babe's.

Sister Wynne stifled a yawn with the back of her hand. She would be relieved when dawn finally arrived and her watch ended. She looked down wistfully at Marianna, sleeping so peacefully now, and wondered for a brief moment what it would be like to be such a beautiful princess. She genuflected, her fingers lingering before her eyes, and asked for forgiveness for the stray thought. There had been too much excitement for the young nun. Her eyelids began to droop.

Something scratched at the door.

Wynne's eyes snapped open as the regular rise and fall of Marianna's breast faltered. With a sigh, then a yawn, the princess' eyes fluttered open as if she had just awakened from a nap.

Sister Wynne forgot about the noise on the other side of the door.

"M'lady, you're awake at last," she said.

Marianna's eyes darted about the room for a moment, at the bare walls, the simple table, chair, and washstand.

"Who . . . who are you?" she asked.

"My name is Wynne—Sister Wynne, of the Abbey of St. Bride."

"Abbey? St. Bride?"

"Yes, m'lady. A young knight brought you to us this very evening. Oh, my dear, we worried so about you."

"A knight. A knight?" Marianna's eyes cleared as she looked at Sister Wynne. "Do you mean Erik?"

"Well, yes—I believe he said that was his name."

"Where is he? Is he still here?"

"He's just down the hall. He collapsed at the front gate and had to be carried to his bed."

"How is he now?"

"Still unconscious, as far as I know. He's in a terrible state, m'lady. The wounds are just horrible. The abbess fears he may die."

"Die?" Marianna's voice echoed the word. She went limp on the pallet, seeming to shrink into herself, trying to hide from some hurt. A faint whisper escaped her lips, so dulcet that Sister Wynne could barely make out the name, "Erik."

Marianna rolled her eyes up and noticed the bindings that still secured her to the bedposts.

"What?" She tugged at them experimentally. "What are these? What means this? I am a princess of the blood."

"Oh—I'm so sorry," Wynn said deferentially. "You tossed about so much that we feared you could fall from the bed and hurt yourself . . ." Her voice trailed off, for it was obvious Marianna had stopped listening. Her face was blank, emotionless. Sister Wynne reached out a hand to her shoulder, but Marianna flinched away.

"M'lady, how do you feel? Are you all right? Here, let me untie those for you."

"I feel so dizzy, so cold." She shivered slightly, and Sister Wynne left the ties alone to pull the covers up further. The princess twisted her body to avoid the nun's touch.

There was another scratch at the door. Sister Wynne crossed the room to place an ear against the rough wood and listen. Breathing labored on the other side, the panting of an animal.

"Some wild beast must have broken into the abbey," she said glancing over her shoulder at the bed. It was empty. The bindings dangled from the bedposts.

"Holy Mother of . . ." she began, and then noticed Marianna standing by the far wall, her arms folded across her chest and her head bowed in a tousle of raven black. "Oh, my dear lady, you startled me," she breathed in relief. She genuflected briskly. "How did you—"

Marianna waved a hand, dismissing her confusion. "It's but a simple trick easily learned from a court buffoon, sister."

"A trick? But how did you get loose?"

"You know, sister," said Marianna, her expression cold, "it's not proper to ask a magician to reveal the inner workings of a trick."

"Magician, or parlor trick?" Sister Wynne shook her head, trying to clear her head. "No matter."

She wondered at the change in the girl who only a moment ago had appeared exhausted and confused. Wynne wanted to fetch Sister Mavis, but with a beast in the halls, her feet remained rooted to the floor. The beast, yes, that was a real concern, not this apparent sleight of hand.

"I think some creature from the forest got through the abbey's outer walls," she said. "Not to worry, it won't be able to get through the door."

"A beast?" One of Marianna's dark eyebrows arched, but she appeared to lose interest after a moment. She strolled about the room and ran her fingers over the table, the walls, and the few other furnishings. Sister Wynne's eyes followed her every move.

"This is an old place, isn't it?" the princess asked suddenly.

The question took Wynne by surprise.

"Well, I've only been here a year. But I've been told that the abbey was built on the order of the previous abbess, a holy woman from the continent who wished to escape the world and lead a life of contemplation. So it couldn't be more than thirty or so years old."

"No, no. I don't mean the abbey. I mean the place. The entire grounds." The princess gestured expansively. "The standing stones incorporated in the outside wall. They were there before the abbey, weren't they?"

"The in the outer wall? I have no idea, m'lady," the nun said.

"Yes, they were, sister," Marianna stated matter-of-factly. "This ground was sacred long before the Judean God encroached upon Albion's shores. They were old when my ancestors arrived in their longboats and first rode across the land in their fierce chariots." Sister Wynne felt a flutter of uneasiness stir in her chest. She felt like the princess was toying with her, asking questions just to hold the nun's ignorance up to ridicule.

"Did you hear me, sister?"

With a start Wynne realized Marianna had continued speaking.

"What? I'm sorry m'lady . . . I was listening for more noise from that animal."

She bowed her head, deciding to be careful until the other sisters drove the beast off and relieved her. *Say as little as possible,* she thought, *and save yourself from fickle royal retribution.*

"I said," the princess continued. "Do you know to whom the stones surrounding the abbey were dedicated?"

Wynne shook her head.

"Honestly, m'lady, I don't see—"

"Then you don't know." A thin smile played Marianna's lips.

"One of the Old Gods, I guess," Sister Wynne said.

"Yes, of course. But which one?" Marianna pressed.

"Saints preserve us, I don't know," Sister Wynne said trying to restrain her exacerbation. "But I believe that you know."

"You believe? You should." Marianna took a step closer to the nun. "What else do you believe, sister? Do you believe that by building a Christian edifice over another god's sacred ground that you can supplant his power? Is that what you believe?"

Sister Wynne's heart ached in her chest at the direction the princess' questions were taking. Murky shadows being tugged from the past made her uncomfortable, and the spider webs in her mind became stickier and more tangled. Wynne had never wondered about the past, but now it appeared to be encroaching unbidden into her world.

"My lady," Sister Wynne countered with an even voice. "This ground has been sanctified in the name of our Lord and Savior that the faithful might devote their lives to continuing the devotions of St. Bride the Wanderer. As far as I know, there have been no priests of the Old Faith here since before the time of the Romans. They were driven off or killed. So the deity of this place must surely have lost interest in it by now."

"Silly girl," Marianna spoke as if to a child, even though she and Wynne were close to the same age. "There are things in the world beyond the reckonings of ignorant scholars and misguided saints. Do you think that all power in this world rests with the Church alone?"

The princess stretched out a slender ivory hand to Wynne, her fingertips beckoning.

"Come with me," she whispered.

Sister Wynne eyed the proffered hand, confused. Yet she wondered what lay beneath the princess' apparent madness. She genuflected, whispering a wordless prayer to Holy Mary, and touched the girl's extended hand.

In a roar of shattering hinges and brutish animal force, the door flew open. Marianna snatched hold of the nun's wrist, and Sister Wynne shrieked in dismay. A huge wolfish creature bounded into the room, broad-muscled under its bristly black hide, its mouth full of dripping yellowed fangs as long as Sister Wynne's forearm. The beast snarled and snapped its mouth open, blanketing the room in a diseased stink.

Wynne struggled in Marianna's grip, but the princess' fingers clamped down like manacles, fingers so cold that Wynne felt her skin burn.

"And what of this abbey, dear sister? Do you think its power will prove potent throughout all eternity? Or will someone come in a distant year and cast it down to erect another edifice? Does another deity await its time to rule?"

Marianna smiled again, this time her mouth was filled with cruel and wicked teeth.

"We must depart."

The beast glanced over its shoulder into the corridor.

Wynne's mind raced for answers, but she was hopelessly confused.

Marianna pressed Wynne toward the door, past the panting creature. The nun gathered her strength as she stepped through the portal into . . .

Nothing.

Beyond the doorway, a black void yawned before her, shapeless and so intensely dark that it bared open Wynne's soul with its terrible blind magnificence. A wind howled from nowhere, carrying with it a fetid stench that choked her lungs. She scrambled to regain the doorway, to gain footing in the cell, but found herself forced out by the princess.

They were not at St. Bride anymore.

They stood alone on a barren wasteland of iron-grey rock that stretched in all directions as far as the eye could see. Gone were the abbey, the cliffs, and the sheltered cove. A uniformly dismal sky stretched overhead, the same color as the rock, but shot through with strange colors like a mad painter's palette. A vicious wind clawed at Wynne's humble garments and flung grains of stinging grit into her eyes. The wind echoed with the wavering, distant wails of unseen voices.

Wynne looked up into the face of Marianna transformed.

The simple clothes supplied by the sisters at St. Bride were gone. In their place, a scarlet tunic draped her sculpted body and her legs were sheathed in breeches of jet-black leather with scarlet boots pulled up to her knees. A sword hung at her side, a common river stone adorning its darkened hilt. Her raven black hair was looped into a single braid over her shoulder. The princess laughed, a heartless, hollow noise, and swept her hand across the bleak landscape; a landscape that went on as far as a teary eye could see.

"What do you believe now, sister?" she shouted gleefully above the wind. "Where's your God's power? Call upon Him, if you can!"

Sister Wynne clutched her small crucifix, pressed it to her lips and frantically prayed in the confines of her mind, all the while trying to shut out Marianna's howling laughter, the haunting wind, and the sharp bite of flying grit against her cheeks.

Father, please. God, Lord Jesus, deliver my soul.

"Go ahead and pray, girl," Marianna shrieked. "Pray all you want! But don't pray to God. He can't help you here!"

The infernal wind, the voices crying in her head, the blasted rock, it all overwhelmed Wynne. Tears streamed down her face and she clung to her cross as if it were a shield.

"Sister Wynne, recently of the Abbey of St. Bride," Marianna yelled at the top of her lungs in harmony with the mounting gale. "I'll show you what to believe in!"

Wynne peered up through watery eyes to see the princess unlacing her tunic. The wind tore it open and exposed a black tattoo on her left breast—a star surrounded by a bird of sickly gray. Wynne cried out with a start. It had not been there earlier that night.

"I believe in *this* power! This power will stand alone when all others are driven from the earth!" The wind whipped to a frenzy, and Marianna's form hazed behind a cloud of airborne dust. Her voice rose over the tempest. "God cannot aid you here, Sister. Look upon your new master!"

Marianna's arm pointed at something beyond Wynne's shoulder.

"Arawn, Lord of Annwyn and master of your soul!"

Wynne turned slowly, her muscles responding as if she were submerged in water, her throat constricted so that she could not breathe. She fumbled with her crucifix to protect herself from the approaching beast. It emerged, huge, manlike, but distinctly familiar, through the distorting dust. She heard the growl of the creature that had tumbled through the cell's door, and the sound chilled her blood.

It came closer; she could sense intense power pulsating from its ravenous form. She frantically thrust out her crucifix, praying again as the creature took the last few steps to stand before her. She screamed, and all her thoughts became a blur of horror. It reached out to her— and she vanished.

Chapter Eight

THE ROAD

THELWYN walked easier now that his feet trod the road. The Romans might have been overbearing bureaucrats and military machines, but at least they'd known how to build a highway—smooth, interlocked stones that had already seen over two hundred years of traffic—foot, hooved and wheeled—and would likely see a thousand more. He glanced up at the sun that even now rode high and noticed that he was making much better time than yesterday, when he'd spent most of the day tromping through the rain-muddied wood along the rugged slopes of the Cambrian Mountains. The smooth paving stones and dry path gave him a much-appreciated chance to shake off his boots.

All the day and into the evening, he probed ahead with wide-ranging senses that extended for miles in every direction. But the clouded results of those probes brought him frustration rather than understanding. As the stars emerged, dotting the sky opposite the falling sun, he finally decided to give his Sight a rest and channel his energy into keeping up his pace.

He drove his weary legs on into the descending darkness. Broken clouds obscured the stars and he lifted his face to sniff the moist air. Rain tonight. He would need shelter soon. He'd already passed the abandoned Roman gold mines at Dolau Cothi and any possible refuge in that place.

There was a disturbance in the winds—faint, yet still far away. Thelwyn gathered his strength and threw out mental probes again. Whatever it was, it moved rapidly. After a few moments, he recognized it as the very thing he was hunting. It was coming directly from the southwest, behind him. He had passed his goal. He did not waste any time questioning doubting his senses—it knew he was here. He readied his faculties for defense.

The Cambrian foothills lay far behind. Ahead, to the left, jutted the peaks of the Epynt, while to the right the bulk of the Black Mountain loomed against the clouds. Between them lay only the open, bleak moors.

Thelwyn searched his memory. He knew this place, there had to be—yes . . . there was an old Roman fort nearby. But it was not his intention to use the actual edifice and its indefensible stretches of crumbling wall. After all, he was but a single old man. Much more important were the two circles of stones next to the fort, left behind by a people far older than the Romans. Power was power, and in a pinch he could tap into whatever residual energy remained. He picked up his pace, his senses shooting out far around him. With luck he would get there with time to spare.

A quarter hour later, Thelwyn stopped at the edge of a ragged ditch, gasping for air. On his left, the fort covered the top of a low rise; two concentric series of earthworks and a crumbling barracks were visible just beyond the gate. Directly ahead of him stood the stones. He paused only long enough to collect his breath and then pushed on across the open ground, alert for any movement.

His acute senses recoiled from the incoming presence, much closer now. It shadowed him as he walked, jogged, and then finally ran the last few dozen paces to the stones. It drew closer and closer, like a panting wolf closing for the final kill—and then he was in.

He leaned back against one of the cool, grey stones and worked his mind to slow his breathing and calm his body. It had his scent. Cold sweat broke across Thelwyn's forehead. Scent? Why would it have his *scent*?

Thelwyn continued clearing his mind as he pulled things from his pack. He stood and placed his hands, palms flat, against the stones, probing them, reaching out and tying together the wisps of power that flowed through them to refill his depleted reserves. He lowered his hands, power crackling in his fingertips, leaving the sharp sting of ozone in his nostrils. Then he turned to face the road. In a burst of shadow, the presence darted from behind the fort's crumbling walls, the wind whipping up in its wake and lightning flashing silently in the distant sky. It skidded to a halt a few paces away on seeing the power in his hands. He raised his staff as the shifting apparition launched itself into combat.

Thelwyn deftly wove strands of power by tapping the ley lines that converged on the stones, his body attuned as no human of this mortal age could bear. His skin tingled and his eyes glowed with an ethereal light as the shadow pounced upon him, a swirl of chaotic blackness that clawed with constructed teeth and talons, shredding Thelwyn's cloak and threatening his flesh.

Energy rushed through his body to his staff, concentrating the flow of power as Thelwyn blocked the creature's multiple mental attacks. Light crackled around him, flittering sparks at first, and then flashes and ribbons of energy surging from the staff in a shattering burst of lightning. The shadow shrieked as the bolts of light tore back its darkness, exposing the foul spirit within to Thelwyn's elemental assault.

The creature gathered its wits and lashed out, a sharp talon striking Thelwyn on the arm. Blood spattered and the staff nearly fell from his numb fingers. He staggered beneath the crush of light in his body as he desperately shut down the flow from the potent ley lines that continued to pulse energy through the hub of stones around him. As he shielded his eyes with the back of his hand, a figure coalesced from the swirling chaos that his attacker had become, a form that shifted and wavered as the entity fought for control of its own shape.

Dropping the staff, Thelwyn knelt and gathered dirt into a shaking hand. His attacker was pulling itself together; razor talons emerged once more from its chaotic shape. The cloud rushed at him, rending his cloak, his rough spun shirt, and opening his shoulder.

Thelwyn's vision blurred as he focused on the power. Energy crackled through his hand and charged the dirt and pebbles he held. They shimmered with energy as he scattered them into the wind.

A shriek shredded the air. Particles of dust and loam clogged his mouth and nostrils as the creature's talons drove through his wards. Then a flash of light blinded his eyes for a brief moment, leaving bright flares in his vision. The attack ended with the final discharge of his spell, and his enemy spiraled into the void.

Thelwyn sank to the ground, blood running down his arm and dripping from his fingertips.

Chapter Nine

KNIGHTFALL

V OICES CREPT into the tiny cell, stirring Erik from a nightmare-haunted sleep—a fitful slumber full of rampaging beasts, fangs that dripped steaming spittle, and frothing oceans of blood. Time blurred as he tried to pull together faded memories that ended abruptly after reaching the abbey. He pushed up on an elbow and looked about the room, a simple monk's cell with no more furnishings than a crudely shaped wooden cross and the pallet of straw upon which he lay. Clearly, he was still at the abbey.

He rolled over, peering through the shadows and wondering if the events of the previous night had been real. The answer lay beneath the thick linen bandages wrapped around his neck. He sat up and slid back against the wall. The cold, damp stone jarred him fully awake.

His mind mulled the question of what had happened to him. Had he become a creature like the blackguard he fought the night before Every fiber of him cried out against that conclusion. Suddenly the faces of his mother and father swam into his mind. Such a fate for their only son would break their hearts. What dishonor had he brought on his family? What curse?

He rubbed his eyes and thought of his father, a man of honor who acted upon what he believed to be right, regardless of the consequences. Fortunately, the proper things to do had not brought ruin to him or his family, as they had to Oedipus, or Cicero. Or had they? The vision of his family, charred in the ruins of their home remained fixed and vivid in his memory. Some dream-spun demon intended to cause them harm and to blame him for their horrible fate.

Erik rose and brushed some loose straw from his torn jerkin. An earthen bowl of water sat near the door. He reached to splash the liquid on his face, but his hands froze, the joints locked instinctively. An intense fear seized Erik's breast, stopping up his lungs in mid-breath. He clutched his hands together and then forced them into the basin, splashing the cool drops onto his face and neck.

His heart felt shredded by the time he finally managed to rinse the grime from his cold skin. The tension flowed out of his body when he finally stepped back and wiped his face dry. Fear of water could be a manifestation of the damnable curse, he suddenly realized.

Am I still the person I was last night, he wondered, *or some phantasmal aberration on a path of destruction and insatiable lust?*

The more he examined the situation, the more his refusal of the Grey God's power appeared utterly hopeless.

Yet this might also be the key, if there could be such a thing, to unraveling the predicament. As the source of the scourge, the Grey God might also be in possession of the cure. Unwittingly, the young knight may have cut off this option when he refused the Grey God's covenant. Yet in his heart he knew he couldn't do otherwise. It was not in him to become a brigand parasite that bled weary night travelers.

He wondered if the Grey Man would renew his offer—for eventually, the secret to making and un-making the hunters of night could slip. Ultimately, the Grey Man became the central figure in this tragedy, for it was driven by his desire to overthrow the very throne of God and all the hosts of heaven. Or, at the very least, the ancient deity intended to carve away part of the Christian realm for himself, the part that was most deeply rooted in his past. Ancient Albion, island of the Mighty, had once been torn apart by games played by the fickle elder gods and their people, the Tuathe de Daanan.

Erik opened the cell door to a babble of merry voices. The corridor was washed with the warm, soft glow of daylight—not bright, but enough to hurt his eyes, forcing him to shrink into the shadows that hugged tenaciously to the corners of the hallway. More from sound than vision, he knew some sort of celebration was underway. He caught a glimpse of a pole, swirling flower garlands, and running children.

May Day was in full swing.

Erik kept to the shadows, wondering where he could find Marianna; she was his first concern. Only she knew exactly who this Grey Man was and what he might be up to.

Erik opened the first door he came to. The room beyond was empty. He tried the next. Empty as well. The third was locked. He rattled the latch and then noticed a shard of iron on the floor. He picked it up. Straightening, he rapped quietly on the door. There was no answer.

At the end of the hallway, two figures appeared, silhouetted against the sunlight—one short and slightly plump, and the other tall and thin. Erik slumped against the door as they approached.

"This is the man who delivered her to you?" one of them, a priest, asked as he brushed at the mud spattered along the hem of his robe.

"Yes, Father Bryce," the woman said. "This is Sir Erik." She then spoke to the young knight. "I'm glad to see you are finally awake."

"What's going on here?" Erik asked.

The dour-faced priest looked at the door and traced his spidery fingers along some deeply etched marks in the frame. It looked as if some large beast had clawed it. The hinges had been repaired with large-headed nails in a makeshift manner.

"What happened?" Erik pressed again.

The priest stepped forward, pointing to the ruined door.

"While you've been recovering, we've had quite a time containing the princess," he said, dour.

"Containing?" Erik bristled. "What in hell's name?"

"Please, my boy, not in God's house," whispered the woman.

"Further defiling a holy place doesn't matter much now," muttered the priest as he opened the door with a creaking squeal of protest from the ruined hinges. He pushed it wide open and waved a hand. The room was dark, but Erik could see nevertheless. The cell was empty, except for a mussed-up bed and what looked like a course grey habit in the middle of the floor.

"What went on here?"

The priest shrugged with forced casualness. The nun's face, on the other hand, paled dramatically.

"We don't know," she whispered. "We left her in the care of one of our sisters. The door and room were blessed and sealed. Before matins, the sounds of some awful creature prowling through the abbey woke us. I thought it some wild dog scrounging about for scraps. But then the howling and scratching began. Sister Rawyn believes it was the same beast that wounded you on the road. We found the door torn open and both Marianna and poor sister Wynne gone."

The woman began to cry, nervously genuflecting.

Erik moved into the room. Other than the coverings on the bed, the room showed no sign of a struggle. He crumpled down on the pallet, his strength failing him.

Marianna was gone? This seemed to reaffirm the notion that little could be done to fight the events tumbling him along like a pebble in a flood-swollen river. Gone?

Along with the princess went any hope of finding out more about this deathly affliction or keeping her from further harm. There could be no escape, no way out of this trap.

He looked up at the two figures in the doorway. The man's face demanded answers that the young knight did not have. Tear-streaked and puffy-eyed, the woman's countenance wanted only the reassurance that Sister Wynne was safe—and that he also could not give.

The priest broke the awkward silence. "What were the circumstances surrounding your arrival with the princess?"

Father Bryce's abrasiveness grated on Erik's patience. The abbess seemed to feel the same way, her brown eyes glaring at his back.

When Erik didn't answer, the priest shrugged. "Shall we go in now?"

"Yes—yes, of course." The abbess waved her hand at him.

Father Bryce stepped carefully into the chamber, as if the floor were covered with shards of glass and his feet were bare. He genuflected, then bent and picked up the habit from the floor. He buried his nose in it, sniffing like a bloodhound, and then handed the garment to Sister Gwendolyn. He examined the walls and floors, pausing at cracks, strands of hair, tufts of straw, and linen threads.

"I don't understand," Erik said to the abbess. "You mean to tell me that this beast snuck in, ripped that door right off its hinges, and spirited two women out again?"

The abbess looked him in the eye—but fear haunted that look. "I don't know. Truly, I don't."

"Of course you don't," sneered Father Bryce. "That's because the witchcraft and dark-magicks are so potent. The beast broke in—possibly. But it did not carry them out."

"What do you mean? Of course it carried them out, didn't it?" Erik asked.

"Did it?" he said. "The nuns saw no creature when came running in response to the noise and screaming. No one exited the room."

Erik looked over the room again. There were no other exits. Now that he was more aware of what happened, he noticed a strange sensation that jangled his outlook of reality, a faint tingling of his nerves that told him powerful forces had operated in this room.

But what mattered to him was that Marianna was gone. Gone, and he didn't know where she had been spirited to, nor how to follow her. Without her aid, he doubted he could find the Grey One, let alone convince the ancient deity to offer him a second chance to strike a deal.

"Sir Erik, are you alright?" the abbess asked. "You must still be weak. You were in a terrible state last night. Perhaps you should return to your room."

"No," Erik said, warding her off. "I just felt dizzy for a moment. I'm really quite all right."

Father Bryce paid no heed to them, absorbed in inspecting and sniffing every last inch of the chamber. He paused, looking at Erik for a moment. The young knight felt an agitated discomfort at the holy man's stare, but the priest suddenly shrugged.

"The beast was summoned here by some arcane call. It entered the hallowed confines and broke the seal on the door. Then with the nuns in a state of uproar, dark sorcery was invoked to escape." He paused and took a breath. "The question is," he hissed through his teeth, "who summoned it—the princess herself, or the nun who watched over her?"

The rosy color of the abbess' cheeks drained as she caught his meaning.

"Don't be ridiculous!" she snapped. "Sweet mother of God, all know the princess to be as noble and pure as anyone born to the royal blood! And Sister Wynne—I cannot allow such an accusation to be entertained. How could you imagine such a thing?"

"May I remind the abbess," Father Bryce's voice was as smooth and as cold as a windswept snow bank, "it was *you* who asked for me. I am merely tapping the skills for which you called upon me."

"Yes, Father Bryce," the abbess responded, still fuming. "I shall keep that in mind."

"Not to worry," he said, turning to Erik. "Now, I ask you again, Sir Erik, what were the circumstances surrounding your discovery of the princess?"

"I didn't just wander around the woods and find her, if that's what you mean. Merrovaine and I spent weeks tracking her. The trail led to a lair of brigands and cutthroats."

"I mean no disrespect to your efforts. Was there anything unusual about these brigands?"

Of course there was, Erik thought as the memory of the Dark Knight standing with a sword through his belly came to mind. However, he didn't want to give the priest the pleasure of hearing the tale. "No, there was nothing unusual about them. They slaughtered the princess' retinue and took her hostage," Erik lied.

"Humph. Nothing, eh?" Father Bryce returned his attention to the room, his arms folded across his chest.

"And what of the beast that attacked you on the road? Might it have been the same beast which broke open the room?"

"I hardly think a mad beast, whatever it was, would sneak into the compound undetected. The one I saw nearly peeled me out of my breastplate," Erik said, letting the priest assume the attacker had been two-legged. "It would have been hard to miss."

"Hmmm. There are forces at work here," Father Bryce said with the self-importance of a Roman senator, returning his gaze to Erik. "It's difficult for me to sift everything out, especially with so much vain arrogance between me and the truth." He glanced at the abbess. "And hostility," he added. "It clouds the aether. I shall require some time alone to meditate. Please leave me now and make sure I am not disturbed. I shall seek you out, sister, when I have an answer for you."

With that said, he turned and plopped on the bed, arms folded and eyes closed. The abbess nervously waved Erik out of the room. She followed, closing the door behind them.

"Where in all of Christendom did you find such a pompous old—pardon me sister—*arse?*"

"I must apologize for him, Sir Erik, but he is the best there is between here and the Eternal City," the abbess said, blushing. "He's from Caerfyrddin and we've had some dealings with him in the past, though even those incidents had been kept to an understandable minimum. Why do you ask?"

"M'lady, I don't question your motives for recruiting his services, but rather ask if he can really be trusted. Caerfyrddin is not wholly disposed to Mattheus, and he may have other allegiances that could cloud his judgments."

Gwendolyn raised a brow. "You have a point."

"Sister," Erik hesitated to ask the question, "are you sure witchcraft's involved in this?"

She genuflected and whispered, "As sure as I can be. There's no other way out. God help me. There's no other way."

They walked together toward the entrance of the abbey's cells. The afternoon sun painfully illuminated the cave's cold stone walls.

"When we found they were gone," the abbess continued, "we didn't waste any time deliberating. We sent some of our order out to look for traces outside the wall and dispatched others immediately to bring back Father Bryce. Needless to say, we found no clues to their whereabouts. Now that Father Bryce is here, we may gain some insight, if we can put up with him that long."

Erik stopped her short of walking full into the sunlight. The glare was bright, causing his head to pound with a hellish pulse. He raised a hand over his eyes and stepped back into the shadows.

"Is something the matter, sir?"

"No, no, sister. I'm just still a little dizzy and need to catch my breath before we continue. Does the High King know about this yet?" His mind suddenly conjured visions of Mattheus riding madly to exact vengeance on the careless unfortunate who had found his daughter and then lost her again.

"No, not yet." she said. "We only sent word this morning that she'd been found. Our messenger won't reach the King until tomorrow evening at the earliest. Now that she's gone, we need to find her again before Mattheus arrives."

The young knight drew himself up, taking a deep breath, and stepped forward to her side to continue their stroll in the sunlight.

Searing pain blasted through Erik's body like a hot iron, obliterating all his thoughts. He clutched his head as he fell to the ground and stifled a cry of pain. Through his watering eyes, Sister Gwendolyn's face swam into view, distorted like the rippling reflection on a pond. Her lips moved, the words filtering through his agony in shattered fragments.

"Erik . . . What's wrong? Mother of God. Can you . . . ?"

He struggled to respond, but could not force out words as he continued writhing on the floor. The abbess shouted for aid. After a moment, urgent hands grabbed at Erik's belt and legs and pulled him back into the caves.

As unexpectedly as it had struck, the pain was gone. Erik went limp, panting heavily. A woman's face appeared in his vision, a pretty face framed in a plain habit.

"I think we can carry him back, now that he's not thrashing about so much. Thank God," Sister Gwendolyn said behind him, where she held his arms.

Erik wiped the tears from his eyes with a shaky hand as his head ceased throbbing. Tentatively, he allowed his legs to take his weight.

"Please sisters, allow me to stand."

He braced against the wall for a moment.

"What happened?" the abbess asked as she caught her breath, brushing strands of brown hair back under her habit.

"I don't know. I honestly don't know."

"I think you'd better return to your cell for a while and rest. You've suffered many ills and aren't fully recovered. Sister Laudine, please take Sir Erik back to his chamber. I'll return later to make sure you're resting comfortably."

The abbess left him with the pretty young devotee, who led him back to his room. She lowered her eyes when he looked at her, shrouding them beneath very long lashes. A lock of golden hair tickled her cheek, and she quickly tucked it back under her habit. Erik thanked her as she helped him lay down on the straw mattress and pulled a coarse woolen blanket up to his chest. The distracted knight barely noticed the blush in her cheeks as she darted from the room with a promise to return and make sure all was as it should be.

Erik lay on the bed, staring up at the rough-hewn ceiling. He raised a hand before his eyes and bent each joint in his fingers, amazed that all the pain was gone and control of his limbs had returned so completely. No trace of the convulsions remained—no lingering after-effects as there should have been.

They had only been walking along. Maybe he really did need to rest, Erik concluded. He *had* taken quite the battering the night before.

His mind drifted to the more important task—Marianna was gone, but to where?

The Grey One. Clearly, he had taken her. Had she gone willingly? Marianna's room showed no sign of a real struggle, but that meant little. There was no clue in her behavior the past few days, either. Her moods ranged from seductive to distant and from friendly to aloof. Confused. Yes, she had appeared very confused last night, but what had happened in the meantime?

She may have given in completely, or she may not have. Erik closed his eyes and tried to imagine Marianna standing before her new master, defiant and fighting for what she had lost. As he dozed off, he thought it a foregone conclusion that Father Bryce would find no answers, either.

Only Marianna held the answers.

Only Marianna . . .

Erik jolted awake. The horror of his dream dissipated as he smelled hot soup and saw Sister Laudine set a bowl next to the washbasin. When her eyes met his, she blushed and smiled.

"Good afternoon, sir," she said with a slight curtsy. "Are you feeling better?"

Erik sat up, stiff. "Yes, a little, thank you."

"Would you care for something to eat?" she asked, her voice melodic. She picked up the bowl, the aroma tantalizing. But when she lowered the soup to his eye level, he was repulsed. The broth looked like blood, deep and red.

"No, no thank you," Erik said gruffly. "Maybe you could just leave it on the table and I'll eat later."

"As you wish," she whispered, poorly masking her disappointment with a smile. She put the soup aside and returned to sit on the edge of the bed, her eyes still lowered. She laid a cool hand on his brow.

"Why, there *is* a heat within you . . . but your flesh feels chilled. This is a strange fever, indeed."

"Indeed it is," Erik mused, half to himself.

"Let me get a cloth to cool you." Sister Laudine rose and reached for the washbasin.

"No!" Erik said firmly and clutched at her sleeve. "No, please, I'll be fine. Honest, I'm feeling much better."

"Nonsense, a cool cloth will clear your senses and wipe away the dirt from your fall."

"My fall?" Yes, he had fallen in the corridor.

"Fear not, I've administered to much filthier men," Laudine said. She disengaged his fingers and soaked a linen cloth in the water. The odd fear crept over him once again, making his skin crawl as if he were a honeyed apple covered with ants. He braced himself against the wall and the boards underneath the straw mattress, all the while struggling against the impulse to snatch the cloth off his flesh.

It was worse this time. Erik's jaw quivered and tremors ran through his arms and legs, but he fought to control each twitch. Sister Laudine ran a finger over his knotted jaw muscles.

"There's no need to be so tense," she reassured. She took the cloth from his head and tossed it next to the washbasin. "Allow me to ease your muscles," she purred suddenly.

Her fingers slipped to the bunched up muscles at the base of Erik's neck, kneading them skillfully before he could protest. His apprehensions slipped away slowly as she worked out the tension.

She continued for a long while, and he began to allow his mind to wander. He heard her gentle breathing and noticed her golden hair had tumbled from under her habit. Her cheeks glowed red and her brown eyes danced in the lamplight like fine pieces of northern

136

amber. She smiled as Erik half-closed his eyes, her hands slipping under his jerkin and tracing the muscles along his ribs and stomach.

"You've the healing of an angel in your touch," he said as she moved around to his back. Through her course habit, Erik felt the soft firmness of her breasts against his spine, and quietly enjoyed the moment. He wondered if Sister Laudine had broken a few hearts when she wed the Church. After a minute, he stretched and turned on his side to allow her better access to the muscles on the other side of his back.

The folds of her habit wrapped around him, warm flesh pressed against his back, and cool smooth hands found their way underneath his belt and into his breeches. Erik could feel her heart racing far better than he should have been able to.

He rolled back over and pressed hungry lips against hers, his imagination seeing the familiar face of Marianna. Yet his eyes still saw the fair face of Laudine, Sister Laudine of the Abbey of St. Bride. Erik froze, the two images superimposed upon each other, his lips lingering against hers.

Her chest heaved with anticipation and she threw a leg over his thigh.

"No," Erik forced out in a choke. No, he wanted to, but—his gut wrenched suddenly, forcing up bile in his throat. His hunger, ever present, longed to be released. "No," he repeated, pushing her off the bed next to her loosened habit.

Tears welled up in her eyes, small diamond drops glistening as they rolled down her cheeks. She hung her head behind her thick tousle of golden hair and pulled the shapeless garment over her slender ivory limbs, covering each exquisite curve.

"I'm sorry, sir. Truly, I'm sorry," she said as she gathered the cord around her waist.

Erik grabbed her wrist and held it tight. "You don't wish to be here?" It was more of a statement than a question.

She wiped her eyes with her free hand then lifted herself to her feet. "No," she replied. "I love God. I desire to serve, but not here, not in a convent." She took a deep breath to calm herself. "I am the youngest daughter of Gyfon of Abertawe."

Abertawe. Gyfon of Abertawe. Yes, Erik knew of him, recalling the grizzled old count, a blond beard streaked with grey covering his thickset jaw. A loyal vassal of Mattheus, though by no means the wealthiest. And here sat his gem of a daughter, disheveled and in danger of having her throat ripped out by a cursed demon.

Erik tilted her face up to his. "Why did your father send you here?"

"I am the youngest of four daughters," she replied sharply. "How can a man of my father's means afford a dowry for so many? So here I am. A bride of Christ."

And in rides a young knight from the court of the High King, a man who can afford a horse and possesses a means to escape this exile with some semblance of honor.

"I cannot—" Erik began as he released her wrist.

"No, don't apologize. I want no pity." She rose and gathered up the soup bowl and washcloth.

"Laudine," Erik said as she opened the door. "Thank you for your kindness."

"I've taken no vows yet, sir," she whispered then stepped into the corridor, closing the door behind her. Taken no vows. Made no covenant. Sweet Jesu, what had he been considering, sliding into the service of the Grey One? Erik hit the wall with his fist, considering what the maid from Abertawe had said about her love of God and her desire to serve as her heart directed her. Amid the supernatural and the bizarre, a girl's open heart shone through the clouds of indecision, and her tears pointed the direction he must take, regardless of the cost to his own soul.

The knight closed his eyes and flopped back onto the straw mattress.

Something made a scuttling noise. He opened his eyes. In the corner of the room stood a hunch-backed, dwarf figure; Erik could just recall seeing it before as if in a dream, a dream most foul.

Eyes glowed red under the dark hood and power burned deep in the creature's body, spilling into the cramped confines of the room. Erik leaped from the bed, diving for his poniard in the pile of his armor. He hefted the weapon between him and the creature.

"Speak, messenger. I thought you were done with me."

It shuffled forward and opened its toothy mouth. Words slithered from its throat without moving its jaws or tongue. "The covenant. Take the covenant, become one with death, and live."

"So you still want me," Erik said. "Do you want me enough to bargain?"

The red eyes brightened. "Do not think to toy with me. Take the covenant and know true power. Swear by the blood of thine own throat that you will serve me."

Erik did not answer.

"Perhaps a little more time, then. A little." The glow died and the creature's orbs became listless, the pupils dilating erratically. It's mouth twitched and slobbered.

"What manner of beast are you?" Erik asked, leaning forward for a better look. The creature wrinkled its nose and its eyes focused.

"Cayl," it grunted, "name Cayl. I go . . . home now."

"Go to hell, you mean."

The beast shook its head. "No, me need go back. Fuddle, fuddle. No can think."

"I ask you again, what manner of beast are you?" Erik asked.

"I—Cayl." It scrunched its eyes into the heavy, puffy folds of its cheeks. "What you do that girl?" it asked.

"What?" the knight genuflected out of habit. "How did you get in here? How long were you there?"

"No warding," the Cayl-creature snuffled. "Oh, not like . . . on other room."

The princess. It knew of her room. "What do you mean, no warding? And I did nothing to the girl."

Cayl held up a hand, gnarled and grey, sharp claws extending from the fingertips. "I—I not." It paused, thinking, its eyes darting back and forth. "I not all . . . all t—t—together m—m—my . . . myself yet." It shook its head again and drops of spittle flew into the air from its mouth. After a moment, it spoke more clearly, "I here just when finished." It giggled. "You toss her to floor."

"Who are you?" Erik asked again.

"I on beach. Remember? I killed then, now new body." It tapped its temple. "More brain too."

"Who do you serve?" Erik demanded.

"Ar—r—awn."

"Who?"

"Arawn," the creature huffed much clearer. "Con—queror of Annwyn, S—s—successor of Havg—gan, L—lord, Master, and K—keeper of the Dead."

"The Grey God?"

Cayl nodded. "You please s—send me back?"

"To Annwyn, or whatever place that was?"

"Yes."

Of all the people in Albion, Erik wondered, *why did the Grey One want a Christian knight in his service?*

"What do you know of this covenant?" the knight asked.

The creature sobered further. "The covenant. You refuse him?" Cayl's eyes narrowed and its voice dropped to a whisper. "Listen. Anger him not."

No? Erik played with that thought in his mind. Would the Grey One rip down the fabric of the universe and wreak vengeance upon a single solitary knight? Why hadn't he already? Realization dawned to Erik as to why the grey god acted through messengers, why the Black Knight had been one of his earthly retainers. He was weak in this world.

"He can't come to get me—not today at any rate—can he? It's May Day, a holy day, and he must either be unable to affect me himself, or he's just too weak anyway, is that right?"

"Yes, it could be so," Cayl said, none too enthusiastic. "But I warn you, whatever day, Arawn very powerful. Accept offer."

"Right, give me the offer. What are the terms?"

"Take you to master, and he make you not to suffer so much."

"Unless he can get out of my life then he can never keep me from suffering," Erik said as he bent over and tickled the creature's chin with the pointed tip of the poniard.

"You not walk in daylight, eh? Maybe he fixes that."

"Don't be ridiculous." Erik snorted. "That's absurd. Of course I can walk in daylight."

He flung open the door and rushed into the corridor. At the mouth of the cave the sun still shone, painfully brilliant; but Erik clenched his teeth and strode toward it.

As he approached the warm glow, queasiness twisted his stomach. He looked back toward the door and saw that Cayl had not followed him. With a deep breath, he continued until he reached the last cell at the edge of shadow and day. Cautiously, he extended a hand from the shadows.

His hand burned with virulence. He snatched it back, clutching it tightly to his body. Through watering eyes, he looked at the fluttering people dancing in the sunlight. They wavered, as if a fleeting illusion—a daydream he couldn't quite reach, no matter how he tried. The nuns' habits fluttered about their faces and shoulders, framing their happy faces in angels' wings. Sister Laudine hung back from the others, her brown eyes meeting his for the briefest moment. Erik turned from her gaze and fled back to his room.

Cayl shrank back as Erik slammed the door and flopped on the bed.

"I tell you," it said, and started mumbling unintelligibly, scurrying for cover that was not there. Erik lunged for him and missed, the poniard striking sharply against the stone floor.

"Arawn, he help you. He give you power. You not hide," the creature squealed.

"Give this to him for an answer!" Erik shouted, throwing the dagger and striking Cayl full in the chest. Blood blossomed from its emaciated sternum and spattered the floor.

"He know you. He always know," Cayl frothed from his lips. "I go, but he send me back. He always send me back." Its voice sputtered, choking and its body dropped to floor. Almost immediately the corpse withered into dust and disappeared.

Erik picked up the dagger from the floor. The blade was stained black where it had pierced the messenger. He tossed it into a corner and began gathering his clothes and gear.

The time had arrived to leave the Abbey of St. Bride.

Chapter Ten

THE GLADE

THELWYN set his pack at the base of a grizzled oak tree, his hand brushing the dew-moistened moss on the trunk, bones still aching from the previous night's encounter. He hoped his foe would never know how close he had come to failure.

He stood up and looked around. This was the right place—a small clearing in the forest, a quiet brook rolling by, the strong oak branches stretching overhead—almost perfect. The only thing out of place was the yellow sliver of a moon, just a few days short of new.

It could not be helped. The necessity of finding a spotless lamb for the divining had slowed his progress. He could have done this at his home, but proximity to the disturbance would help bring a more accurate reading from the augury. Hopefully, the accuracy granted by proximity would surpass the disadvantage of having missed the prime conditions.

He tethered the lamb to the tree and opened his bulging pack to withdraw a small bag of white powder. Muttering incantations under

144

his breath, he sprinkled the powder sparingly in a circle near the stream's bank. Next to the outline he set a stained bronze bowl. Away from the circle, he built a low fire and set a kettle filled with water over it. Then he untied the lamb, petted its ears, and led it to the circle. Softly patting its neck, he withdrew a knife from his belt.

In one swift, smooth motion, he drew the knife across the lamb's throat, catching the beast as it fell and directing the flowing blood into the bowl. When the stream slowed to a trickle, he laid the body down and opened its belly, letting the entrails squirt out so he could read the portents.

As he studied the gruesome signs, the stars wheeled by overhead in their eternal paths. If anyone had been watching, they would have thought the old man had turned to stone.

Hours later, he began to move again.

Thelwyn gathered the entrails in his arms and dropped them in the kettle. He sprinkled a red powder into the mixture and it burst into brilliant orange flames, sending up a column of thick smoke sprinkled with flickers of light. This he also read as the night wore on and the moon dropped toward the western horizon.

Finally, in the pre-dawn darkness, he rose and paced to get blood flowing through his stiffened legs and joints. He pondered what he had seen. There had been a good many things, and if he had been any other man he would have wondered if the fates were playing a cruel joke.

An evil power was approaching; a strong power that could not easily be stopped by the mortal humans that populated the world these days. Scattered, disorganized armies of iron wandered Albion, while on the continent larger forces of Franks and other Germanics fought over the bones of old Rome; and all the while, this old adversary girded for battle.

Although it was a foe Thelwyn had never before encountered, he had seen its works and knew something of how to counter them. Yet he feared his knowledge would not be enough without a strong legion behind him. The Children of Danu had long left this world in their swift ships that traversed time and space. They would not return to save Albion or the world.

The mage leaned against the oak tree, suddenly feeling weak and inadequate. His eyes watered as he looked into the sputtering fire and thought over what he'd seen.

There had been two young acolytes in the temple of the Eastern god. Thelwyn had always thought it strange that believers would make buildings to protect themselves from the elements that their god had created. In that temple, the blood of their deity's son had been spilled to the ground, and the black crack in the earth had opened to receive it.

It was risky to use the power of a foreign faith for one's own end. The Grey God must have been desperately scouring this world for scraps of power, like a starved dog beneath a day-old feast table, to be willing to chance a conflict of cosmic strengths. Thelwyn shook his head—this had occurred quite some time ago, and the visions had not shown how strong the god had become in the meantime. Perhaps he no longer required the blood's strength. If that were the case, Thelwyn's powers would be inadequate to stem the tide from the Otherworld. His life had been long, and he had learned many things since his birth centuries before, but a method for killing a god remained in the realm of the unknown and beyond the deeds of the heroes in the long forgotten songs of his people.

He sank to his knees. Fatigue crept into his ancient bones, but his keen mind had already focused on a purpose. Resistance; there was no alternative. Failure would allow no second chance. If he failed, he would die, his memory obliterated from the world by the chaos that was to be unleashed.

He felt a twinge of regret for leaving Merdydd behind, but the boy was better off tending animals and the village folk. He knew just enough of the healing arts to remain useful until Thelwyn returned.

If he returned.

With a heavy heart, Thelwyn collected his things, packing them carefully away. Deep inside his soul, a faint glimmer of hope burned, for he had seen that he would not be alone on this mission; there was another, a youngster from the south, come to fight the darkness, even though Thelwyn did not yet understand how much this boy was involved. The nameless youth was somehow the key to the struggle, and all Thelwyn had to do was find him.

From what the mage had seen of the lad, finding him should not be difficult. He was not hiding his passage, and neither was the Grey God's creature that followed him—a probable sign of the Arawn's weakness.

Thelwyn's presence was known, that was clear; the attack could not have been coincidence. The mage idly wished for help, for a companion of equal power to himself, at least. But he wistfully conceded that there was none to be had . . . indeed, there had not been for a very long time. The Celts had seen to that millennia ago. He sighed.

Still it was Beltane, and for at least a few days he stood a chance alone. He would need that chance.

The young warrior would pass not far from where Thelwyn now sat in the moss and leaves, but that would not be for more than a day yet. The mage decided to proceed to the place and wait, using the time to shore up his reserves and gird himself for the coming struggle.

He flipped his pack over his shoulder, took a deep breath, and pointed his steps Southward.

Chapter Eleven

THE WESTERN SEA

BLAINE sniffed the salt air, puckering his mouth with distaste. He had never liked the sea—not in life, and certainly not in death. At least as a specter in a constructed body he could control the terrible fear of water that clung to the Higher Dead. He wrinkled his nose and turned to Magwyn, who leaned against the rail at his side.

"Why have we been summoned back to Annwyn by sea? Specifically by sea?" he murmured.

Magwyn turned his face into the watery spray heaving over the rail and onto the deck. "M'lord, I believe he alluded to leaving behind the proper clues, or some such thing, but I have not been able to put together what he meant by it. Could someone have found us out?"

"Who knows?" Blaine answered nonchalantly, though the questions gnawed at him. "I suppose that could well be possible."

Blaine pushed his senses out across the sea—yet his mind was distracted, working over the events of his recent, stinging defeats. He'd still not informed his master that he had been beaten back by the old healer and that Marianna had been spirited to the abbey despite his best efforts. If Arawn knew already . . . no, he could not know without a report from an agent in this realm. He knew of no other save one—and that one could not know after Boca's confinement. Still, Blaine had his suspicions, and they were not comforting.

The large fishing boat cut through the grey waves, its deck heaving up and down with each roller. Thick grey mist, typical to Annwyn's clime, hung about the hull as the ship pushed through the aether of the Between into the Realms of the Isles. It was ironic that Blaine no longer needed a ship to travel, yet had been forced to use one.

He had debated not answering Arawn's summons. But he thought better of such folly. The Grey God would find out that plans had gone further awry, and there would be no plane of existence where Blaine could hide from his reach. In the end, he decided it was safer to obey Arawn's command and be done with it. After all, Arawn was a god—lord of the dead. Blaine had forsaken all other options to take up Annwyn's service, and no refuge remained to him. He found very small solace in the fact that if Arawn had wished to punish him, he could have already done so. Small solace, indeed, when the Grey God still might.

The Dark One would not be pleased with the outcome of events, but there was a possibility that Blaine could put the plan right. He clenched his fists in a purely theatrical gesture, now that he possessed no reflexes in the literal sense, and thought of what he would do to the young knight who'd unraveled his carefully laid designs. The young knight that brought misfortune—and something else. The boy possessed something familiar, though Blaine knew that he'd not met the boy before his capture.

A fog bank lay low against the water, a great pile of vapor with the appearance of rolled lead. Four mortal crewmen scurried through the rigging, their shapes silhouetted against the grey sky as they called to each other in their pidgin dialect.

They were the reason Blaine had chosen to travel in a form, rather than as disembodied specter. The need to return to the other realm would soon arise, and he did not want to give his men the impression that he was less than fully and bodily present.

What a rabble of superstitious slugs, he thought. He doubted he could control them effectively as a mere spirit.

For this reason, he could not disclose their destination, so he manned the helm himself. What man in his right mind would willingly sail to the land of the dead?

"There's something off the starboard bow," Magwyn's nervous voice broke into his thoughts. The castellan was not used to the watery path they took to the nether realm. Blaine turned to look, a thoroughly unnecessary gesture since his mind was probing in all directions. He recognized the spouting, white-capped plume coming out of the water.

"Seleanric," he said. "A sea dragon rare to Annwyn's waters. Pretty far South."

"It's the weather," said a new voice from behind him. Magwyn spun on his heel, but Blaine did not need to. Arawn stepped forward, the slender form he had chosen swathed in a thick, black robe that billowed in the wind. "It's getting colder."

The god faced the wind, his nostrils flaring as he breathed.

"M'lord," Blaine ventured, "could you have anything to do with that?"

"That is possible," Arawn replied. "I am not pleased."

Magwyn glanced nervously at Blaine. The dark knight remained outwardly impassive, although it was useless—Arawn could see into his mind.

"I was on my way to inform you, sire," Blaine said, bowing for added effect.

"Oh, you were?" Lightning flashed across the god's steely eyes. "That is not what I perceived. Please, enlighten me."

All pretenses melted away as Blaine steeled himself for the report.

"Sire, the young knight made off with the princess down the beach. I pursued, but had to leave him in her hands while I dealt with the old priest . . . the old man is from the elder faith. He beat back my attack. When I returned, I was too weak to prevent her from being taken to an abbey."

"I know. I have already reclaimed the princess," Arawn declared.

If Blaine had had a body, he would have been chilled to the marrow of his bones. How did the god accomplish such an act so easily? Why involve Blaine at all?

"Make no mistake," Arawn continued coolly, "it was no simple matter, and one for which I should not have had to expend valuable energy. I grow weary so soon after Beltane."

Blaine took a step back to the rail. He knew it was futile, but even with a constructed body a few things were still instinctive.

"I assure you, sire," he said, bowing his head, "I will make every effort to carry out your wishes. This knight, this Erik—he was fortunate, nothing more. A completely random circumstance."

"I cannot tolerate servants who are ill-prepared for such random circumstances. Anyone could have stumbled upon you; a more experienced warrior, for example." The god's voice remained low and measured. "My plans are in ruin due to your *circumstance*, and I've had to take drastic measures as a result. To attempt a Crossing at this time—I stole her away from a Christian abbey before dawn and have not been able to function until now! Your *circumstance* has unleashed a situation of which only the Fates can foresee the result. The carefully woven strands of wyrd have been ripped from the fabric of my kingdom by your *circumstance!*"

"My lord—"

"Enough!" Arawn waved his hand and Blaine was muted. His lips continued to move frantically, but he produced no sound.

"Magwyn."

The castellan jolted erect and faced his master.

"Magwyn, you will take this vessel on to Annwyn."

Blaine screamed silently from the rail, unable to move his constructed body. Magwyn avoided his gaze.

"Yes, sire. Umm . . . what of Lord Blaine?"

Arawn regarded Blaine casually.

"Do not concern yourself with him."

The god waved a hand in Blaine's direction again and his constructed body was blown away by a fiercely shrieking wind that no one else felt, blasted over the waves like so much dust. Blaine's contorted face lingered for a moment, his disintegrating mouth shrieking epithets no one could hear.

At last only a dim spark remained, like a far-off star covered in soot. Arawn stretched out his fingers and snatched the spark from the air, tucking it away in the deep folds of his robe.

"No more mistakes. They won't be tolerated. Be warned for the last time, castellan. We can still seize the currents of reality and bow the fates, but we must act swiftly. I will supply you with a new master when you reach my palace."

With that, the Lord of the Dead disappeared.

Magwyn stood frozen for a moment, the sea spray stinging his cheeks as the vessel continued to plow the waves. At length, he shook his torso and gathered his robe tightly to his body, warding off a sudden chill. Then he glanced over at the crew, who hung motionless in the rigging, fearfully distant from the exchange between men and god. Magwyn would feel much better once this voyage was over.

"Rhys!" he called. "Rhys, come take the helm."

Chapter Twelve

CRY OF THE HUNT

THE ABBEY'S WALLS melted into the haze of oncoming night as Erik rode through the gloom. The woods were still as he rode through, but for the barest rustle of wind through the tops of the trees. Erik's thoughts distracted him.

Where did you hie away to, Marianna? he wondered. *Spirited out by your new master to a place where not even Father Bryce could track you?* He genuflected and bowed his head into the darkness within his soul, pulling up his cloak to cover his face. *Sweet Jesu, keep her safe if you can.*

He spared a glance over his shoulder as the abbey's wall merged into the shadows of the trees. St. Bride had been meant to provide refuge, not more torment and supernatural tampering in his life. He feared God's ears probably remained deaf to those who had betrayed life, as had the princess; and the question of his own salvation gnawed at his breast.

Could the Church offer grace to one inducted unwillingly into this undead fraternity, and could he escape the curse of blood thirst?

Did he truly want to? Was it really necessary? *Maybe I am a threat to no one,* he thought wistfully. His aching gut and problem with light might be from loss of blood and battle fatigue.

He shook his head and reached down to pat Hadrian's neck, tangling his fingers in the horse's dark brown mane. There was no use trying to fool himself.

The night moulded into an extension of his mind, bringing in a flooding awareness of everything that moved around him. The darkness teemed with animals emerging from their lairs to participate in the hunt. His body tingled and seemed to become light, almost ethereal, as excitement and anticipation of the slaughter coursed through his innards.

Suddenly, a sound strummed every chord within him: the kill— the whimper of a dying beast accompanied by the noises of a hunter tearing into its victim. His wet tongue running across his dry lips jerked him back into himself. He was repulsed, enthralled, and hungry.

No, he thought, *I'm not one of them; I'm not a creature driven to leeching off the lives of man.*

He rode through the night toward Loughar, continually wrestling with what he had seen and experienced. Life. Death. New life. It was clear that he still didn't understand the entire scope of the events that had transpired over the past few days. He had been cut adrift in a vast sea, the expanse of which he could only imagine. Where the capricious currents would take him, only the Heavens could guess; and they weren't wont to reveal themselves.

The moon rose high, casting pale beams of light through the forest leaves, which in turn threw twisted shadows all around. They danced a pagan faery ritual as he rode by, animated by his motion through the dark. Deep among the gloom and woodland shades, he heard the crackling of twigs and scuffling of leaves. He pulled his sword from its scabbard and reined Hadrian to a halt.

The noise stopped.

"Who's there?" he whispered. Almost without thinking he tried probing with his newfound senses; but either he wasn't good enough at manipulating them yet, or something blocked him. With renewed vigor he thrust them out again, as if they were an extension of his sight.

They were thrown back at him.

Hadrian threw his head against the reins and pawed a hoof on the damp turf. With no other choice, Erik sat waiting. Eventually, a creature emerged from the shadows, and Erik raised his blade.

"That's far enough."

The creature stopped and muttered under its breath, pulling its familiar black cowl about its shoulders.

"Things be afoot this night. Aye, they be afoot and the living shall be swallowed up in the damned." Cayl looked up at the knight with those glowing, coldly intelligent eyes of another, greater presence. "Beware the scavengers of the night—enter the covenant. Become one with life and death."

"To Hell with you," Erik shouted. "Be gone!"

Cayl stumbled as the spark of otherworldly malevolence faded from his eyes. Erik's nose wrinkled at the scent of its unclean body. Marianna must have been desperately hungry to taste this beast's flesh.

He thrust the tip of the sword under the black cowl, lifting Cayl's face towards him for a closer look. Pale yellow eyes blinked back.

"In truth, what sort of demon are you?" Erik demanded.

"I'm not a demon yet," Cayl laughed. A quivering grin stretched his gaunt lips. "I hope to be one of the Master's special ones." He shook his head and brushed dark spittle from his chin with the back of his hand. "Now, of course, it may help if you gave me a good response to deliver this time."

"No. Tell him I won't join him! No matter what he pulls to try to force my hand. I won't be part of this." Erik grimaced from the hunger in his gut. Deep inside his own flesh he could feel the slow, stagnant pulse clotting in his veins.

"Is that all?" Cayl slobbered, a little surprised. He shuffled back from the sword point.

"Yes! Unless you possess the courage to tell your lord to leave me alone and return the princess to her father where she belongs."

"Oh, he wouldn't like that. He'd torment me until he sent me again. Please don't make me take that back."

"I don't care what you do, just leave me alone. Be gone!" Erik booted Hadrian to a trot.

"No!" Cayl shrieked. "Don't leave me here. Not alone in this place. Send me back!" His frightened eyes darted nervously from one side to the other.

"Why?" Erik pulled back on the reins and Hadrian halted, but continued to shift nervously beneath him. "You've done nothing but torment me with your blithering drivel and foul stench. I'd like nothing more than to see you miserable—look at it as a gift from me to you." Cayl stared back with pained eyes. "Damn you! Why die just to return to someone who regards you as nothing more than a pawn?"

Cayl shrugged. "I'm just that way."

"Well, if it stops you from tormenting me, then so be it. Hold up your head."

He charged Cayl, Hadrian's hooves pounding the path and shaking the creature's smallish frame. When his blade sliced through its neck, he heard a laugh burst from the crumpling body. Its head spun through the air atop a fountain of black blood. With the sticky black nectar drying on the blade, Erik urged Hadrian to a gallop, hoping to regain the mesmerizing peace the night had instilled before the intrusion.

But such peace was elusive. Everywhere he looked he saw blood—honeyed mead to quench a gruesome thirst. His stomach grumbled.

The sharp sound of crackling branches snapping under shod hooves and the heavy breathing of the sweat soaked horse beneath him faded as his sharpened senses focused on the vibrant sounds of the night. He had to forget himself; he had to find a release for the pent up rage in his chest. Further and further, his mind pushed into the forest and into the night, flying away from the visions of the cursed disease he bore.

Motion, halting and cautious. His senses tuned to something nearby. A fox's paws padded through the rotting leaves that layered the forest floor, stalking the scent of a nesting bird. The diminutive predator made no sound except for the thumping beat of its heart pulsing hot blood through its smooth muscles. Its eyes narrowed; instinct focused through the excited ache in its tapered skull. Even before the kill, anticipation of warm blood stimulated thin drops of spittle rolling off the ends of its—Erik's—tongue.

He opened his eyes, shaking his head for a moment in disbelief, only to find himself again caught up with the predator, with the fox in its hunt.

The bird slept in a nest of thistle and twigs, hidden in the underbrush. Through red tinted eyes, Erik could see each feather rise and fall with its breathing. One false move and the bird would vault into the air, leaving the empty gnawing in the fox's tightly wound gut. One paw carefully moved forward, and then another.

Muscles froze—the bird had stirred. As stiff as a statue, the fox patiently waited for the unwitting quarry to doze again, to slumber off into dangerous oblivion. The inner flames of anticipation stoked hotter with each passing moment, temples pounding out the rapid beat of the hunter's heart. Muscles relaxed once more as the feathers ruffled and the bird drifted back to sleep. The nose twitched, the bird's scent tingling every fiber of the fox's taut body. Just a few more steps and the feathery neck would lie bleeding between sharp teeth.

A horn blast shattered the night, rousing the doomed bird to premature flight.

No! One with the fox, Erik howled his disapproval into the sky, chasing after the last fading echoes of the piercing notes that were fleeing through the trees.

He reached out instinctively for the saddle horn and straightened himself. Everything was a blur. Gradually, the fox's surroundings vanished away, leaving Erik again on the path, staring at Hadrian's withers, and swinging with the horse's gait. His clenched fist trembled with frustration at having lost the bird.

Sweet Jesu, this cannot be happening. The union between man and predator. He sat up straight, realization spreading through his flesh with a disgusting exhilaration—Marianna was bound with the black wolf in the same manner.

Hadrian skidded in the loose stones on the path. He snorted, pawed the earth, and shook his mane in a shower of lathery sweat.

"Easy, easy," Erik said, patting the horse's neck and cooing soothingly in its bent ear. Then he noticed what had caught its attention.

Two small, fiery eyes peered out from the underbrush at the side of the trail, piercing through his skull and into the depths of his head. The still-hot passion burst into his mind again, threatening to engulf him in the flames of primal lust.

He dug his heels into Hadrian's ribs and shot past the lurking fox. Burying his head in the musty smell of the horse's withers, he avoided contact with the beast's eyes; yet the presence of the predator tore at his insides as if he were leaving behind a long lost friend. The foul feeling in his chest told him there was no escape from this or any of the other fates in store, and that this wild ride into the night was only a temporary withdrawal from the friendliest of his adversaries.

The stars stared down at him dispassionately. The trees reached up their twisted arms to snatch the luminous sparks from the sky, vainly attempting to throw the world into total darkness and despair. His vision of the forest changed to a wilderness of bestial apparitions. The forest, the underbrush, the animals—all conspired to keep his soul in their nocturnal clutches.

He slowed Hadrian to a walk. They traveled through the dense forest until everything blended into the night; the darkness mercilessly sucked at Erik's very being, pulling at bottled-up passions.

Was this how the Black Knight Blaine began his own bloodthirsty career? The creature that lay in a distant courtyard with his face dissolved and a lance through his chest hardly resembled the natural creation of a mortal mother and father. Yet that desperate hunter, twitching as whatever animated its foul form departed in death, had seemed strangely at one with the night.

The crisp note of a hunting horn resounded again through the darkness. Erik tried to gauge the direction. The eerie echoes scattered off the treetops and into the expanse of the open sky above. Something rustled in the underbrush. Almost before he could register it, a figure burst into view.

"Merrovaine?"

The Anglan knight stumbled, twisting his head over his shoulder as he fell to his knees. Dark mud caked his shredded surcoat and tangled hair while broken links of his mail coat jangled loosely about. He drew a mad breath and toppled on his face. Something akin to a sob shook from his body. When he looked up, chips of broken branches and leafy undergrowth clung to his beard.

"And what sort of specter might you be?" he choked. Then abruptly he chuckled, a raspy noise in his throat. "Another ghoul come to torment me before I reach Mattheus? Reach him I shall—I shall!"

Erik leaped down from Hadrian to kneel at the knight's side. Cradling the man's bruised head, he whispered, "It's me, Erik—Erik of Birkenshire."

"Erik?" Merrovaine asked. "By God, is it really you, lad?"

"Yes, yes, of course it is."

He brushed the strands of filthy hair from the other's gaunt face. Merrovaine's eyes stared up, glazed and unknowing. "Look at me," Erik demanded. "Look!"

Through the haze in his pupils, the Anglan knight focused and a wan smile twisted the corners of his lips. "Yes, of course it is you. I wondered—" Terror drenched his eyes, his body tightening spasmodically. Merrovaine pushed him away. "You must get on your horse and ride! Ride, I say!"

"What? I'm not going to leave you here. Come on. I'll get you up in the saddle and we can return to Mattheus together." He tugged at Merrovaine's shoulders, but the knight thrashed his arms madly.

"No!" he shrieked. "You must go. Go alone. Fly to Mattheus!"

The knight's mad eyes flashed. "There are foul things in the land! You must make Mattheus aware. Hurry! Hurry now, before they catch up. Before they find me."

"They? Who? Are the brigands chasing you?" Erik grabbed

Merrovaine's arms, dragging him toward Hadrian. "Come on, now. We can still get away."

"No, no! Get on your horse—flee!" Crazed spittle flew from the knight's lips as he shook his head, voice dropping to a dramatic whisper. "They're not human!" His gaze jerked back to the trees beside the trail. "Oh God, they come!" he wailed.

The horn blasted this time not far off, shrilling through Erik's bones with an icy clarity. Merrovaine crawled away, his fingernails clawing desperately at the dirt as his legs flailed up and down.

"Damn," Erik hissed.

A large four-legged shape crashed through the underbrush. Long, yellowed fangs protruded from the wolfish black snout of the hellhound, dribbling strings of saliva from their pointy tips. Black tufts of fur jutted from its knotted, hunched shoulders. Fiery red eyes smoldered as it examined first Erik, and then Merrovaine.

Another dog-creature arrived, followed by three more. They warily looked the two warriors up and down, as if they did not know what to do with them—or simply couldn't decide which of several gruesome ends they would inflict upon them. Erik pulled his sword from its scabbard, the weight of the spatha in his hand suddenly feeling very inadequate.

The horn sounded once more—shrill, harsh, and much closer. The dogs moaned in response, lying down in panting heaps, their eyes never leaving Erik. A creaking noise whispered through the woods like a soft funeral dirge, steady and plodding. The snapping of branches grew louder, as did the huffing of large animals working against a heavy burden.

Erik raised his blade to a guard position, waiting, though he had the feeling the steel would be insignificant against the specter that stalked the Anglan knight.

Four dark stags, black as midnight, emerged from the shadows, muscles straining in the harnesses about their necks, the leather pulled tight. Above their twisted antlers stood a great figure in an elaborately decorated war-wagon.

Atop the huntsman's head sat a dull steel helmet with a set of magnificent antlers affixed to it. Through two narrow slits a pair of malevolent eyes burned. A thick gray beard flowed from what could be seen of his solid, square, pasty-colored face, down his broad chest and across the thick, shaggy gray garments he wore. In one meaty hand he gripped a set of reins, and in the other a large, twisted

hunting horn. When he laughed, the ground shook, causing even his terrible dogs to cower from him.

The Huntsman reined the stags to a halt and stepped down from the chariot, his footfalls firm with the authority of distant thunder. From inside his chariot he pulled a cruelly barbed, iron-tipped spear and playfully hefted it in his hand.

"Do you intend to interrupt my sport?" he inquired dangerously. "I'd heard mention of a rebellious night stalker in my wood. Blaine should have been more careful."

"Are you all in league together?" Erik muttered.

The Huntsman's lips pulled up into the semblance of a smile. "That depends on what you mean by together. Sometimes interests flow together, sometimes they do not."

Merrovaine began babbling, froth dripping from his lips, "Save yourself, Erik—just flee . . ."

Erik hung his head. The sick twisting in his gut, the fierce hunger of the hunting dogs, the desire of the Huntsman—all injected a black flame into his limbs. He looked into Merrovaine's face, horrified that he couldn't find there the man he'd known only a few short days ago.

Sweet Jesu, he thought, *how I wanted to rely on his strength and his courage.* But the older man lay trembling and whispering; a crushed shell of what once was the pride of the German kingdom of Angland. *Merrovaine, you cannot trust me to ride at your side.*

"Come now, whelp," the Huntsman sneered, "It should not be hard to leave the lost. He's not one of us—he lives." When Erik hesitated, he added more ominously, "You must choose whom you will stand with."

Choose—choose between life and death, between day and night. Choose . . . choose you this day. "Choose you this day whom ye shall serve," the warrior-prophet had said, "but for me and my house, we shall serve—"

"No!" Erik screamed. "Damn you all! I'll not become like you!" He braced his feet, prepared to stand and die with Merrovaine. If anyone possessed the power to kill him, there was no doubt it was this Huntsman. "Run me through, if you can. Do it!"

The hellhounds growled impatiently, sniffing at Merrovaine. Satiety tempted Erik to pounce on his former mentor himself, to rip open his throat and drink deeply. To drink until he could swallow no more and his belly was swollen, thirst sated. He dizzied and staggered forward.

The hounds rushed past, pushing him out of the way and throwing him further off balance. He swiped at them with the spatha, hitting the hindquarters of one, but the beast followed the others in its flurry of carnage.

Merrovaine shrieked as links in his mail coat cracked and his flesh was torn. Sobbing, Erik threw himself into the fray. He clawed one beast by the scruff, ripping the snarling hound away, but another shouldered in to take its place. He thrust his fingers around another's throat, crushing down on its windpipe and then tossing it aside. The beast tumbled to the ground, only to roll back to its feet and dive anew into the kill.

Under the unrelenting assault of the wild teeth, Merrovaine was shredded into a quivering red mass. Blood spattered Erik's face and arms as he fought to fend off the hounds.

Through the entire melee, the Huntsman stood silent. Merrovaine quieted, his shrieks fading to whimpers, then to whispers. His suffering ended when Erik thrust his blade through the press of hounds and into Merrovaine's chest. One of the hellhounds lowered its head and lapped at a pool of blood—blood that streamed everywhere.

Erik sank to the earth, putting his head between his knees, but he could not hide from the Huntsman's laugh. His mirth mocked Erik, for he too was stained in Merrovaine's blood, stained as surely as Judas the betrayer of God, the deed sticking to his smeared hands and face.

The Huntsman bounced his spear from hand to hand, musing over the kill, while his dogs tore into Merrovaine's flesh. "You can be at peace," he said. "To many, death can be a kindness, a gift, and you could be the angel sent to bear the boon of relief."

"No!" Erik leaped at the Huntsmen, who dropped the tip of his spear. The barbed metal penetrated Erik's breastplate, but he continued pressing ahead, not caring for himself. The lance entered his chest and pierced through his back.

The Huntsman laughed and twisted his weapon. Erik shrieked in agony as the Huntsman effortlessly lifted him into the air and tossed him into the brush.

"There will come a time when you beg for the Grey God's offer of service. You will beg but none will hear," the Huntsman said.

Then he raised the horn to his lips and blew. The dogs responded to the cue with nary a whine and left their kill to crowd around the war wagon. The Huntsman cracked the reins and the stags threw themselves against the harness. Pack and master disappeared, leaving only the dead behind.

Erik remained in a bloody heap for quite some time, unable to move. His thick blood oozed from the wound to the muddy ground. Eventually, he twitched and searched his chest, but found no mortal wound—though a gaping hole remained in his ruined breastplate. A chill rose from his gullet as he realized the Huntsman could have ended his life with a surer strike to the heart, as he himself had done to Blaine.

He struggled to his feet and looked at Merrovaine's lifeless form in the trampled muck. The Anglan knight was unrecognizable, torn and bloodied. Erik called Hadrian and, after a search through the nearby woods, found him with his reins tangled in the brush. He cut Hadrian loose then took his blanket from the gear tied to the saddle.

He knelt and wrapped Merrovaine's corpse, strapping the blanket in place with the Anglan knight's belt.

Under the twisted trees, Erik laid out the corpse beneath a hastily constructed cairn, wishing as he stacked the mossy stones that he could have lit a pyre, as befitting the valiant old warrior. As he fitted the last stone over the grave, a realization dawned on him. There was but one way to end his involvement in this, to keep himself from becoming what Blaine and the Huntsman were. He had to die, that the foul hunger would not consume him—to ensure that a day would not come when he, too, would slaughter good people for his own enjoyment. Such a sacrifice might pay for the blood he'd already spilt, possibly even saving his soul in the eyes of the Lord.

He threw himself into the saddle, slapping Hadrian's withers with the reins. The horse trotted up the trail.

His resolve could waiver, as this path would leave Marianna in her current state. Honor and fealty made his course bitter to swallow, but she would still have hope through her father, once Erik died. He hoped the king might be able to deal with the horror that had taken his daughter. The Heavens knew he had more resources on which to draw than Erik did.

The village was already awake as Erik approached along the narrow track that opened to the cleared fields and mud plastered huts, though dawn had not yet come. People rushed about their early morning labors. Dogs howled and yapped occasionally through the rising mist, punctuated by the dinging of a cow's bell.

Erik felt the growing urge to flee, to run and hide as a horrid nocturnal outcast. His tongue licked across dry, cold lips as he thought of the slaughter he could perpetrate against these villagers. He shook his head as Merrovaine's gruesome, mutilated face came to mind, glazed eyes locked into where Erik's soul should be.

"No," he muttered, "please don't haunt me." It was then he realized that he was truly no longer fit, nor safe, to dwell in the company of humans. A wild beast dwelt within him, aching for free admittance to the henhouse.

"What's wrong? Are you hurt?"

He straightened, unaware that his eyes had been closed. Hadrian had stopped in the middle of the village, and next to his chest stood a scraggly youngster with two pails of milk sitting by his feet.

Erik looked about for a moment then back at the child. "What place is this?"

"Tywiford," the child said. "You look tired, Sir Knight, and there's not a finer inn in the whole kingdom than the Red Rose."

"And just how would you know this?" Erik asked. "Have you traveled the length of the realm?"

"Well, my father owns it; and he's the richest man in the whole village!"

"Ah, and that bucket is for the morning porridge, right?"

"Of course." He drew himself up to his full, rather short, height.

"I am the official master of the stables, and I get a copper a month."

"A noble title indeed." Erik laughed, but his mirth cut short as a beam of light broke the night's hold on the countryside. He needed shelter. Reaching into his belt pouch, he pulled out a copper and tossed it to the child. "There's another in it for you if you take good care of my horse while I rest."

The child's eyes went wide. "Yes sir! I never had a knight's horse in the stable before." He ran ahead to herald the arrival of a warhorse.

The innkeeper was cordial and quick in his work. Before the sun flooded the earth with its light, Erik had locked himself into a very plain, windowless room with strict orders that he not be disturbed before nightfall.

Chapter Thirteen

SECRETS OF THE KEEP

DESPITE HIS LONG NIGHT at the monastery in Llanelli, Aldonzo rose early and dashed about Loughar, fussing over last-minute preparations and fretting about the thick fog that had rolled in during the night, which delayed their departure until early afternoon. Finally, as the sun was westering and daylight aggravatingly wasting away, the ship cast off. The young prince paced up and down the deck during the few short hours until sunset.

The following day his burst of energy was but a memory. He slept until mid-afternoon; when he arose, his aching muscles paid the price for the cramped accommodations, while his stomach launched into its own twisting and turning.

At the very least, Kien could have made sure to fit the place with decent bedding. Aldonzo said nothing, though, for he knew the way the party looked at him when they thought he didn't see, and the way they talked when they thought he didn't hear. He winced as he stretched his arms into a finely tooled leather jerkin, and then flexed his shoulders and drew his cloak more tightly about him as he stepped from the ship's cabin.

The ship pitched and he stumbled across the deck, his boots skidding on the slick wood. He grabbed at the mast, missed, and desperately grabbed for the rail. Abysmal weather, as usual. Cold, clammy, and a persistent shade of gray—certainly not divine portents for success. Not that the weather anywhere in Britain suited him, but the sea aggravated the drab to an unbearable level.

He heaved himself off the aft rail, wiped his chin with a sleeve, and turned to face the bow. Nothing rose above the gray waves or fell from the gray sky ahead of them that differed from what they left behind. An occasional settlement on the shore appeared, a small hilltop fort or two, with endless grey forest between. He clenched his fists. The chance to find this Black Knight character and put things right with Marianna had lit a fire in him, but that now dimmed beneath pangs of boredom.

Something else bothered him as well—concern for Mattheus. It surprised Aldonzo, for he wasn't usually afflicted by such attachments. But the strain affecting the King had begun to break through the man's battle-hardened exterior. Aldonzo worried not simply because of the obvious problem of succession to the throne, but because of the unexpected affection he'd developed for the old man.

A seagull swooped for the deck to snatch some piece of refuse dropped by the crew before another screeching rival could grab it. Aldonzo sympathized with the gull, flying around and around searching for some small bit of flotsam before another took it. He thought of some of the other men searching for Marianna and cursed himself for hesitating to commit to it himself.

What kind of husband would he make, swearing oaths in front of God and King, with that sort of attitude? What kind of future king?

What if he was too late?

Aldonzo pushed that last thought from his mind. If he arrived too late it would serve him right to play second fiddle to another's victory; not to mention that there was little he could do about it now. He tried to take his mind off his worries by watching the rest of the crew go about their activities.

Weylin, in particular, constantly drew his attention. Not that he did anything very unusual. On the contrary—he seemed perfectly relaxed, considering the importance of their mission. Aldonzo wondered why the man occasionally smiled to himself when no one was watching. He could make absolutely no sense of the smug grin.

Weylin stood in the bow, looking ahead of the vessel, stiff as a statue lashed into place for good fortune. Aldonzo realized with a start that he had been in that position for quite some time. The prince squinted beyond the other man at what passed for the horizon. Gray. The world turned grayer and grayer, like an old beggar's knotted beard.

"Damn the mist," Aldonzo cursed softly. There was nothing visible but a blur where the sea met the sky and traded waves for winds, neither element gaining or losing color in the contest. It was as if they sailed in a limbo of shapeless dreams, with their only link to reality being the rocky shadow of the coast to their right and the sparse hearth fires glittering through the windows of a half-visible hut or two.

Nothing moved on the shore save the birds. Aldonzo mused that the inhabitants must be laying in wait for some as-yet-unfathomed event to summon them from their huts. He chuckled to himself, hoping they weren't waiting for spring. It was already here.

Weylin's head moved—first to the right and then ahead again. He was looking for something. Was it something from the charts he had, something that no one else knew about? His scrutiny intensified, and he leaned forward for several seconds until the lookout atop the mast called out and a large, regular shape appeared on the coast in the distance— a keep.

The shape became more distinct as they sailed closer. The donjon itself sat upon a low hill, surrounded by the usual collection of stables, servant's quarters, and other assorted outbuildings. Around the entire complex a wall had been thrown up, built of dirt and sheathed in stone and wood. The builder had taken great pains to erect solid fortifications, though Aldonzo had no idea who would have wanted such a God-forsaken spur of rock.

But these thoughts scampered to the back of Aldonzo's mind as two details of the site riveted his attention. First, the keep was old. The edges of the blocks were well rounded from the constant abuse of the sea; the walls were crumbled and overgrown in places with weeds. Certainly, the harsh climate of Britain would accelerate the deterioration, but by his guess, the fort was an early example of this type of construction in Britain.

The second detail held even more significance, and Aldonzo congratulated himself for spotting it. The fort had not been actually built on the coast, but rather on a small, narrow-necked promontory jutting out from the nearby beach. He eyed the wooden causeway that crossed the shallow water to the beach, the fort's only approach from land.

Rumors of a stronghold off the coast . . .

The strange words in Merrovaine's message that had perplexed the King's Council at Caerleon came back to him in an instant when he saw the bridge.

Aldonzo slapped himself on the brow; the location appeared nearly perfect. The place sat just out of catapult range from the narrow beach, and only reachable from one side. Off the coast, indeed! His chest rose in elation as he sucked in the grey, misty air.

This had to be the place, he thought. But as they approached, his hopes were dashed. The place looked *more* than aged; it was in an advanced state of decay. Ivy snaked along the walls, pulling stone from crumbling mortar and bark from wooden upper ramparts.

He stepped to the starboard rail, shushing the crew around him so he could listen better, but heard no sounds emanating from the walls. A wisp of thin smoke drifted lazily over the ramparts. It must have been a cooking fire, he deduced. The thieves could have been a roving band, given to moving from place to place and with no means to maintain, or hold, a fortified keep. If this was the place, and the smoke rose from their camp, then fortune indeed smiled upon the expedition.

Aldonzo motioned to Kien and then hurriedly explained, in hushed tones, the need for silence. The captain agreed, and within moments the only sound of their passing was that of the wind whistling in the rigging. Slowly, the ship bobbed in the currents and drew near to a small pier on the promontory's shore.

The captain motioned for the crew to take in the sail, and the ship glided in. Sailors gingerly moored the craft, all the while scanning the walls for sentries. Two archers stationed themselves in the bow as a precaution, but no one appeared; no one challenged them, no one demanded they halt.

A few heartbeats later, Aldonzo stood on the dock with a small contingent of men-at-arms. His fingers tightened on the hilt of his sword, and he took a brief moment to look over his troop and the dock. A handful of sailors remained aboard the ship to stand guard.

Kien laid a hand on Aldonzo's shoulder and leaned close to his ear. "I don't like it m'lord. It stinks of death."

Aldonzo nodded, his nose wrinkling at the odor as well. "I don't know what to make of it. I suppose we'll find out when we get inside."

Kien waved his men up the dock to the small door in the seaward wall. They advanced cautiously with drawn swords and took up positions on either side. With the deftness of experience, a few of the soldiers forced the door open and slipped inside. One reappeared in the doorway and motioned for the rest to follow.

Inside the dank, dark walls the temperature dropped and the light faded to nothing, but Kien forbade lighting torches lest the light give away their position. Each man laid a hand on the back of the man in front of him, and they slowly advanced down the narrow corridor. Aldonzo's nostrils filled with the familiar odor of nervous perspiration intermingled with the stale stink of decay.

A glimmer of light appeared ahead as they rounded a bend and found a door ajar. A courtyard lay on the other side. From their narrow perspective it appeared deserted.

Kien conducted a quick head count and then sent a man out to scout beyond the door. Silence hung thick in the air, for they dared not even breathe. As Kien's men stood motionless, Aldonzo fidgeted, listening to his own fears ringing between his ears and the surging of blood in his throat, until at last the scout returned.

"M'lords, the place is empty," he whispered. "There be signs of a recent fight. Bodies everywhere." Aldonzo picked up an odd, barely noticeable inflection in his voice.

Kien did as well. "What's out there?"

The man hesitated. "M'lord, you need to see for yourself."

He led them into the courtyard.

The stench of death hung in the air like a tangible vapor. As the scout had reported, there were bodies scattered around the yard in small groups, as if an attack had broken into small individual combats before victory—or defeat—had been accomplished and the survivors had fled.

As Kein's troops explored, it became apparent the place had not been looted, for the telltale signs of everyday life remained relatively undisturbed: the barracks, stables, storage shelters, even the mess kitchen from which the smoke emanated. Many of the combatants still bore serviceable arms and even money pouches.

The scout took Kien by the arm, with Aldonzo following, to one of the farther groups of bodies. He pointed to one corpse in particular, lying a short distance from the others as if it had crawled off before dying.

Aldonzo stepped over the other corpses and bent down for a closer look. The flesh was stretched gray across the bones as if the body had rested in a grave for years before finding a place here. Kien rolled the corpse over and Aldonzo gasped at the contorted face with its black lips stretched in a grimace, baring canine teeth. A gaping wound bisected the body's gullet and a wooden shard was buried in the corpse's chest.

Aldonzo genuflected hastily.

"The bastard must have thought himself an intimidating bugger," Kien muttered. Aldonzo thought he saw something small and white squirming in the flesh before he turned to vomit.

Kien's men whispered at this new discovery, many of them genuflecting and desperately muttering various saints' names. A short, sharp command from their captain silenced them. As Aldonzo wiped the edge of his mouth, he noticed even Kien's voice remained subdued. When he finally lifted his head, he saw something lying near a very large, very dead black horse.

"What is that?" he asked, pointing feebly to something half hidden under the beast.

Kien waved over two men and together they pressed hard against the stiff animal until they pulled free a battered war-board.

"By Saint Michael," Aldonzo hissed, "it is familiar to me."

Kien held it in front of him and nodded. "Aye, m'lord, the green griffin and black mace on a crimson background. It's Birkenshire."

"Sweet Jesu, what happened here?"

Kien shrugged. "M'lord, I don't know. Heaven appears to be the only witness, and I don't expect anyone there to talk."

Aldonzo tore his eyes from the shield, shook himself then allowed his gaze to wander over the walls.

"What happened here?" he whispered. "Birkenshire, what happened here?"

His eyes caught Weylin skulking away from the rest of the men, who appeared more fascinated by the gruesome remains than with searching the rest of the keep. The mapmaker slid through the great hall door and disappeared.

Merrovaine, Birkenshire, and now you, Weylin, Aldonzo thought. *Too many secrets—far too many secrets.*

He brushed back his hair, drew up his chest, straightened his belt, and said, as deeply as his voice would allow, "Have the men keep looking for some indication of what happened here." His eyes remained fixed on the door where Weylin had vanished as he hurried to follow the man.

Kien barked orders, his ringing voice bringing some semblance of discipline back to the crew, who scattered like hounds on a scent. The captain then noticed Aldonzo's attention focused elsewhere.

"Excuse me, m'lord," Kien ventured and quick-stepped to catch up with him, "but what are you looking at?"

"Eh? I'm not sure." Aldonzo's curiosity was piqued. "But we shall see. Follow me?"

They crossed the yard to the hall. The door opened easily, and they stepped into an interior dappled with light that shined through the arched windows high in the walls. Tables and benches were scattered about—fighting had occurred here also. In the gloom on the far side of the room, another door stood half ajar.

"Weylin came in here," Aldonzo whispered. "Did you notice?"

"No, m'lord. Did he come in here alone?"

"Yes. I think we must find him to discover some of the missing pieces to the mosaic."

"Ah, you mean before he finds what he's looking for," Kien said.

The captain's remark struck a chord in Aldonzo. That had to be what had occupied Weylin since they left Loughar.

"Yes, exactly," he replied. Aldonzo started to step forward, and then stopped. Suddenly his years spent in a practice yard seemed frighteningly inadequate. He caught the grizzled veteran eyeing him expectantly. "Uh—you know more about this than I do."

Kien graced him with a curt nod and took the lead. They hurried quietly through the debris-strewn rooms beyond the hall, weapons drawn, with their free hands on their kits to muffle the rattles. Kien stopped a few times to cock an ear or sniff the air before they'd press on. Aldonzo marveled that a human could be so aware of his surroundings that he could track his quarry like a bloodhound.

The trail led down into the dungeons of the keep to where a lone torch sputtered feebly in a small guardroom. When they drew close to an open door leading to a hallway of cells, Kien motioned for Aldonzo to slow his pace. They tiptoed the final few feet to the portal.

Weylin's voice hissed from the passage beyond. And, in the depths of this damp place of rotting death, someone answered.

". . . I know not, master," a shrill voice sniveled. "There was much talk of departure. Everyone down here seemed so afraid."

"Afraid of what?" Weylin demanded.

"I don't know," the voice pleaded desperately. "But, but when he left, I don't know exactly, but it wasn't long after that the smell started."

"Smell? What smell?"

"Didn't you smell it when you came in? It's death! It's the smell of death. It's all around us. It's in us with every breath. Death." The voice whispered now, and Aldonzo almost leaned through the doorway to

hear. "And the fighting—oh, by the Grey God, it was horrible! They couldn't stop them, you know. I heard them down here, screaming and howling. They just kept coming and coming at them. They didn't know what to do. They struck them with their swords, and nothing happened, and they were screaming and crying . . ."

"Stop it, man!" Weylin said angrily. "You're not making any sense."

"The creeping dead! Didn't you know? Didn't you see? They looked just like any man, but then quick-like they just rotted away to husks. Insane, they got, and turned on the rest of the men, and the fighting—oh, the fighting! They're all damned! Every single one of them—damned!"

"Stop it! We found one of the creeping dead out in the courtyard cut to pieces. The others must have had some effect on them."

"No, master, no. T'was the sun that did them in. The sun! They can't walk in the sun! That's what it was. Nothing else could stop them."

"Shut up, idiot," Weylin said harshly. "Look, there's only one thing I need to know. Where's the girl?"

But the other voice only picked up where it left off. "It must have been the sun. It must have. Do you think it's possible? By the God, I hope! That'd be the end of them, yes."

"Damn you man! Listen to me! Listen!" Weylin's voice strained. Aldonzo heard the sound of fist striking flesh, and a muffled whimper. "Where is the girl? Did they take her with them?"

Aldonzo exchanged a glance with Kien, the object of this conversation no longer in doubt. But as the captain poised to enter the hallway, a faint sound came to their ears from above—the clash of steel. Another fight had begun.

Kien eyed the door they had just come through then looked at Aldonzo. The prince nodded a reply.

"Go see," he whispered. "I'll take care of Weylin." In a heartbeat, Kien disappeared, and Aldonzo feared that he wouldn't be able to find his way back without the soldier's help; that is, if he survived the encounter with the mapmaker and his hidden ally.

Weylin spoke again in a cloaked whisper, and Aldonzo could not make out the words despite pressing closer to the door. The cartographer sounded nervous now, as the noise of the battle above grew. A muffled grunt emerged from the cell, followed by the thump of something hitting the floor.

So much for Weylin's shrouded ally.

The prince placed himself squarely before the door, bracing himself for action. Weylin appeared with bloody dagger in hand. At the sight of the prince, he stopped short, his mouth a circle of surprise.

"My lord Aldonzo!"

"Where's Marianna?"

"I beg your pardon? How should I know?"

"Don't snivel at me, worm," Aldonzo replied. "How much did you sell her for? Eh? How much?" He raised his slender blade to Weylin's throat. "Whatever the price, I hope it's worth your life."

"Now hold, my lord." Weylin held up his hand as if to ward off an annoying fly. He recovered his composure and his demeanor changed.

"There are forces at work here beyond your ken."

"Pah! I can deal with you."

"Yes, but I am the smallest part." The cartographer's eyes flicked briefly to the door behind Aldonzo. "I had very little to do with any of this, my lord. No. Please, hear me out. We needn't be enemies." His voice dropped to a conspiratorial hush. "I have been denied my payment. You want the princess; I want my reward. Together we can get what we want. Divided we will both be denied—we could both be dead."

Weylin suddenly lunged at Aldonzo with the dagger outstretched, but the cartographer had been too long a scholar; he was unskilled in the use of his weapon. While no paragon of swordsmanship himself, what the prince lacked in technique he made up for in fervor as he fell on the older man, hacking wildly at the dagger and letting loose a bloodcurdling war cry.

Weylin's hand flew into the air, fingers empty and the dagger clattering to the ground. The mapmaker froze at the sight of his own blood spurting from his arm, and Aldonzo, hot with passion, slashed at the man's throat.

Weylin stood for a moment, struggling to speak through the torrent spilling from his neck. Then his eyes glazed over and he crumpled to the floor.

Aldonzo stepped back, his hands trembling. He howled at himself in rage for allowing passion to rule him in this briefest rush of battle.

Weylin was dead; his only link to Marianna was lost. Dazed by his own thoughtlessness, he retraced his path out of the darkness. He mechanically opened the door to the courtyard without noticing that the sounds of battle had stopped.

When he stepped outside, his jaw dropped. The number of bodies strewn on the ground had grown, and a score of men stood around them. Too late, he realized that the bodies on the ground belonged to Kien's men and that he recognized not a single face of those standing.

Then something struck the back of his head.

Chapter Fourteen

THE DEAD CITY

ARAWN STOOD upon the battlements surrounding his palace, gazing out over the gray expanse of the Western Sea. Far below, over the bustle of the city around him, he could see the boat that had brought Magwyn out of Britain bobbing gently by a pier in the dockyard. It was empty for the moment, but before long it would depart the misty isles of Annwyn to carry Magwyn and a new agent back to the fortress so recently vacated by the bungling Blaine. The thought of having to send his former right arm to the mortal world brought a snort of disgust to his lips, which drew the attention of his youthful companion, who strolled idly along the fortifications a short distance away. She turned her head, delicate and so finely shaped, framed by raven hair that had recently been cut just shy of her shoulders.

Arawn sensed her gaze upon him. He beckoned and she walked back to him, each step measured and even, giving her the appearance of gliding over the cold stone.

"What is it, my lord?" Marianna asked quietly.

"Oh, I was thinking of my wayward Blaine."

Marianna's face clouded, but she covered it quickly with a neutral smile. "Does he trouble your thoughts, my lord?"

"Never more than slightly. I merely find it a nuisance that I must expend so much energy picking up the shattered pieces."

"Surely he could not have been that clumsy?" she said. "He served you for so long."

"Oh, he did well enough. But his petty desires and ambitions clouded his judgment in my time of greatest weakness. Mortal spawn continually overestimate themselves, and he was no less susceptible to that flaw—even after he was dead. Once he overstepped his bounds, he made the error of underestimating all those around him, including his enemies."

Marianna's usually smooth brow knitted into sharp creases. "He was attacked?"

"Aye, my dear, that he was." He looked at her intently, reached out and stroked her cheek. "He was attacked by not only his own folly, but also the ambitions of a rival. One could almost write a tragedy out of it. Desire and the treachery of the most trusted."

"Someone turned on him then."

"Someone bought his captain with silver. Imagine—coin used to betray a god's plans." He slammed his fist down on the stonework, sending shards flying with the force. "One of my own, of all mortals, one of my own! I was not cursed with one ambitious fool, but two." He fumed at the grey sky, causing the clouds and mists to twist and curl, and he clenched his fists spasmodically.

"Fortunately, not all is lost. I have set other events in motion, and I will yet gain what I desire. I am much too close to fail now."

Marianna was silent for a moment. She moistened her ruby lips as she watched her new lord's eyes scan the sea. At last, she spoke again.

"May I ask what it is you seek, m'lord?"

Arawn sighed.

"Look down," he commanded. "Watching the teeming denizens of this city, you'd not think anything amiss. You'd never suspect I had lost the better part of my power. But there are signs, if you look closely."

After a long pause to scrutinize the streets, the princess asked, "What signs, m'lord?"

"Ah, child," Arawn said wistfully, "not long ago, only the span of a very old man's life, there was a man by the name of Arthur who styled himself king on your island." His eyes returned to the sea and he clasped his hands together. "He ruled over a number of my faithful, but was himself given over to the Christian God. To secure his hold over his paltry kingdom, he sought to demonstrate the strength of his God over me. He tried to break the power of my priests in his domain."

Marianna's voice hushed to a whisper. "King Arthur . . . how?"

"He hunted them down; had them killed as unclean, unbelieving pagans. But that was not all. He needed to do more to squelch the common faithful. He needed to show them that I was impotent."

The Grey One paced down the walkway a few steps. "I had a cauldron—a great black iron kettle as tall as a man and twice as much across. It had many properties; for one, it was an endless source of food. But it also had stronger, more arcane abilities. The cauldron could raise and control the dead. So, the mortal stole into my sanctuary and fetched the cauldron right out from under me."

Marianna said nothing.

"When he returned to Britain with his new prize, his power was demonstrated. Since then I have weakened; for with the cauldron in the hands of a Christian king, my people lost faith and converted to the new god. My power in the other realm was . . . set back."

"Couldn't you take the cauldron back?"

"No, my sweet child, it would not be so easy for me. We gods are not as mortal man. I suffered badly during those years and have recovered slowly because so much power was stripped away. If I *could* have brought the cauldron back, it would have given me a tool to draw believers together once again. Converts would follow and strength would flow from the power of their faith. Blaine was tasked with the search, to find traces of the cauldron or a remnant of the faithful, but even he showed signs of rebellion without my firm hand over him.

"In any event, what little searching he did proved fruitless. Then the fortunes changed. Events transpired that allowed me to regain some measure of power and take a more active role in my interests. You, my dear," he reached out and cupped her chin in his icy hand, "you are part of that."

"And the others, m'lord? What part were they to play in this?"

"That is not for you to worry about. Blaine has been controlled. Shortly the others will also feel the bite of my rein. There are new complications and possibilities that might try to thwart my efforts, but I will overcome them. With a measure of help from you, that is."

Arawn dropped his hand and turned back to the sea. "You had better go back inside. There is a storm blowing in. Storms in Annwyn are not safe for the living or for the dead, my dear."

Without a word, Marianna retreated into the massive, brooding stonework like a dismissed cur.

The Grey God did not watch her. Rather, he looked down into the streets and furrowed his brow. Soon, he would regain his rightful position, though he was no longer the master of the cauldron. But he could now master the graal, once again strengthening his stranglehold over the minions of the dead. The power of his devotees would grow as well, providing him with the faith of believers to work his will beyond the confines of Annwyn.

He chuckled at the irony.

Arthur had thought to defeat a god, but now the man moldered in an unmarked grave, his soul departed to his own eternal reward, and Arawn remained free to use the most sacred Christian relic for his own purposes.

He sobered. Annwyn itself worried him the most. He needed complete and total control over the dead once more. He must be the master of his own house. Bustling through Annwyn's crowded streets were the myriad generations of faithful dead, going about the tasks intended to occupy long eternities. Each had a place, a purpose, or a punishment. Except recently, one or two had strayed. An occasional wild one would do something to stir up trouble. For seventy years he had been blasting these into oblivion while trying to maintain a solid grip on the others, but it was only a matter of time before his threats and reputation would erode too far.

Annwyn remained the City of the Dead, but by no means did it rest in eternal peace.

Chapter Fifteen

ON THE WINGS OF
ANGELS

THE MAN'S ODD QUESTION took Erik aback for a
moment. "Have ya seen annathing like the creepin' dead
afore?" the man repeated, looking at Erik intently, as though he had
vital information to impart.

Erik licked his lips beneath the cover of a raised wine cup. *By any
of the gods who'd have me,* he thought, *I've seen more than he'd ever
want to know.*

But the man hadn't been talking just to Erik. In his drunken
stupor, any ear pointing vaguely in his direction would do. Yet, for
some reason, his babbling amused the young knight. He and the
others in the inn truly had no understanding of the sickness they
called undeath. Besides, the dead that had chanced his way lately
didn't creep, at least not much.

"Tell me, sir" Erik said, peering at the man through narrowed
eyes. "What could you know of these things?"

The man leaned forward, a twisted smile on his lips. The smell of cheap ale filled his breath as he spoke through broken teeth.

"Hell, I've seen them a-walking the moors north of me fair country. Aye, true be the words . . ." He wagged his head and stuffed his face into his tankard. "Comin' out of their filthy, rottin' graves jus' as soon as the sun sets, with the moon risen on their 'eels. Then— then, with bodies a' stinkin, the dead goes out to do the work of the devil. Aye, I saw it with me own eyes, I did, an' I'll never forget the sight. It was . . ."

The drunk's red eyes went blank and his head dropped to the table. At least his sleep would end with a headache the following morning, his befuddled mind forgetting all about the previous night's misdeeds.

Not so the damned, the young knight thought.

When Erik closed his eyes, Merrovaine's torn face seared the inside of his eyelids, a constant reminder that he was nothing more than a thrall to the passion consuming his gut. He knew a lust not even heady ale could satisfy.

He tossed a few coppers on the table. Pulling the tattered cloak about his shoulders, he quickly departed the tavern and stood beneath the cold, dark sky.

I can trust myself no longer amongst the living. He knew the slightest provocation could drive him into a ravenous bloodlust that would refuse to be sated. The disgust he had felt so strongly watching the corrupted Marianna tear into living flesh rose like bitter bile in the back of his throat. Not only did her bite curse him to be offensive to God and man, but now to himself too.

I am the foul rotting dead, he thought. *I am the creature who dwells in darkness, unable to walk by day. My kind drove men to drink themselves into a stupor, women to shut up their windows and to bolt their doors with fear, and*

children to shriek with terror at shadows.

He looked at his pale hands as he untied Hadrian's reins from the tether post. To him, by the fleeting light from the tavern's windows, they looked bloody. Yes, they were bloodied, though he'd not sunk his terrible mandibles into living flesh. Yet. But he was powerless to save Merrovaine from the slaughter, to keep the Anglan knight's blood from staining the ground. He feared that soon he would become one of the feared dead because he would be powerless to fight the urge.

He swung up into the saddle and, with a press of his heel into Hadrian's flank, galloped out of the hamlet. The night was alive, tingling his skin like the comforting caress of a secret lover. Forbidden, and therefore all the more desirable. The fingers of the darkness embraced him and refused to release their grasp.

He closed his eyes, giving Hadrian his head down the broken Roman road that traced the countryside. Did the road lead to Rome? He doubted it, but if it had, he may have been tempted to press in that direction rather than to Mattheus' stronghold in Caerlon. What did it matter if he arrived at court in a week or a month? Marianna would still be missing and just as diseased as when he left her. For that matter, what could any of the physicians of Albion do for her in any case?

Curiously, as he sped down the road, something began to unfold in his mind—a vision of sorts, not unlike the one he'd had after Marianna had wounded him. The difference this time was that he still had control of his limbs; he tightened his fingers on the saddlebow.

Before his closed eyes a pale light appeared, opening up a dreary scene of shifting shadows. A familiar presence emerged from the coalescing mists—a figure in black, whose smooth walk and shapely hips he knew all too well.

"Marianna," he murmured. Though riding at a full gallop, he stepped into the vision to stand before her, to reach out a hand to her. Her pale skin was smooth and white as snow against the black of her garments, and her eyes were brilliant gems of blue.

"Where have you been? I thought I'd lost you."

Marianna's laugh rang sharp.

"Do you miss my love bites, Erik?"

He wanted to feel his fingers around that smooth throat, constricting life from her body, but that was as denied to him as love.

"Did you really think a gaggle of foolish fanatics could control the power in me? The strength of Annwyn reached into your precious sanctuary and ripped me free." She smiled girlishly, but the flash in her eyes belayed any appearance of childlike innocence. "Think, Erik, an eternity of nothing but our love, intertwining together forever."

"Twisted together in death during the day," he replied petulantly, "and hunting innocents by night. I can't. I hate what you've become, what I—"

"You hate me?"

"No! Not you. I hate what we are—the rot in my gut, this wretched craving that I can't control."

"Take the covenant, Erik. Truly cross the great gulf between life and death. We have an eternity to love each other. An eternity."

"An eternity of love? Is that what you call this nightmare? How many more are going to die before you realize what you've done?

People like Merrovaine, who were just trying to find you and to bring you back to your father."

Her beautiful face turned away.

"My father is an old fool. One day he will die and leave me, as would you if I hadn't taken steps to assure your survival."

Erik took a step forward, clenching his fists. "Survival? Is that what you call skulking through the night, sniffing out fresh blood, and running from the dawn to keep this nightmare from ending?"

"It doesn't have to be that way, Erik. We could come here to Annwyn, where I am now, and settle in a small keep, with our own vassals, and never have to be separated again. The hunger is satisfied here. We could live as noble guests in the court of a god, and yet still have a home of our own on some quiet outer isle."

"Just what I've always wanted—to be a duke in Hell." He began walking away, and the vision shifted in the grays and shadows.

"Don't go, please," she begged.

"I'm not going to continue this way."

"What—where are you going? What . . ."

Marianna's voice trailed off. He was riding madly through the night again, his mount in a lather beneath him. He pulled back on the reins and Hadrian, heaving heavily, slowed to a walk.

Marianna—deluded Marianna. There couldn't be any peace for night's own creatures. Now she'd slipped from his clumsy fingers like sand and he'd accomplished nothing. Merrovaine had died for nothing. Mattheus, Erik's family, his people, they would all die for nothing!

Everyone dies—even God died; yet Erik could not. A clean death was denied him. Was he going mad? Mad . . . yes, he was mad, and the madness ached through his skull.

He rode down the old road as the night whiled away, mulling options, trying to pull out the simple alternatives from the unencumbered, insane tangents of what he perceived as fate. He found his despair growing. He could arrive empty-handed at Caerleon, bearing an ungodly disease and news Mattheus probably already had. Not only that, but he couldn't be trusted in the midst of the warm flesh at court.

Could he risk even the long ride to Birkenshire, in the hopes that the dark visions would prove false? The knowledge that he could easily kill many people en route from Cymru ended that thought.

Death . . . was death denied by this dangerous kiss? Yet the answer might be found there. The thought came clearly; his true death could possibly end this vicious cycle. At that moment, he almost envied Merrovaine for his quick passing—no time for thought, or philosophical reflection, no choice.

Yet he would have to act wondering if the pain of his curse would indeed be severed with his demise, for in God's eyes he'd be twice cursed: first by Marianna's bite and second by suicide. His own actions could end up giving his soul to the very Grey God that sought him so fervently.

He turned off the road into the depths of the forest. He knew of a place some distance away that would do well enough. The dark trees reached down with twisted limbs, trying to rip him from the saddle and thwart his scheme. Not caring, he let them tear his skin; there was no pain. All around other creatures of the night stirred, returning from the Hunt for the comfort of their own woodland lairs and crypts.

The angular lines of a jutting hill rose up out of the trees to the east. Erik dismounted and, grabbing the reins firmly in hand, led Hadrian up the rise. The growing light of the new dawn warmed the eastern horizon, though as of yet not a single ray of light had broken the damp mists and cool night air. The tingle in his spine warned of the impending approach of the first shot from Apollo's bow that would be the harbinger of his doom.

The ground rose to a rocky crag overlooking the Tywi valley three hundred feet below. Before him lay western Cymru, veiled in darkness and mist. The remains of an old Roman outpost stood here, probably built on the ruins of a Celtic hill fort after some long forgotten battle. The victors' defenses now sprawled in crumbling abandon, grown over with tangled seas of green ivy and weeds.

Erik carefully guided Hadrian through the gaping opening in the outer wall and into the central courtyard beyond. Amid the ruins, he prepared himself.

He dumped his saddle, travel packs, and bedding in a jumbled heap as he stripped Hadrian of his tack. As the sun crept closer, he took out an old bristled brush and worked the dirt and sweat from the horse's coat, keeping his mind focused with each sweeping stroke.

His hand trembled when he ran his fingers through Hadrian's mane, twining the stiff, black hairs around and around nervously. The horse nuzzled him, and, suddenly feeling like a little boy, he wrapped the steed's head in his arms.

"I know you trust me," he whispered into the horse's ear, rubbing the soft fur inside. "If I could I'd do something else, my friend, but I can't."

Up until that point of his undead existence tears had been elusive, but now they scalded his eyes and cheeks. *My horse—my Hadrian.* In his fifteenth summer he'd named his horse after his childhood hero, the greatest of the warrior kings of old Rome. His boyhood friend had become his comrade in both battle and death here on a barren hilltop so far from the fertile green pastures of Birkenshire.

Still cradling the noble head, he pulled his long dagger from its sheath and quickly drew the cold steel across the trusting throat. The great beast jerked and tried to pull away as the blood poured from his great heart. Erik struggled against the perverse hunger welling up in his stomach as the horse's strength ebbed into the dirt.

"Easy boy, easy," he said, stroking the beast's head. Hadrian twitched, and the precious life drained from his eyes. The horse's knees buckled and Erik sank to the ground with him, clothes drenched in blood.

Erik wailed in despair at what he had done, sprawling across the steed's warm body for a long moment, fists knotted in the mane. His newfound senses protested, screaming at the wasted blood soaking into the ground.

"Together, my Hadrian," he choked, "together we'll ride through the gates of heaven." He lied to himself, knowing the words to be false. More likely, he would ride through the gates of hell on something else.

When Hadrian's great heart ceased beating, Erik sat up, wiping his face with a bloodied hand. A faint glow had begun to chase along the horizon, ever so slightly. He stood up, intending to face the end on his feet, head held high. But such defiance was short lived.

Beams pierced the sky, and a bolt of light shot directly onto his chest. His flesh crawled as the shaft heated his tunic. Other shafts of light followed quickly, colors bursting all around him, blinding his eyes. He threw up his hands to cover them. Strength flowed from his limbs with each passing moment, as Hadrian's blood had a few moments earlier. Soon he was reduced to writhing on the ground in the gore-soaked mud. The sun struck relentlessly, driving light into all exposed flesh— searing out the evil, the overbearing darkness.

There was nowhere to run, no shelter. His horse could not carry him to safety. He clawed the ground, throwing up clumps of muck and dirt to cover his burning flesh.

"What's this?" a voice said, swimming through the waves of pain that washed over his body and mind like a swollen torrent.

"Go away," Erik growled. He looked up, trying to focus on the figure blocking the sun. Two large wings shielded Erik from the morning light. *By God,* he thought, *either an angel has arrived to bear me up to Heaven, or some demon has come to suck me down into the Pit.*

"Be gone—leave me to die."

The creature bent over. "I've never seen one such as you go to such great lengths before."

"Then leave me to it," he snarled, lashing out with cramped hands.

The creature reached out its wings, haloed in light, and shadowed Erik from the sun. Everything went black.

"Erik. Erik Caius Aurelianus"

He turned in the direction of the voice, but couldn't see who was calling him.

"What do you want? Must you torment me to the end?"

There was a stirring and something emerged, mounted on some sort of shadowy beast. He gasped. An armored figure with a large closed helm covering his face sat astride *his* horse.

Hadrian, Erik thought, pained. *How could they catch you, my innocent? Did they rob your death of any sanctity?*

The warrior laughed. "Take the covenant, become one with the dead. Your love awaits you."

"No! Just leave my horse and go!"

"You have no claim over the beast, just as you no longer have claim over your own body."

He raked his spurs into Hadrian's flanks, flicking drops of blood into the air, and they charged.

Hadrian's hooves thundered as they bore down on Erik, and suddenly dark black wings spouted from the beast's shoulders. The horse transformed into a smoldering nightmare. Now a monster, he sprang into the air, his hooves narrowly missing Erik's head. The warrior lifted his helm, revealing a mirror of Erik's own face as he flew by.

"No!" Erik screamed as blackness poured like a wave over him. "No!"

Blackness descended with a silent crash.

The snapping pop of twigs feeding a fire and the flickering of shadows greeted his eyes. With a start, he realized he had been dreaming. It was dark in the fortress courtyard, but he had no problem focusing on the figure huddled over the small flames. Grey hair hung down from his head, curling around his face. When he stood, his great grey wool cloak fell swirling down about his ankles and a thin bony hand reached back to push the folds out of the way.

"Who are you?" Erik forced out.

The man turned to face him. From his body, Erik could feel the pulsing of life; but not like in most people. The intensity of his life force made Erik's eyes water and his empty stomach churn with want. A long, grey-streaked beard swept down from the man's face, a continuation of the dark, bushy eyebrows bordering his intense green eyes. His features, though rather sharp, bore neither animosity nor cruelty in them.

Erik sat up from a pile of leaves, brushing them from his tangled hair. His fingers caught his attention. The flesh on them hung from the bones, scorched black, with some sort of pus running in a sickly yellow trickle.

The man read the horror on his face. "The lesser wounds have already healed," he said. "Your hands clung to my shoulders as the sun hit my back, but be assured they are by far the worst of it. Now if you come over here a little closer to the fire I will wrap the flesh so they heal better. At least, I think they will."

"Who are you?" Erik asked without moving.

The man bent to pull linen strips from a pack. "I am Thelwyn."

"An old name," Erik whispered. "So you dragged me from the hill. Couldn't you let me die?"

"Do you think you'd be in peace now?"

"I don't know. But anything must be better than an eternity of this."

Thelwyn walked over and began smearing salve into the wounds of Erik's hands. Then he wrapped them with a well-practiced skill. "Why did you choose this way of life in the first place?"

"Choose it?" Erik felt the man start at the venom in his voice, but he did not pull away. "You think I had a choice?"

"Undead such as you reproduce only with those consenting to cross the threshold." Thelwyn stood. "Didn't an undead creature lead your soul across the veil of death of your own free will?"

"No," Erik spat. "It wasn't of my own choosing."

"Hmmm . . ." Thelwyn muttered as he sat in the pile of leaves next to Erik. "I didn't think this breed of undead propagated itself on the unwilling. This is a worrisome development. How did it happen?"

Erik looked into the man's face and saw, deep in his eyes, the kind of understanding that could draw out the entire tragedy. He avoided the man's eyes as he related the betrayal of Marianna's fall into darkness. The intertwining worry for his family and for his personal wellbeing jumbled in with his guilt for betrayal of vows and honor. Eventually he sat back in the leaves, covering his face with his arms to hide his shame.

After a few moments of silence, Thelwyn asked, "Does your King Mattheus know that his daughter has been dragged to Annwyn?" "If not now," Erik muttered, "then he will soon." He rolled over and stared at the dampness of the wall.

Thelwyn sucked in the cool air between his teeth and let it out slowly. Then he rose and walked over to the fire, where he stooped over the flames and threw something into a pot simmering on the cherry-red coals. Steam puffed into the air and a pungent scent stung Erik's nostrils. Thelwyn fiddled with the concoction for a few more minutes and then stood up once more, pouring the pot's contents into a small earthen cup. He wrinkled his own nose and brought it over.

"It seems to me," he said, "the first thing we need to do is take care of that hunger. Drink this down and it should take the bite out of it."

He insistently pressed the cup into the knight's hands. Erik gulped down the nasty draught without giving himself time to either think on it or taste it. As soon as it entered his stomach, a warm sensation began to dull the voracious pangs. The pain remained, but the intensity grew bearable.

"What is that foul mess?" he asked.

"Oh, an ancient recipe from the land of the Greeks that dulls the senses. In your case I had to triple the ingredients. Now, if that will keep you from feasting on me, I believe we have much to talk about; and the sooner we do, the sooner we may begin."

Chapter Sixteen

A WARNING

S'ISTER MAVIS closed the door to Gwendolyn's cell and sagged against the wall. "Abbess, we must do something about Father Bryce."

Gwendolyn looked back tiredly from the window where she'd been watching the sunset bleed rosy smears along the edge of the horizon.

"Is he eating again?"

"Again? He never stopped! If he keeps on at this rate there'll be nothing left by midsummer! How much longer is he going to be here?"

"I don't know. He still hasn't figured out what happened."

Sister Mavis harrumphed. "At this point, I'd be surprised if he could figure out anything beyond the shortest route to the pantry."

"Now, sister, whether or not we approve of Father Bryce, he is still our superior and he deserves our respect." The corners of her lips turned down into a frown, something Mavis had seen entirely too much over the past three days. "But you're right. He does seem more interested in the proper procedures than in problem solving."

"I'll say. How best to devour a lamb is procedure du jour. The sooner we're rid of him the better. It's not just his eating. It's his whole demeanor."

"I think he's just trying to hide that he's not any wiser about this than we are," Gwendolyn sighed.

"Then he should admit it and stop acting like he knows so much more than he does. It would make him easier to tolerate."

Gwendolyn turned back to the sunset. "I think—" An urgent rap on the door interrupted her.

"Abbess Gwendolyn!" said the voice of one of the younger nuns. Mavis opened the door to a wide-eyed slip of a girl, not more than fourteen winters old. "What is it, child?"

"King Mattheus has arrived!"

Mattheus waited outside the abbey gate with four dozen soldiers, their leather-and-chainmail coats concealed beneath gray woolen cloaks. All their weapons were similarly wrapped in innocuous bundles on their saddles with only the hilts protruding, ready to be drawn at a moment's notice. The effect was of an armed band trying to draw little attention, but to Gwendolyn they looked like common highwaymen.

The hardened soldiers parted before her to where Mattheus waited, mounted on a massive white warhorse that exposed the entire 'innocent traveler' ruse as a lie. She bowed her head to him.

"Sire."

Mattheus nodded an acknowledgment, his face gaunt and drawn and his gray hair and beard wind-swept and unkempt. The king had urged his company to travel quick and light, and probably hadn't rested since leaving Caerleon.

Her throat caught at the thought of telling him his trip was in vain.

"How is she?" Mattheus asked, wasting no time with formalities.

Gwendolyn took a deep breath before answering. She could feel all eyes upon her. "She is not here, my lord."

The look in the King's eyes almost broke her heart. Life suddenly drained out of him as his chest sagged and his head drooped. Gwendolyn thought she saw his lips quiver.

"She was here," Gwendolyn added. "She arrived in the company of one of your knights. She was ill—deathly sick, and we cared for her. But in the middle of the night she . . . umm . . . disappeared."

Mattheus appeared to return from some other place. "Disappeared? *Disappeared?*" He drew himself up, and when he spoke again his voice carried a note of authority. "Exactly what do you mean, Abbess?"

"Perhaps it would be better if you and I discuss it in private, sire." She turned back to the gate and reentered the abbey grounds without checking to see if he followed.

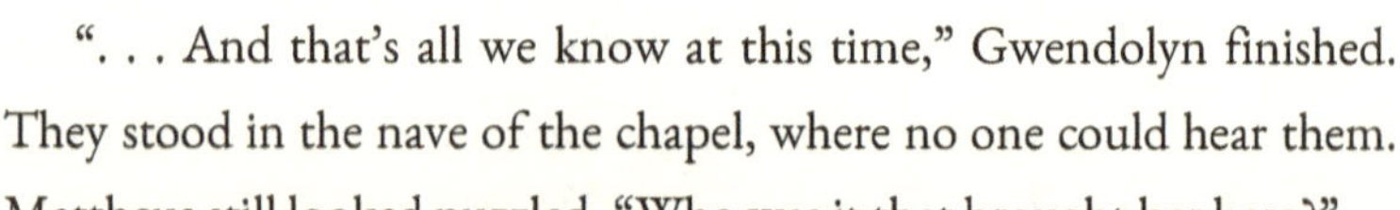

". . . And that's all we know at this time," Gwendolyn finished. They stood in the nave of the chapel, where no one could hear them. Mattheus still looked puzzled. "Who was it that brought her here?"

"His name was Erik," Gwendolyn said.

"Was anyone else with him? An older man? An Anglan?"

"No, my lord. He came alone, with the princess."

"What did he do after he had delivered her?"

"We tended to him in one of the cells. He was in bad shape, covered in wounds and bruises. I fear there was a terrible fight before he actually escaped with her, though he didn't say where he found her. He didn't awaken until almost the following evening. There was so much noise outside from the Mayday festival. Even the princess needed rest, you know. She was chilled."

"She was ill?"

"Her body was clammy and cold, and she was lost in fits of screaming. We did what we could. When it appeared that she'd calmed down we left her in another of the cells . . . under the care of one of our sisters."

Mattheus noticed her hesitation. "What of your sister?"

"Gone. Some sort of beast broke into the compound and when the sisters heard the noise, they found that both of them were gone. No blood, no struggle—just gone. We have no idea what happened to either of them."

"Do you think your sister might have stolen her?"

Gwendolyn shook her head once sharply.

"You said Erik was still here that afternoon, though?" the king asked.

"Yes."

His eyebrows drew together as he tried to sort the events out.

"What does this Father Bryce think of the whole affair?"

Gwendolyn snorted. "He's still piecing it together."

"So we really don't know anything, do we?"

"No, my lord, we do not."

Mattheus nodded and walked slowly out of the chapel, his head bowed and arms crossed as if he were trying to ward off the grief hovering about him. Gwendolyn followed him to the door of the chapel and watched him cross the yard toward the gate. Halfway there he stopped, tilted his head to the sky and bellowed a wordless cry. Surprised voices on both sides of the wall rose in response, but he took no notice of them. He bowed his head again and walked on through the gate.

General Reeves passed the command to the men—they would camp here tonight, and ride back to Caerleon in the morning.

Word spread quickly about the re-disappearance of the princess; no one relished the thought of going back empty-handed. None wore that emotion more plainly than Mattheus himself. So visibly did disappointment crease the monarch's face that it pained Reeves to even look. Once the troops had erected his tent, the king withdrew silently into it.

Above, the gathering clouds obscured the stars. Few of the men lit fires that night, as if the dark mood settling into the camp would stifle the flames. Eventually only a single fire in the center of camp fended off the darkness, tended by sentries who used it to chase the chill from their backsides.

A light shower started after midnight and grew rapidly into steady rain. The sentries stalked the camp, grumbling to themselves or to each other about the dismal weather and the fruitless mission. So intent on his complaints was one guard that he missed the arrival of an outsider until he felt something brush by his shoulder.

"Wot the bloody hell!" he cried and spun around, spear at the ready. He almost impaled the wisp of a teenage girl dressed in rags who had ambled past him. "Sweet Mary mother o' Jesu, girl, what are you doing out here? Can't you see this is an armed camp? You don't jus' walk into it like a marketplace, now."

His voice trailed off when she ignored him. The girl plodded ahead as if in a trance. She stumbled into camp and would have walked into the fire had the bewildered guard not rushed to grab her shoulder. She stopped easily in her tracks, not moving further. The soldier called over the master-of-arms.

"Hey, what is it . . . who have we here?" the older soldier asked.

"Dunno," said the guard. "She just walked in as pretty as you please, like we wasn't even here. What d'you make of her?"

The master-of-arms eyed her up and down. She looked like a beggar, like she hadn't eaten in days. Her clothes were disheveled and dirty, torn in a few places; her hair lay tangled and matted to her scalp by the rain, and her eyes were distant and unfocused. She didn't blink when the guard passed a hand in front of her face.

"Looks to me like she's in Rapture."

"Don't talk like that!" warned the guard.

"What's the matter? Got the spooks? She's just a girl!"

"Aye, but there's something funny about her." The guard stepped in front of her and stooped a little to look her in the eye. "Missy? Can you hear me?"

Not an eyelid flickered.

"Here, let me try," said the master-of-arms. "Hullo, there, missy," he said in as friendly a tone as his gruff voice allowed. "Is there someone you'd be looking for?"

There was still no answer.

"I dunno, mate," he said to the guard. "I think she's gone batty."

"Mattheus?" the girl said faintly.

Both men bolted upright. The guard almost dropped his spear.

"What was that?" he stammered.

"King Mattheus?" the master-of-arms echoed. "You're looking for the King, missy?"

The girl looked around but still seemed unfocused. "Mattheus' men?" she asked groggily.

"Aye, that we are, missy. Can we help you? Do you need something?"

"Need? Need Mattheus." She took a few faltering steps in the general direction of the king's tent.

"Hold there, miss," the master-at-arms grabbed her arm. "You'd better let me go with you. You wouldn't want to see the King unannounced, would you?" he nodded at the guard to get back to his post.

"Now I'll just go along and tell him you're here. What'd you say your name was?"

"Mattheus," she repeated faintly.

"No, miss, I don't believe so. You see, *he's* in the tent there. Now, what is *your* name?"

"Marianna—"

"Alright, Mary, we'll just go see the King now, if he's still awake."

"No!" The force of her refusal caught the soldier by surprise and she yanked free. "Not Marianna! The Princess . . ." Her voice trailed off as the spark faded from her eyes.

"Princess? You know where she be hiding?"

"Gone. She is gone to us. She is in the hands of another."

"Another who? Is she a prisoner somewhere? Tell me where! By bloody hell, girl, tell me where!"

"I don't know . . ."

The master-at-arms growled in frustration. "Have you seen her?"

"Oh, God have mercy!" She trembled.

"You have! When? Don't fear, missy, you're safe here. When did you see her?"

"No, not safe! Not here, not anywhere! Another has her! Another has her and she is his, oh God, she is his. She is lost to us. We cannot save her. She has gone to him willingly and we do not have the power to bring her back. She will rain death upon our heads! Don't you see?" Her voice rose to a shriek, and voices from around the camp grumbled as the rest of the soldiers awoke.

"Don't you see?" she shouted. "She belongs to the Grey God! She—I have seen a vision." Her voice suddenly dropped to a hush. "I have seen Christ upon the cross. I have seen Mary weeping, her face in the dust to catch drops of blood. I have seen—I have seen—" her voice faltered, "The Lord God trembling upon His Throne!"

By now the other soldiers had emerged from their tents to see the commotion. They gathered around the girl, but when they opened their mouths to ask questions the master-at-arms impatiently waved them silent. He leaned closer to her and tried to sound reassuring. "Is there anything else you saw?"

There was a long silence. He thought that she hadn't heard him, and was about to ask again when her lips moved. "The keep."

"What keep?"

"By the sea, to the West. Half a day's ride down the coast."

"Alright, miss, what did you see there?"

"I saw—I saw his servants. They were leaving, preparing a ship . . ."

"Leaving? When?"

"I don't—I don't know. I don't—" She suddenly fainted, and he jumped to catch her. She felt light as a feather in his arms.

He looked at the bleary, surprised faces around him. "Don't just stand there like boles on a log!" he growled. "Bloody hell, somebody get the King!"

Chapter Seventeen

THE CORSAIRS

ALDONZO didn't dare look up from scrubbing the deck. Ever since the previous evening, when he had been dragged aboard this miserable tub, his stomach had been turning in continuous knots. But he didn't dare vomit. He'd seen a very graphic example the previous evening of what could happen if he did.

There had been an old slave aboard who'd suffered badly at the hands of the pirates—battered and bruised, cursed and tormented constantly. The extent of the abuse had been obvious to Aldonzo from the moment he had laid eyes on the wretch. But in the midst of the evening mess the oldster suffered a fit of coughing that ended in a vomit of bright red blood splattered across the Captain's plate. Fearful that he suffered from consumption (not to mention outraged at the slave's audacity to spit up on the captain's food) the pirates killed him on the spot before he could infect any others in the crew. So Aldonzo fought down the waves of nausea that washed over him. There was no telling what the pirates might think he could have.

He held no illusions why he, alone out of the entire expedition, had been kept alive. All the others had been merely soldiers. Even Kien, stout, dependable Kien, had been nothing more than another trooper to them. Aldonzo, on the other hand, was different—he was ransom material. He was nobility, from a rich, landed family with ties in both Britain and Gaul. The pirates knew well they could expect a healthy reward for his safe return.

Ha, he thought bitterly. Qualify that 'safe' return to mean simply in one workable piece. They beat him thoroughly to find out who he might be, and, much to his disgust and shame, he told them. He'd always imagined that in such a situation he would be filled with iron-willed resolve to oppose his foe, who would have to kill him before anything of use could be revealed. *Some hero,* he thought ruefully. But he had never imagined reality to be so brutal.

His left hand throbbed in its rough bandage where they had severed his finger to remove his ring.

So it was that when the lookout reported the sail of another ship, Aldonzo just kept his head down, his right hand scrubbing despite the splinters and lye, his left cradled against his chest. He fervently hoped the ship approaching would be one of Cynric's war vessels. But even that hope hung by a thread. The Anglan king possessed little by way of a navy and lacked sufficient skilled sailors to use even what he did have. And even if he had, they seldom ventured this far from land.

He kept at his work, removing the accumulated filth of regular neglect, working his way aft from the stem to the mast and listening to the shouts and orders around him. Yes, it was a trader's vessel and, yes, it attempted to evade this vessel crawling with unkempt reavers. The other captain probably knew this ship for what it was even before it sailed into smelling distance. Slow and cumbersome, the merchant's ship would be no match for the faster raiders' vessel. All around Aldonzo, the brigands prepared themselves for yet another plunder, yet more death.

From his position by the helm, the first mate shouted orders, and the distance between the ships closed. Aldonzo glanced up. The other ship teemed with passengers—Saxon settlers in search of a new life in Britain.

The other sailors hustled women and children below the decks. The crew and male passengers strapped on leather-covered bucklers and hefted weapons, arming for the impending attack.

Aldonzo put his head back down and slowly crept across the deck to the starboard side, away from the other ship. Deck crew cursed and kicked him as they ran past whether he was in the way or not. Others heaved ropes up from the hold and tied on the grappling hooks. Then the brigands clustered so tightly on the port rail that the ship heeled from the weight.

Due to an unfavorable wind, the fleeing ship wallowed a bit, wind spilling from her sail, and the pirates cut through the waves to close the distance. Aldonzo's stomach churned with apprehension. The helmsman appeared not to be as skilled as he had thought, taking an unfavorable approach, but it only prolonged the gut-wrenching anticipation of the inevitable, and Aldonzo's innards had had about all they could take.

A great shout broke from the pirates as the grappling hooks sailed through the air to the other ship's gunwales. Some caught, some didn't. But enough held to allow the raiders to start hauling the ships together by hand.

The defenders wasted no time hacking at the ropes, but the pirates constantly pitched out more hooks as archers picked off the defenders. Steadily, the ships rocked closer together, and with a great crash and grinding they struck sides. Brigands poured over the bulwarks to the other deck. The Saxons made a fight of it, but Aldonzo, peeking over a coil of rope, saw they would not be the victors of the brutal engagement.

There were only a few experienced seamen on the Saxon ship; most of the rest were only farmers and had no sea legs. Their difficulty in keeping their feet on the pitching deck proved to be fatal. The Saxons briefly rallied near the afterdeck, but the stand was cut short when those pirates occupied with finishing off the Saxons in the fore completed their task and moved rearward to reinforce the aft contingent.

The entire battle lasted only minutes. Then the real killing began.

The pirates swarmed down the companionway to the hold, rousting out and dragging up the remainder of the passengers. Aldonzo watched in disbelief as the reavers slaughtered the aged and infirmed out of hand and dumped the bodies overboard. They hauled most of the children back over the gunwale of the raiders' ship, like bawling young calves, to be sold later as slaves. Those that were too small, too weak, or in poor health from the sea voyage, the reavers dispatched with chortling delight, sending them to sea with their kin.

The air filled with the screams of the survivors as they watched their families fall gutted to the deck before them. Then the blood-grimed victors raped the wives and daughters. Several times Aldonzo watched a pirate finish with a girl only to kill her, an act that elicited spirited displeasure from whomever stood next in line.

Fights broke out, causing more injuries and deaths than the fighting with the settlers. Aldonzo cringed against the rail, stunned. True, he had battle experience. True, vicious acts were committed by victorious armies; he had always believed these acts justified by the right of victory in combat. But he had usually observed battles from the rear guard, surrounded by other young nobles and an elite guard force, the soldiers usually more disciplined than the common troops. Reports of such activity after the battle invariably came second, or even third, hand.

He realized that he had entertained very childish notions of war. He'd always imagined that when the day came for him to lead a victorious army into a vanquished town, the young women would give themselves to him willingly, having been overawed by his valor and skill in the battle that slew their lovers. But here, now, in the middle of the open sea, women shrieked and wailed at the deaths of their men, the enslavement of their children, and the violation of their bodies.

He scrambled up, his feet slipping on the deck, and hung his head over the rail as what little was left in his belly came up in a knot of wretched pain.

Eventually the sun sank in the west and dropped below the blood-frothed waves. The debauchery continued, accompanied by renewed plundering of the Saxon ship, until both the hull and its dead were picked clean. The pirates hefted the last of the survivors over to their vessel then put the other ship to the torch and cut it loose to flounder away. It drifted on the sluggish current, smoke billowing into the sky as the flames ate ravenously at the spars and rigging.

This new destruction occasioned another wave of celebration by the raiders, and casks of just-plundered wine were opened. Some of the more popular girls were retrieved from the hold and brought back up on deck; a few of the other prisoners were brought up as well for other forms of entertainment.

Aldonzo, forgotten for the moment, slipped forward and huddled down in the shadows of the stern. He tried closing out the sounds behind him. The waning moon rose to port.

The ship headed south, though he doubted anyone remained at the helm. The moon's silvered reflection spread out on the waves like a precious trail to freedom. For a moment, he conjured a mad notion of vaulting over the rail and running up the phantom path to the moon itself, catching it before it rose too high above the waves, and then riding it to some place far away in the west.

But the idea didn't really seem so mad after all; indeed it was probably very close to the truth. Probably the only way he would leave this boat would be by Heaven's Trail.

Chapter Eighteen

A Storm In The Knight

BOOTS CHURNED into the rich, muddied earth, turning up the countryside like a plow being pulled by a mad horse. Dark worms, their bodies split open, wriggled senselessly. Bands of vagabond warriors carried torches over their heads, the burning brands illuminating pale faces with hollow eyes. Damp leather slapped against their legs. A horn sounded through the grey mist that clung to the valley—the horn of the Hunt.

A building lay nestled in the swirling fog, a villa, built long ago by a Roman patrician named Marcus Julius Aurelianus, offspring of the House of Magnus. He had served as a commander of horse under Honorius in Thessolonika and, with his eastern gold and booty, had returned to Britannica to buy land, build a home, and raise a family. His progeny grew up on the estate to march under the banners of the Western emperors of Rome, Uther the Pendragon, and Arthur, High King of Camelot.

An aged man cared for the villa now, hair streaked white and blue eyes dim. He stood in the gardens to look at the stars, as he had for many a night since his only son had left for court. Genuflecting, as was his habit, he prayed for God to speedily return his son.

Caius smiled as his daughter waved to him from her window and blew out the oil lamp that sat on her windowsill. He reached up to scratch a long thin scar that ran across his cheek from the base of his ear to the corner of his mouth—the most noticeable of his battle marks.

The sound of the horn echoing across the green pastures caught Caius' attention. Servants lit lamps and hustled about, unsure what to make of the noise. The old man had heard the awful sound too many times to be uncertain; he strode to the main hall, where his long slender cavalry sword hung over his chair. Pulling the blade from its scabbard, he pushed past his steward, who tried to slap a banded breastplate over his master's chest as he ran out the villa's main door.

A group of men tumbled out of their cottages and assembled in the courtyard, banging around as they shrugged on boiled leather coats and iron plates. Most of them were old men beyond the season of battle or young boys milling about nervously, eager for their first taste of blood. Caius directed his retainers into some semblance of order. Their carelessness rankled the soldier in him.

Tendrils of fog clung to the hills, deepening with the sinking moon, stretching the shadows into murky nothingness as the rhythmic tromp of lead-studded leather sounded in the dew-covered fields. Wild eyes flashed in the torchlight and cold blue iron clanked against buckles and plate.

Fire flared as oil-soaked grain caught the heat from passing brands. Still the marauders continued to forge ahead to the heart of the estate, penetrating the undefiled pasture and fields. The rape had begun.

The fog soaked red, bleeding with the flames and scorched blood. *Blood of my blood,* Erik thought.

"It has finally begun," said a voice in the dark, a familiar voice— a voice Erik despised. "Now is the time to take up the sword and bleed the land."

Mists swirled again about him as a void coalesced into visible form. Erik suddenly realized that he had no body.

The form took the shape of a man, a tall grey man, whom he recognized from earlier nightmares. Atop his head sat a narrow band of iron—a plain, unadorned crown. He reached out to Erik's essence and the knight trembled, waves rippling through his unbeing like a pond—not in fear, but in horrible anticipation—for as the Grey God clenched what was left of the essence of his soul, he knew he had been here before. The shade spoke most clearly through dreams.

"I have waited long for one such as you, Erik of Birkenshire. One who would taste death with such relish and do my every bidding. Finally, you are here, stripped to the barest of threads and ready to fulfill your destiny."

Visions fluttered into view, and Erik had no eyelids to shut them out. Life, death, the thousands of years Albion had known bloodshed and war. Celts, Romans, Picts, Gauls, and countless other peoples marched to bleed themselves like fatted cattle in the war-torn land.

Fire spewed from the earth and legions of monstrous deformities spilled from the cavernous bowels of the nether worlds, waging war with a man wielding a two-handed sword at their head. Erik had never seen such a weapon before. Great hosts of humanity fell in his insane path. Gouts of red-hot insects spewed from flying beasts that swooped down in a buzzing roar, causing the inhabitants of the land to run to their crumbling buildings for cover.

Erik saw himself wielding the sword with terrible fury as streams of blood flowed from beneath his booted feet. The sky darkened and the earth shook with the savage blowing of brazen horns and the steady booming of leather drums. His unbeing shrank back from this scene, but the grey man held him in place, and laughed.

The vision dissipated like a wispy morning fog and he stood alone in the familiar fields and hills of Birkenshire

"No!" he shouted. There had to be an end to all this, a way to keep this from concluding with his family's death. But if this was the same vision, he already knew the outcome.

He ran. As he climbed the knoll to his father's villa, he saw the faint curl of smoke rising and smelled the putrid stench of burnt flesh.

The villa lay smoldering, black and charred.

He pumped his legs hard and fast, thinking to stop the carnage, as he dashed recklessly into the sooty destruction. Warm, shamefaced tears washed his face as he searched the ashes, calling all the time for his family, yet knowing their brutalized bodies lay hidden.

Metal-studded boots had tramped desecrating tracks in the churned dirt and remains.

"Father! Juliana!" He found himself rubbing his filthy hands across his face. "Damn you!" he shrieked heavenward. "Why do you torment me like this? Show your face, or are you so ignoble as to cower in shadows, behind skirts and messengers? Face me yourself!"

The earth quaked, throwing up rocks, dirt, trees, the villa, and even the reddening skies; all of creation flew up in a chaotic mess, splintering and cracking above the groans of unseen voices.

Erik stood in the grey mist, the shadows thick and long—all around nothing but darkness and the disparate sounds of the unseen voices. Again he ran, but the mist clung to him, weighing heavily on his limbs, keeping him from shrugging free.

Arawn appeared, his laugh resounding over the groans, and his hands still grasping Erik's throat.

"Truly do I speak when I say time has passed for you, Erik of Birkenshire. You walk the Valley of Immortals, in a form not understood by common man. You're one who hungers for godhood. Yes! You hunger deeply, beyond the reach of human medicines or potions. You've felt the power, the grip of the Nether in your body and mind; I am part of you and you a part of me."

"I don't feel any closer," Erik gasped. "Your offer disgusts me more now than before."

But Erik could feel that Arawn knew his growing hunger, and even fed the lust himself, somehow. Arawn's steely grey eyes pierced into and through the young man.

"Take the covenant, truly be in the realm of power, of life eternal, and all will be released to you. Take the blood and become my arm, my eyes, my being in the world of man. Swear this to be so by the blood of thine own throat. Become mine."

"I despise you, as I despise now my own flesh. By God, I hate you. I'll never become your leech."

All around them burst the sounds of battle, drowning out the pitiful groans. Banners of crimson and gold dipped in the mists and blood. The din of warring weapons crashed back and forth, as mighty breakers against Albion's rocky coast, with the flooding press of bodies and armor. An undercurrent of moaning burbled subtly beneath the horrible crescendo of war.

"I have given you the power to wrest control from the chaos shrouded over your world, power to crush all beneath your heel.

Swear the covenant to me, make complete the significance of your being." Arawn's grip tightened.

"Again, I say no to your face, demon, or whatever you are!"

"Swear to me!" the Grey God howled, and Erik felt his existence slipping away like the embers of a quickly dying fire.

The sounds of battle stopped.

The mists thinned and broke as Marianna appeared, clothed like a fair angel—but he could see the venom of death in her. Within the trappings of finery he saw only the shroud of a corpse.

"Erik," she hissed softly, "I told you about the true power. This is living with the gods. I lie not! This is as close as a human can ever get to godhood."

"No, Marianna," Erik answered. "You justify being part of Hell. This is not godhood we're cursed with. It's a prison that one cannot escape by dying of starvation, or slitting of wrists. You're no better than a flea or a leech, lying in wait to drop on something warm."

"No, Erik, you've not seen what I've seen, been where I've been! There are worlds beyond our own, realms, kingdoms of great wealth! We can tap that power and reunite our own crumbled world, restore what once was. Think of it. The Romans couldn't keep order Maximus grasped for it but became overwhelmed. Arthur was merely a fleeting dream. But *we* could rule eternally in an empire stretching from Albion to the deserts of the East."

"And lead mankind in a bloodletting orgy? Marianna, no, this is not what you want. Please, don't be seduced by this."

A large ornate scepter appeared in her hand; a sharp-edged ruby raven perched atop with its wings spread.

"This," the princess said, "this is the power promised if you but take up the covenant, if you become one with the Honored Dead."

"You already know the answer. God be my witness, I will do all I can to free your soul. I see now that this is what I must vow instead of the Grey God's covenant."

"No! You must take the covenant; feel the blood over your lips and across your tongue. In blood there is life from death."

Erik could see the glamour being woven to soften her features, to trick his senses into perceiving something not there—her lost innocence.

"Damn it, Marianna! I will find you. I will come and wrest your soul from him."

"Erik!" Crimson rivulets of blood ran from the corner of her mouth. "I've tasted blood! I'm damned without you!"

"I will come for you!" The vision shredded into strips of torn fabric, fading into memory. A voice spoke, wrenching Erik's soul with anguish.

"For the last time, Erik of Birkenshire, Knight of the Realm, Chosen One of the Grey God! Take the covenant of blood, become one with life and death!"

Rain was falling in buckets from the black clouds by the time Erik had revived sufficiently to move. He looked around. The smell of damp, rotting leaves hung sweetly in the air, mingling with thin smoke from the small fire and brewing potion that he knew would be there. The old mage, wizard, or whatever he was, had large sprigs of forest herbs, roots and plants already hanging on makeshift racks that he'd lashed together.

"How long?" Erik asked groggily.

Thelwyn answered without looking. "A day and a night and another day," he answered amiably, "since the ruins."

Thelwyn bent over the kettle and ladled out the potion in an earthen cup, passing it to Erik and urging him to drink. The rosemary and honey tasted foul against Erik's perverted tongue. He handed back the cup and noticed for the first time his hands had been unbandaged and the terrible burns inflicted by the sun were nothing more than thin lines of white scars. He pressed his back up against the damp wall and took in a deep breath. The throbbing remained in his stomach, but the pain no longer crippled his midsection.

"I see you appreciate the effects of my little brew," Thelwyn mused as he knelt beside him, his knowing eyes examining Erik's wounds.

"I must say, I wondered while you slumbered what the dreams of the undead must be like."

"Don't wonder," Erik replied. "They really aren't worth wasting time over." He looked out at the drops of rain falling and splashing in puddles. "I can feel the sun behind the clouds."

Thelwyn smiled. "Couldn't fix that, I'm afraid. All the elixir can do is dampen the hunger pains. But your body healed itself rapidly."

"I'm sure things would have been better if I'd died."

The mage rubbed his nose, considering his words.

"Death is such an un-final act. It blurs life and flesh, soul and body. A corpse, cold and stiff, becomes dirt, which renews life, and the essence of man is cut loose into the eternities." He took Erik's cold hands into his warm fingers. "Feel the life flow; feel the transfer of my body warmth, as surely as I feel you sucking at it. Make no mistake, you have been taken across the threshold of death, in a manner no man should ever experience. But where would you be if you snuffed out your existence in this plane by melting like a lump of beeswax in the sun?

"You think it must get better, but the voices of other damned wraiths would tell you otherwise. Many mortals hope to escape the uncertainty of another plane by remaining. They cheat themselves and lose their souls in the process. Then if the unthinkable happens— like a nail run through the navel, a splinter of wood shredding the heart, maybe a head cut off, or sunshine—there is no hope for a better existence to come."

Erik stood up. So there it was. The sentence was endless torment in some nameless hell where the knowledge of Christ and hope of salvation held no sway. Satan and all his demonic hosts could never have devised a crueler torment. Somehow he had slipped from a Christian deity's care into the murky shadows of pagan legends with only an eccentric hermit to rely on.

He sat down again and wondered what would happen if he approached the bishop of Birkenshire for advice. Would he be able to drag the lost sheep back to the fold, or would he consign a lost soul to damnation? He could see him; his miter on his head, grey locks about his face and a look of terror in his eyes.

Hell, I'd have been terrified of myself, Erik thought. *I must look the mad man in my bedraggled, bloodstained garments—lost in my own native-born land.*

No, the thought continued, *I could not be turned away from home.* Yet, if the dreams were true, his father might not even be alive to give refuge. There could be no quest for Erik with a pagan, not until he returned to Birkenshire and found out.

"I'm going home."

"No," Thelwyn waved his hand as if he were dismissing a peasant. "It is unthinkable. We must follow the portents. This is not a game we can start tomorrow. There are forces scouring the land, even as we speak, trying to find where I've spirited you. And if they find you, then what? They'll find me, and I don't want to lose that edge over the Grey Lord."

The bite of anger rose in Erik's body as he listened, fighting to overcome the dullness of the medicine; it strained to be unleashed upon this wizard, this magicker who had trapped it. If Erik willed it to, it would roar forth in horrible fury. But he did not wish it; at least, not yet.

"Look," he snarled instead, "I must return home. That's all I know. I must see to my family's safety, and then I'll find Marianna."

Thelwyn stomped a foot, a remarkably childlike gesture for one so old. "No. I've explained to you that by helping me, you will find the means to release not only the whole of Albion from this blight, but also your family and Marianna."

Erik turned away from him.

"I go to Birkenshire. Do not keep or hinder me."

"We must begin the journey. He is too powerful here for me to mask our movements much longer. As all men who bear iron, you are impatient—and this is always the path to undoing. Once we hie away to the sea then there will be time to ponder our situation, but first we must get there, not cut a trail deeper into Albion."

Erik swallowed hard, pushing an empty knot down his throat.

"I must go to Birkenshire," he said without blinking, afraid the charred and ruined nightmare faces of his family might appear inside his eyelids. He looked at Thelwyn, noticing for the first time how haggard the old man appeared, his tired eyes staring at the popping fire. Thelwyn picked up a twig and poked at the coals.

"All right," he murmured. "We move quickly. Then will you come with me?"

"Maybe by that time you will tell me where and why."

"Maybe," he said, but from his voice Erik also heard the unsaid. *He can find you in your dead dreams, so I dare not tell you, lest He hear as well.*

At nightfall they broke into a nearby stable and stole two horses. The steed Erik selected shied away, its nostrils flared wide in fear. Out of instinct, he made eye contact with the beast, and it calmed.

This is no Hadrian, he thought to himself. This poor creature had not witnessed the bloodletting, had not carried him in battle, and did not trust him. It only feared him, and Erik found that he relished it.

Night clothed them, as well as Thelwyn's eldritch magic; and while traveling, Erik experienced a strange freedom from the watchful eye of his netherworld tormentors. The respite seemed to strengthen his senses as they galloped. The mists and black trees groped toward the stars with naked limbs extended, vulnerable and sensual in the still dance that stood unaltered from before the time of the tramping Roman legions. There was oneness between him and the black trees, both reaching upward, unable to touch the sky, anchored as they were

to the heavy stuff of the earth.

Soon, night passed into day; they hid and waited. Dark cellars and damp caves shielded them from prying eyes and the sun.

As time wore on, Thelwyn's face appeared strained from the exertion of continually hiding them from unseen enemies while pushing a brutal pace. When they were forced to rest, Erik restlessly paced back and forth, marking the days by footprints pressed on top of each other.

Four days of travel found them finally riding through the rolling green hills west of Birkenshire. The forests gave way to cultivated fields, orchards, and cattle tracks. During the race through Albion, Erik had imagined feeling relief at the approach of home, the familiar scents of the trees and summer flowers, the babbling of the brook, the knoll where he first played knight as a boy and listened to tales told by Demetrius of similar hills in far-away Greece; but comfort was denied. A dark cloud hung over the place, as if the entire world were alerted to the threatening nightmares slavering at their heels.

Impatiently, Erik booted his spurs into the horse's flanks to hurry the pace.

They crested the hill before the villa and he held his breath, expecting the stench of burnt flesh and spent ashes to pinch his nostrils. He stood in the stirrups. Nestled at the hill's base lay the sprawling villa, darkened and quiet, not so much as a candle flickering in his sister's room; it was her habit at times to stay up late and read a book or write to her friend Diana at the court in Exeter. The pillars, the tiled roof, the trimmed garden, and the whitewashed walls all looked frozen in time, unchanging and familiar. He bit his lip in anticipation and charged down the slope.

"Father! Mother!" he called while rapping loudly on the main door. "Juliana! Are you here?"

A spark flickered inside through an upper window. Feet shuffled across the floor and creaked down the steps. The latch inside squealed as it was pulled back.

A crack appeared between the door and frame and an old dry voice asked, "Who is it?"

"Gunther?" Erik pressed his face against the door. The servant breathed laboriously on the other side. He must have rushed from his comfortable bed to reach the door before Erik could awaken the entire household.

"Gunther, it's me, Erik."

"Erik?" The door opened slightly. "Is that really you, Erik Caiusson?"

"Yes, yes, it's really me! I've just returned from Gwent and I must see Father."

Gunther swung the door open wide and squinted his milky, misted eyes. He looked greyer than Erik remembered from less than a year ago, his back bending with age and his face haggard and wrinkled.

"Saints preserve my moldy hide!" he exclaimed. "It must be you, I can recognize your voice, though you sound older. Gods, life a' court has made a man of you."

Erik knew Gunther couldn't see him, but the old man had always read more from sounds than most literate people could read from a written page. Gunther reached out a gnarled hand to Erik's face then withdrew it suddenly after a light touch.

He genuflected and said, "Be gone, whatever you might be. I'll not invite the likes of you in this house."

"Gunther?"

"No, be gone from here, shade, you've no right to torment the living!" He tried to slam the door closed, but Erik threw a shoulder against it. Gunther shuddered. "No, be gone, be gone, be gone!"

The old man fell to the floor inside the villa, sobbing like a child.

"Gunther, I've not come here to harm anyone, God knows I'd never hurt you." Erik knelt at the threshold and reached for Gunther, but an unseen barrier kept him from extending his fingers into the house. The old man looked up, his face flushed, strands of hair sticking to his cheeks and his lips quivering.

"No," he moaned. "The dead must not visit this house, please go . . . you can only bring doom to us all. If you have any love for your own flesh then be gone quickly."

"Gunther . . ." Erik knew the old servant spoke the truth. "Yes. Yes, I'll be gone, but I must know if everyone is all right. You'll never understand, Gunther. Never can you know the dreams I've had. I need to know that everyone is safe."

The old man shrank back deeper into the entryway, squinting through milky eyes.

"Go back to your grave, go back and sleep as the dead should. Nothing you do can keep hearts from breaking or make them rest easier at night. I know not what ghoul's possessed you, or if you are my master's son. But I do know you must not bring the curses of the dead into this place. Go and we'll mourn your passing!"

Erik looked past Gunther into the dark room. He could make out the tables his mother had brought as part of her dowry from Scandia, the intricate serpent bodies intertwined in curving legs and the flat unadorned surfaces with earthenware basins and glazed cups. The great fireplace at one end of the room smoldered with dying ashes and smelt of fresh bread and burnt meat drippings.

The windows in the back of the room were flung open to the night air of the inner courtyard and the shadows of bending fruit trees that Erik's mother had doted on like they were part of her own brood. Many a summer night Erik had climbed out his bedchamber and, with an arm full of precious, juicy treasures, settled into the fresh rushes that Gunther scattered about each evening. He had lain in this room and watched the embers of the fire snap and blink red, throwing little sparks into the air. This room was the heart of the villa.

Behind Gunther, a traditional tapestry hung on the wall. The peaceful figure of a Roman-styled Christ playing a lute to the sheep had been woven in the fine linen, the colors faded and barely perceptible in the dim light.

"Is Father here?" he asked as his eyes traced the familiar holy figure.

Gunther sobbed, not responding to the inquiry.

"Damn you, old fool!" Erik snapped with such sudden venom that he startled even himself. "Tell me Father sleeps in his own bed." His shadow fell across Gunther as he filled the doorway. There was no reason for the rage, but it welled up from its potion-induced slumber, full of bitter gall and the desire to snap the frail body into bloody pieces. Gunther was merely fulfilling his duty to protect Caius as best he could, and Erik ached to kill him for not answering.

Throwing his own inner reservations aside, Erik yelled through the door.

"Father! Father!" he called. "Thelwyn—that door, right there. Check it for me."

Thelwyn stepped over the sobbing man and stopped at the closed door of Caius' chamber. Erik had never been bold enough to barge into his father's private room after the door had been closed. The latch clicked beneath Thelwyn's touch and the door squeaked open.

"It's empty," Thelwyn said.

"Damn you to hell, Gunther," Erik raged, trapped outside his own

home. "Where are they?"

Thelwyn raised a finger to his lips as if Erik were a child and then placed a hand on Gunther's shoulder. "Listen to me," he said. Gunther turned his face in the direction of Thelwyn's low yet very powerful voice. "There are forces at work here that you cannot understand, and we have not the time to explain. We must know where Erik's family is. Are they safe? Allow your master's son this much."

Gunther's mouth quivered. "Then will you return to your resting place and leave this family in peace?"

"I have no peace to impart to them," Erik said, grabbing hold of the door frame, his fingers knotting. No peace at all. How could he promise a frail old man that he would not bring destruction on his own house, when the tragedy was already well into the second act? "But I will leave."

Stroking Gunther's few remaining grey locks with his fingers, Thelwyn bent over to meet the servant's milky gaze with his own active, vibrant eyes. "This son of Caius needs to see his father so that his body may find the peace of the grave. Strong vows of love and devotion have been exchanged between father and son, vows that transcend even death. We implore you to please tell us where they might be so that duty may be fulfilled."

Gunther sobbed anew, tears running from his puffy eyes through the age-old crags and crevices in his skin. 'Duty' he understood.

"Oh, how much we've loved the boy. We loved you so much. Now you come back to us dead. How can this be, how did this happen? God save my soul for telling you. Oh, Lord have mercy on us all." He smeared the back of his hand across his face. "I tell you this that you might be able to go to your heavenly paradise, in the care of the soldier, Saint Michael."

"Get on with it," Erik hissed under his breath.

Gunther's trembling hand raised and a crooked finger pointed west. "Caer Baen," he whimpered. "Caius has gone to the town to raise men to defend the fields from thieves."

"And Mother? Juliana?"

"Yes, yes, they too."

Without another word Erik turned from the door and mounted his horse. Thelwyn whispered a few words of comfort and then followed.

<hr />

Caer Baen lay dark, a stark blotch in the rolling Birkenshire countryside. Squared Roman walls crumbled into the smoothing green of moss and ivy from years of intermittent neglect. A torch guttered, giving off a smoky light from the gatehouse.

Erik led Thelwyn off the road to the stream that ran south of the town. Roman tiles protruded from the bank, just as he remembered them; as a child he had hidden inside the cool tunnel here during a game. The ceramic surface was slick with green scum and slow, almost stagnant water. They climbed inside, the sound of their dripping and splashing boots echoing into the darkness. Thelwyn's hand grabbed Erik's shoulder in the dark.

Just inside the walls, the tunnel rose to the surface. They stopped under a drainage hole covered by a rusted grate. Erik pushed, pulled, and pushed some more, until the corroded metal began bending and warming in his hands. One of the bars in the grate snapped and he peeled it back, twisting the rest of the grate loose. He wriggled through and reached back in to pull Thelwyn up.

They crouched in the shadow of Caer Baen's church, a thick-walled Roman government building that had been converted to Christian worship sometime before the reign of Theodosius. Clinging to the building's black outline, Erik scanned the nearby wall for sentries and then scurried in the direction of the quarters that his father kept in town.

They skirted the marketplace and, undetected, reached a walled garden, beyond which was the rear entrance of the dwelling. The tops of heavily laden fruit trees stretched over the upper stones, branches bent. There was a gate along the back wall that Erik had snuck out through many a night as a youth. He found a small branch and slid it through the crack between the gate and the frame. A quick jerk and the portal creaked open. He motioned Thelwyn to follow quietly. No matter what changes may have occurred to his body; Erik still felt uneasiness at the prospect of being caught and enduring his father's sharp reproach.

When Marianna and her father had visited Birkenshire a year ago, they had stayed here in this house, where they could entertain the bishop and townsmen. Erik had begged his father to allow him to stay with him at the inn just down the dusty road. The night after the royal entourage arrived, his father had sent him to bed early, that he could arise before the crowing cock and help in the final preparations for the feast—but there had been other things on Erik's mind.

He hadn't seen Marianna when she arrived in town because he had ridden with Gunther and Petros to the villa to make sure the calf had been butchered and the other food readied for a wagon back to

Caer Baen. When he returned, his friends babbled with descriptions of the princess—her dark raven hair, blue eyes, and breasts pressed up tight to her blue gown. According to them, Venus returned to Britain. Pagans, Erik had thought, but when he saw her for the first time, a warm prickling started advancing up the back of his neck and up over his scalp. She was far lovelier than they'd described, and his heart pounded faster and faster with each of her movements. Then she had smiled at him.

Later that day, at the joust honoring the royal visit, Erik had withdrawn from the lists to find her. Fearing his voice would crack like a child's, he asked if he could bear her colors in a squires' match. She consented, laughing merrily. That evening, after the bruises and scrapes of the lists, he glanced at her during the feast and she blushed ever so slightly across her sculpted cheeks, a faint brushstroke of color, probably noticeable only to Erik. When the troupe of performers began their tricks and songs, the princess excused herself, tossing Erik a quick glance. Of course, their eyes met.

The brick ovens were still warm and smoking from the feast, though all the servants had long before retired to their homes for the evening. They met in the quiet and exchanged only a few words, but they were not important, merely chatter, until someone's footsteps creaked the floorboards. She leaned over and kissed him quickly before darting off. Later, once his parents were asleep, he had slid through this very gate to spend a few fleeting moments with her. He had known at that moment, when she kissed him a second time, that he loved her.

A branch swatted his face. The green, dark leaves rustled softly as he peered through them at the open windows in the house. No lights. Moving very slowly, he stepped up to the back door. Hearing nothing within, he pushed it open. Again he was unable to cross the threshold. Thelwyn elbowed him aside and, upon seeing that the way was clear, grumbled an invite for Erik to enter.

The main hall smelled musty and unused. *Mother must have agreed to come here on short notice,* Erik mused, *or else she would have sent someone to open the place up and let fresh air in.*

He hesitated, his hands falling to his side.

What would he do, or say? If old blind Gunther recognized him for the creature he had become then what of his father? He knew Erik better than he often knew himself, or so he said. They were kindred spirits, Caius and Erik, bound together by more than flesh and blood. He scanned the dark, some part of his mind hoping his father would stumble down the stairs on his way to the kitchen for a piece of chilled fruit, or strip of mutton, as was his habit. How often father and son had sat up during the night at the small table near the ovens, cutting open day-old bread and hacking up the remnants of an earlier meal, talking about the sale of a ram or the bolt of cloth purchased from the continent.

Sometimes Caius had spun a mystical tale of Maximus Magnus, the Spaniard who came to Briton as a common soldier and sailed away with a dark blade to conquer the city of cities, Rome. More often, though, he told of Arthur and his reign, stories that had been passed on to him by his own father, who had been a young man during the chaos following the High King's death.

His grandfather's dusty blade, given to him by Constantine of Cornwall during the civil wars—a time when the very fabric of Albion had been pulled into bloody strands of ruin—lay over the mantle of the fireplace. Caius explained the weapon's place as an ornament with the story of how it was made during the wars by local craftsman who used inferior metals, and had lost the art of fine steel. Now, there were only a handful of quality blades on the whole island; one Caius bore, and another he had bought from a Syrian merchant for his only son. Erik rubbed the dust from the cool, dull steel. This was all that even the king could afford during that tumultuous time.

A floorboard creaked as someone stirred upstairs in a bedroom.

Erik could not stop himself from rushing to the stairs. A faint light flickered down the corridor as someone moved from one of the rooms to another and then disappeared as a door closed. He hurried to the top of the stairs and stopped. She stood before him shrouded in black, her face pale and white. It was a young face, a familiar face.

"Mother." The words seemed strange, for she was obviously too young to be the woman who had borne Erik, yet they were right. She smiled sadly, her bright eyes brimming with tears. Her gaze penetrated into his flesh, as if searching what had been her son for the resting place of the soul. Her mouth formed a silent word as she turned away.

"No." He lunged for her. *No, you cannot die during this time of trouble,* he shrieked in his mind. His fingers clawed at nothingness as she faded away. "God, oh God," Erik sucked in the stale air, leaning against the cool plastered wall. "Mother, take me with you!"

He noticed Thelwyn gazing at him from where he stood halfway up the staircase. From the puzzled look on his face, Erik knew he had not seen the shade. Before he could say anything, a shriek ripped through the closed door.

"Juliana?" He threw his shoulder against the door and stumbled into the candlelit chamber. His sister knelt beside the bed on which his mother lay, tears streaming down her flushed face as she held his mother's white, gaunt hand against her breast. His mother's eyes were closed, and her flesh looked as if it were being pulled into the pillows under her head. Thelwyn shouldered past. Erik knew before he even placed a hand on her brow that she was dead.

Juliana looked up, startled. "Erik? Is that really you, Erik?"

He nodded, not knowing what to say even as horrific thoughts rose in him. He looked away from her trusting, pained eyes, before she saw the horror in his own. Juliana buried her face in his shoulder, startling him from his thoughts. She clung to him for comfort, but what comfort he could afford was cold and wicked—totally and completely. He stroked her hair and wrapped his other arm around her, his body trembling from her warmth. "Where's Father?" he asked.

Juliana sniffled, her eyes misty wet. She wiped back a tear and said, "He went to get the bishop. She has been ill for weeks since you left." She wiped her nose with a handkerchief. "She's gone—she's gone."

Thelwyn nodded and folded their mother's arms over her still chest.

His mother had passed to a place where an undead monstrosity had no right to follow. Erik's jaw stiffened with a mixture of remorse and anger. He let Juliana go, stalked over to the shut up window, and flung the shutters open. The cool, humid night air whispered across his face. Juliana crumpled to the stool beside the bed and cried with her head buried in her hands.

Torches flickered on one of the streets, glimmering wraiths bobbing up and down with shadows as men tramped through the alleys between the houses. Erik leaned out the window for a better look. Father was returning with a small delegation from the cathedral. He cringed. Under scrutiny from all these people who knew him intimately, he feared discovery.

The group reached the front door and Erik's father pounded on it with his fist. Juliana jumped.

"It's alright," Erik said. "Father has returned."

Juliana rose and ran down the stairs, her slippered feet creaking each board. Erik looked out the window once more and saw Caius greet Juliana with a bear hug, and wipe her face with a caring hand.

"Has she departed yet?" Erik heard him ask, clearly already expecting the answer.

"Yes," Juliana replied. "Come, Father, Erik has returned!"

"What?" he said as he stepped from sight into the house.

The stairs rumbled under Caius' weight as he bounded up them and burst into the room. He looked quickly at his wife and genuflected. Then calmly, acting as a man who had already prepared for the worst, he turned to Erik with a smile.

"I welcome you home, son, even though these are not the best of times." He reached out to wrap his son in his strong embrace, but Erik took a step back.

"We need to talk, father," he said quietly. "I don't think mother's death chamber is the best place for us to do this." Caius raised an eyebrow and looked his son up and down, his eyes lingering on his still blood-blackened attire. "All right," he said, sensing the urgency in Erik's voice. He turned back to his wife's body, pulled the blanket down from her face, and kissed her pale brow. Then he motioned for Erik to follow him through the press of people at the door. Thelwyn started to move in the same direction, but Erik stopped him.

"Allow us to be alone," he said, nodding his head to the townspeople.

Thelwyn shrugged and said, "I was wondering about the changes in services since I last witnessed a Latin ceremony." He stepped back into the shadows, allowing the bishop and a priest into the room.

Erik noticed the silver on the bishop's body and unwittingly shied away as his skin began to tingle. The bishop looked oddly at Erik, shook his head, and began the rites for the dead.

Caius took Erik by the elbow and steered him down the stairs into the kitchen.

"What is it that's important enough to take a husband from his own wife's deathbed?" His gaze was firm. Erik tried no glamour; this was his father, his flesh and blood. If he did anything unfamiliar, Caius would notice, he would find out.

Erik told him everything. The tale flowed from his lips, horrid and unnerving, even for him. The color drained from his father's face as Erik recounted the origins of the curse and the desire to flee from this life by slaying his horse and waiting for the sun.

Erik finished his story and waited for a response. Caius said nothing. He just looked at his son, his jaw trembling and his fists clenched.

Finally, as if a torturer dragged it from his lips, Caius said, "If what you say is true, and you are now some dark creature, then you must hide. The day is nearly upon us. Go to the cellars and wait for me. I must tend to my wife."

He turned without another sound and left Erik standing alone.

Erik paced the damp cellar impatiently. The sun was well to the west before Thelwyn opened the cellar door and entered.

"We must leave," he said. "There's tension here, beyond the death of your mother. I sense it in the bishop and the other men of the town—even in your father."

"What?"

"Don't you see? You are no longer one of them, your family or your village. You are unnatural."

"But this is my father, my sister! For the love of God, they are my family."

"No longer!" Thelwyn said firmly. Then more gently, "No longer. They expect death to take your soul from your body, leaving the husk for them to bury in the soil of the Cross. Buried and dead, they can then move on in their own way through the grief. But there must be a finish, a death, to end it in their hearts. They don't expect you to return as a walking corpse, dragging a pagan healer in tow and whatever other curses have attached to you. You are no longer your father's son."

"No. No!" Erik raged. "I am Erik Caius Aurelianus. He cannot have taken this from me. I must keep this!"

"And you would have, if we had not come here. We must leave at dark so we can make a dash for the coast and catch a ship. To linger here would be disastrous."

"But I must speak with my father, warn him—"

"You have told him, you can do no more."

"I can," Erik started. He heard something pawing or clawing at the door. It stopped for a moment then scratched again at the wood in a flurry. Erik rushed to the door, but withdrew his hand from the latch when he felt the sun's warmth heating the other side.

"Here, let me," Thelwyn said, shouldering past. "It's probably nothing more than a scavenging cat, or at worst a rat." Erik stepped

241

back. It could very well be something worse, he thought, though he didn't sense the presence of the grey master. He drew his sword and waited in the shadows.

Thelwyn cracked the door open and a narrow head peeped in, looking up at him. The creature's eyes darted back and forth, the eyes of a predator, familiar eyes. As the beast timidly pushed its sleek body between Thelwyn's ankles, its red fur glinted briefly in the sunlight before it scampered into a dark corner. Thelwyn shut the door and moved closer to the animal. It snarled, baring white teeth.

"Damn. It's a mad fox," Erik said, quite aware of his own foolish words. This was the same woodland creature that had stalked the bird on the night of Merrovaine's death. He prodded the beast with a booted toe and it pawed back, a growl in its throat. "Just what I need, a damn fox tracking me the length of Cymru." Though judging from the animal's muddy fur and gaunt body, the task had been difficult for it. Erik turned his biting words on Thelwyn. "Tell me, magic man, why in the name of Mary is it following me?"

The old man rubbed his chin. "Well, many an undead of your sort attract a natural creature that acts as their ears and eyes during the day and a stalking companion by night. Most attract beasts that reflect their dark personality—a skittish but hungry wolf, a night-flying bat, or a snake that gorges itself to survive. I must admit you are the first I've seen to attract a fox."

"Terrific, an outcast with a lap dog," Erik said threateningly with boot poised to kick it. It did not flinch.

"I suggest you rethink that," Thelwyn said. "It could be extremely painful to you, and at this point we need all your faculties intact."

"Great. Just . . . great," he spat, swiping his foot at the fox. "Just keep this away from me."

Thelwyn reached down to the fox and crooned soft, deep guttural notes. The creature relaxed. He slid his fingers under its belly and lifted it into his arms. "Sleep now," he said. "Rest from your journey."

The fox slipped its narrow head into the crook of Thelwyn's arm, keeping its eyes warily on Erik. The look in its eyes clearly stated, 'you did not choose me and I did not choose you.'

At least they had an understanding.

There was a muffled rap at the cellar door. Thelwyn motioned Erik to stay back and, covering the fox in the folds of his robe, climbed the steps and opened the door. Juliana slid inside and pushed the door closed behind her. In one hand, she held a small oil lamp.

She peered into the darkness and said, "How can you stand to stay down here in this cold and damp place? You'll catch a death, you will."

Erik merely smiled.

"Are you running, Erik? Did something happen at court?"

He stepped up to her and kissed her forehead. She had their mother's fair northern features, her blue eyes innocently taking in the sight of her only sibling as if he had been gone a lifetime.

Erik tried to force the truth out of his mouth, for he wanted to plead with her to run away, leaving this curse far behind. But he didn't. He felt himself weaving a glamour over her, reinforcing the vision of her living brother—an illusion that would have been much more difficult to sustain against Caius or Gunther. She was his sister, and for selfish reasons he wanted her to continue thinking of him without all the burdens he had placed on his father.

"No," he said. "I'm not in any trouble at court. I just need seclusion for a while." He took her hand and squeezed it reassuringly. "How did mother die?" he asked.

"Sickness," she answered, burying her head into his shoulder. "She just got sick; fevers, cold sweats—then delirious. But she's always been so healthy."

Thelwyn raised an eyebrow. "It's here, too," he hissed.

Just then the cellar door opened again. The sunlight was no longer directly on the door, and had become a filtered glow as the sun began to slip down to the western horizon. Erik moved Juliana to block the light and tried to focus his eyes on the figure in the bright haze.

Caius closed the door behind him. In his clenched fist he held a crucifix, the one usually around his wife's throat, a fragile wooden cross with bands of silver around the ends. Erik could feel a faint pulse from it, a power like in the bishop's holy symbol. He suddenly wondered why he had not felt it at the abbey. His senses flared as they centered on the source of the power—not the symbol in and of itself, but the seeming extension of his father's soul into the object, his faith holding open a window to somewhere at the point where his flesh touched the inanimate wood. Heaven, perhaps?

Erik let Juliana go, his whole being focused on that window which could very well have been a portal between earth and the beyond. He froze when he realized the magnitude of the power Caius held, the memory of the searing sun still fresh in his memory and on his scarred flesh.

"Juliana," Caius said evenly, "I need to speak with Erik and this man alone." Juliana opened her mouth, but his look made her quiet.

"We'll talk later, dear heart," Erik whispered to her. She nodded and then gracefully walked over to their father and kissed him lightly on the cheek. His eyes half-closed at the touch, and then she was gone beyond the door into the daylight.

"Now, we talk." His voice quivered. "I know not what thing has been done to the body of my son, for if what you have said is true then my son no longer exists."

"I exist, Father," Erik said. "I loathe this. I want nothing more than to end the torment both to myself and to you. But I can't." He faced his father squarely. There would be no lies, no deception.

"You can no longer be mine," Caius muttered flatly. Suddenly his years seemed to weigh heavily upon him. "God would not allow such a horror. I can only thank Him that your mother didn't live to see it." He raised the cross in front of him. His hold on the power was very focused, though Erik knew full well it was his first time using it as a shield. "My own flesh and blood would not shrink from the holiest emblem in Christendom. If you are truly my son, then take up the cross and kiss it."

"Look," Erik said, anger clawing its way past the effects of Thelwyn's most recent potion. "I explained to you everything that happened. I cannot kiss it while it is in your hands." Caius lowered the crucifix a bit.

"I've lied to you on nothing. I've no desire to keep anything from you." Erik pointed to Thelwyn. "He can verify everything I said as truth. He found me when I tried to end this curse and my life."

Thelwyn said nothing, but nodded.

"Damn you," Father sputtered, lowering the cross. He could feel the blazing power falter. "I could never do as the bishop said. He wants me to hold you at bay until he arrives with some village men so they can test you for themselves. God, if you did not look so much like my own son."

"I am."

Caius staggered back against the damp cellar wall, his eyes remaining on Erik all the while. "What do you intend now?"

"Father, I'd be free of this curse if I could."

Caius looked at Thelwyn, seeing him as if for the first time.

"And you? You'd have him traipse out of this country in search of what? An old wives' tale?"

Thelwyn's strong eyes met his gaze. "Nay, I'd have him bring back the power to stop this plague, to seal up the curse."

"You mean the sickness that plagues the land these past days?"

"Indeed. It is a sign of the growing power of the Grey God—"

"Enough!" Caius said. "I've a belly's fill of pagan stories. This is a Christian, God-fearing house. By the Saint, I've no easy answers, but he'll not be cast forsaken on some distant shore, parted from fellowship with the Church. He's my son."

Caius straightened and placed the holy symbol into his pocket.

"What do you require?"

Erik looked down at his pale hands, thin pink scars twisting around his fingers as a reminder of both his vulnerability and curse. They trembled slightly and he thrust them suddenly against his sides.

"Father," he hissed, "go tell the Bishop that I desire to have the unclean spirits cast from my body—I wish to end this curse."

Chapter Nineteen

THE MONTE

F'ENYAS POURED himself another mug of ale and squinted his good eye at the young man sitting across the table.

"I've got a problem, lad," he confessed.

Aldonzo pursed his lips and didn't say a word. He knew that any problems Fenyas consulted with him on boded ill for himself. Besides, the prince could not take his eyes off the ale. He'd been on the pirate vessel for an eternity, and it had been even longer since he'd had a good stout drink. His mouth watered, so he kept it shut. The last thing he wanted was to show weakness, or receive another beating.

Just the other day, he'd caught a glimpse of himself in a stagnant water barrel right after the last thrashing and had almost fainted from the sight. The fact that they were holding back on him because he was worth ransom money provided little comfort. That could change at any time. As a matter of fact, he suspected that was the reason for this conversation, and his already uneasy stomach fairly roiled. He may not have been much of a navigator, but he knew enough to realize what it meant when the sun rose above the port bow every morning.

"The problem I've got, laddie," Fenyas rumbled on, "is that I'm not sure just how I'm supposed to get in touch with your kin. You know, to, uh, let them know you're alright, that is."

Aldonzo stifled a painful laugh of contempt for the pirate's churlish attempt at subterfuge. After all the questions and beatings, he expected Aldonzo to be ignorant of his true purpose? He wouldn't last a day at court in Septimania. Some noble's daughter would have a squire slip a dagger in his back before he even realized someone hated him.

"Have any ideas that might help, laddie?"

Aldonzo shook his head, but only once. The motion sent his head spinning; if he had dared, he'd have reached up to stop it. He hated the sea and he hated these men. He'd never get used to either one.

"Come on, boy!" Fenyas' voice dropped to a low growl. "I don't have time to fool around. You know what will happen if you become more trouble than your worth?"

There was fuzziness in Aldonzo's head that had been growing for several days from the seasickness, lack of food and drink, and work followed by harsh abuse. Yet in spite of all the torment the words cut through to the center of his awareness like a Roman gladius through his cracked ribs. He shook his head to clear it. Fenyas misunderstood the gesture.

"Hah! You don't, eh? Well, let me tell you all—"

"No, wait!" Aldonzo held up his hand. It was no longer the finely manicured appendage it once had been—he hoped for a moment they'd take it off at the wrist for his interrupting. One of Fenyas' mates in the shadows of the cabin looked wickedly eager. "Give me time to think. It's been such a long time since I've been home."

Think? Think of what? Most of his people were in southern Gaul. The pirates likely would make landfall somewhere near the northern Frankish kingdom of Nuestria, and relations between his people and the Franks were not always the best. He could end up ransomed to another lord who would in turn ransom him to his family, if he lived long enough. Aldonzo had a sudden vision of being loaded on a merchant's wagon, carted from town to town looking for a bidder. 'Lord for sale! Lord for sale!' the wagoneer would cry. 'Two denarii for a young lord! Are there any offers?'

"Think if you must, laddie, but make it quick!" Fenyas took another long wet pull on his ale, blew some foam from his lips, and wiped his stubbly chin with a salt-stiffened sleeve. "I wouldn't care to keep a popinjay like you around much longer."

Aldonzo's mind whirled in circles. He could only guess where they were; the last land he'd seen was a line of sheer, mist-covered cliffs that he suspected was Land's End in Cornwall. He wasn't sure though; his British geography had always been sorely lacking.

They had been in the channel for some time, though it had been days since he'd seen a Briton merchant. Reflecting on the slaughter he'd witnessed the last time they did, their absence was not unwelcome, even if it meant a lengthy venture in unfamiliar water for the hostile crew, too long since a plunder—just too long, period. The crew acted edgy, and Aldonzo felt it. Doubtless Fenyas could too, which would explain his rush to dispose of his catch.

It didn't help to try recalling the shores of Gaul. Until his arrival in Albion some months ago, he hadn't cared the least whit what the world was like north of the Massif, and his knowledge of northern Gaul was about as extensive as that of Britain.

Except for one thing.

"Come on, boy. Time is wasting." Fenyas glared at the prince for another moment, then motioned to one of the crew standing nearby. A wicked bit of steel appeared from a tattered shirt.

"Wait!" The last thing Aldonzo wanted was for Fenyas to bring out his 'toys' again. A thought floated about aimlessly in the back of his head, a fragment of memory from a conversation not so very long ago.

"What?" the pirate snarled.

Aldonzo racked his brain. What was that place? For God's sake, he had told Mattheus about it. When? A week ago? Maybe longer.

"Ach!" Fenyas spat, slamming his mug down on the table. "Forget it, laddie, I've no more time to waste. Mac Nir!"

"Monte Tombe!" Aldonzo forced out in desperation.

"What?" Fenyas said.

"Monte Tombe, off the Frankish coast, near the spur of Armorica."

"And what is that?"

"A place where . . ." Where what? They could deliver him to the hands of the Franks? What would be the lesser of the two evils? To pass into the power of a semi-Romanized Frank lord that would know who he was and use him for some political advantage? Or to stay here and . . . he brushed that thought quickly from his mind. At least in Gaul he could get off this blasted boat.

"It's a place where you can contact my people."

"Ach! Now this is what I've been looking for." Fenyas sat back down and slapped a square hand on the table. There was a wicked smile on his face as he poured himself another draught. "Tell me about this Monte Tombe."

⸙

Aldonzo lifted his eyes to the sky, looking for some miracle from on high—an angel, or a warrior saint; anything to aid him in pulling off this deception and to keep him from sweating the proverbial blood.

The ship's leather-covered curragh departed with Fenyas and a couple of his henchmen bearing a note written in Aldonzo's own hand to whatever Frankish lords they should find. The thought of scribbling the Latin script brought a smile to his cracked lips. He'd written it because the pirate Fenyas was illiterate—a small victory, but a victory nonetheless.

Still, fear gnawed the pit of his stomach like a starving cur on a soup bone. He questioned his own plan endlessly. It could either work for him, or kill him. The plan was simple in design; the actual execution would be the problem.

Execution . . . bad choice of words, he thought to himself. He looked pensively at his feet. The heavy manacles clamped on his ankles posed a threat if he jumped overboard too soon.

The night sky was clear and bright, showing a few hours past midnight. Soon, very soon. Growing battle nerves drew his stomach up in a tight knot, which only aggravated the constant nausea. He knew he would have vomited if there had been something in his stomach to bring up.

251

Aldonzo closed his eyes and tried to relax. There would be no sense trying to escape if he got himself too sick to even stumble. He put his head in his hands and leaned against the rail to conserve his strength. The shadow of the boat glided across the starlit bay.

They had arrived only a short time ago, dropping anchor in the waters to the south of Monte Tombe, between the jutting rock and the shore of Gaul, where a river wound down to the sea. Scanning the coast of the mainland, Aldonzo recalled that to the left lay Neustria, to the right Armorica. Not much of a choice—between the cutthroat Franks who despised the Visigoths and the ever-warring continental Bretons that despised all Germanics with equal fervor—but he decided these options were far superior to staying on the ship.

He looked over his shoulder briefly at the bulk of the Monte, rising out of the water like a brooding sea god, a huge cone of rock just over a fifth of a Roman mile wide and almost three hundred feet high. It wore a forest mantle, like a thick cloak of invisibility.

After a short time the curragh passed out of sight and the crew settled in for the wait, bedding down across the deck. Aldonzo, attempting to make himself as inconspicuous as a prisoner could be, sank down in the shelter of the windward rail. He allowed himself to doze off, confident that when the time came, he would awaken.

In time the sideways rocking of the ship slowed. Aldonzo awoke with a start. The first glimmerings of dawn lit the horizon, but his stomach knew that was not why he had awakened. The vessel was settling.

He glanced around and mouthed a silent "Hallelujah." Fortune finally looked to be taking an interest in him. Only a pair of pirates were in sight, teetering against the mast, apparently unable to decide whether they were too tired to stand watch any longer, or just too drunk. Aldonzo stretched his arms casually, rubbed the back of his neck to ease a nagging muscle, and stood ever so slowly.

One of the pirates looked his way. He returned a blank stare until the pirate shifted his gaze back to the serene shore.

Aldonzo walked gingerly aft, following the anchor cable to the windlass, where he quietly slipped the lynch pin. He continued to the mast; the deck here sloped down to its lowest point above the water. Once amidships, he leaned on the rail and pretended an interest in the gulls diving out of the sky for their breakfast. All the while, he kept an eye on the water. As the sun broke the horizon, lighting the top of the Monte in a burst of color, the ship's keel bottomed out with a lurch that threw the two lookouts to their knees.

Aldonzo breathed a quick prayer and vaulted over the rail to land knee-deep in the receding tide. He stretched out on the water and, kicking his feet along the bottom, allowed the current to sweep him away from the craft on a line between the Monte and the Frankish shore. Shouts and curses echoed above him as slumbering reavers were awakened by their own shipmates rolling onto them down the listing deck.

The current carried him a few dozen yards before the water grew shallow and left him in the sand, but it was a head start. By the time the pirates discovered he had slipped over the side, he was on his feet and shuffling away across the wet sand.

The brigands poured over the rail, howling and shrieking as they slogged after him, and he increased his pace toward the Monte. If he could reach it quickly, he might even avoid Fenyas' return from the mainland.

He looked back a second time and huffed in relief; not so many were chasing him as he thought. Some had stopped and stood gasping for breath in the swirling ankle-deep water, but most were milling around their beached vessel, as if they could get it floating again by merely scratching their lice-infested scalps and shouting at each other. A stalwart few kept up the chase, but they lagged behind him, slowed as much by the wet sand as he was by his manacles.

Aldonzo's heart pounded in his ears and throat, and his churning legs burned like fire. But the thought of the pirates' renewed hospitality kept him going like a Greek athlete.

He looked back once more to see that the few pirates still in the hunt were not doing any better than he in the clinging sand. One limped like a lame mule, and another pressed on by holding his sides. One of the pirates stumbled and fell in the slogging sand. He tried getting back up, but the sand sucked him down as he thrashed and called out to his mates.

Aldonzo kept running, now watching the sand fearfully, hoping he trod the right kind. The wooded slopes of the Monte drew closer and closer and with each painful step the sounds of pursuit grew fainter. Aldonzo stumbled breathlessly up a short slope to the first of the trees and collapsed, gasping in a heap among their tangled roots.

Distant voices filtered through the Monte's shadowy boughs.

Aldonzo pulled himself against a tree, took a few deep breaths, and staggered further up the Monte. Moving deeper into the wood, he selected a likely looking oak with accessible branches and pulled himself painfully up to a high vantage point. In the distance, the pirates buzzed around their vessel like hornets as Aldonzo settled onto the wide limb of the ancient tree, the leaves thick about him, deep and green. He leaned his back against the trunk and sucked in the cool air of freedom.

The pirates cast lines and attempted to drag the ship to deeper water, but soon they abandoned the effort and tossed the ropes aside. One of the mates had managed to muster a few brigands into a search party and seemed ready to strike out for the Monte when Fenyas returned, stalking across the sand like a man possessed by fiery demons. Aldonzo cringed into the oak's comforting embrace when the man's hated voice reached his ears. The pirate chief had returned bloodied and alone—the Franks clearly had not thought much of his offer and the crew paid bloody hell for his rejection.

Finally, the pirates struck out for the Monte to search for their flown captive. But as the first few reached the trees there was a distant sound of rushing water that grew louder and louder with frightening speed. The tide was returning in mighty foaming waves, much faster than it had left. Fenyas, standing high on the aft deck, howled for his men to return. The pirates tumbled from the woods across the sand, nearly exhausted from struggling with the chase, the boat, and the chase again; but some of them managed to reach the boat before the crashing water did. Too bad for them.

Unfortunately for Fenyas, when the boat had been stranded it had heeled over in the direction of the returning sea. A large wave at the head of the tide slammed over the rail, swamping the boat and propelling it across the sand at the pace of a horse's gallop. The anchor windlass Aldonzo had released spun out yards of line like a furious snake as the wave carried the boat away. Men, supplies, rigging, and timber from the hull were thrown into the foaming tide, bobbing on the surface in a scattered trail behind it; other men shrieked as they were thrown from the deck onto the sand ahead of the vessel, to be crushed and drowned a heartbeat later. Survivors desperately clutched at fragments of timber as they were washed out into the distant bay.

Aldonzo rolled back into the tree trunk and laughed until tears came and exhaustion finally stole over him.

Later that evening the tide receded once more, exposing the bare white sand to the shore. Little trace of the ship remained; only a few shattered timbers and an occasional limb protruded from the smooth surface. Aldonzo waited as long as he dared before striking out for the mainland.

Despite the calm peace of the puddled strait, the walk filled him with fear as he thought of the cruel Fenyas and wondered on his fate. But he walked easier now that his bare feet finally tread solid ground again. He continued up the beach to a meadow a few hundred feet inland that was cut by a road, where a small train of wagons rumbled along through the night. Aldonzo's stomach growled.

Politics with the Northern Franks be damned, he thought. *I'm hungry.*

He stepped onto the road and waved his arms to catch the attention of the lead driver. The man reined the draft horse to a halt and hopped down. He looked Aldonzo up and down, slowly and carefully, and his gaze stopped for a moment on Aldonzo's feet.

Aldonzo's blood drained from his face with a chill when he realized he still had the manacles on. He stammered out an explanation in a Germanic dialect the Frank would understand when the man cut him off with a few coarse words.

The man spoke Celtic.

Aldonzo tried to cover up his blunder by launching into the Celtic dialect of southern Cymru, mixed with Latin. He had clearly made a mistake in crossing the strait, and had come ashore on the wrong side of the river. He wasn't in Neustria at all; he stood stripped to his chest with rusty manacles on his legs in Armorica. As he squinted past the drivers, the back of his neck prickled as he saw the cargo the wagons carried.

Slaves.

He turned to run, but too late. The driver's hand clamped down on his shoulder and a rope was thrown around his chest. Aldonzo's protests were quelled with a few sharp blows to his face as he was trussed unceremoniously and tossed into the back of the wagon, bound for Brest.

Chapter Twenty

At The Gate

UNDER THE WANING MOON, a small force of soldiers galloped through the splashing sand of the beach at a punishing pace. Waves and salty spray spurted from beneath their mounts' hooves as they thundered into the surf, their attention on the two figures that led them.

One was Mattheus, High King of Gwent. He had been terribly anxious since Sister Wynne had wandered into the middle of the camp the night before, dazed and confused. He had readied immediately to leave St. Bride, snatching up snippets of information from the mad sister and the partial map Weylin had left at Loughar, bent on charging down the coast to find this keep that turned up at the heart of every lead.

But calmer heads had prevailed when Lord Reeves convinced Mattheus to have a good night's rest, a full day's preparation, and a fresh start at sunset. A king, any king, gallivanting through the countryside without a fresh escort would not solve the problem,

Reeves had insisted. It would put the entire kingdom at risk. And the men needed rest after the long ride from Caerleon to the abbey. It served neither Marianna nor the realm to have the king feathered in the back by an arrow in hostile territory.

But now the time had come and they were on the trail. Next to the wild-eyed king charged the young scout who had ridden ahead to verify Sister Wynne's ravings. He'd returned late in the afternoon with a positive report of a fortified manor just a few hours' ride up the coast. Now he led the party, his fresh mount beginning to flag under the exertion.

Lord Reeves rode behind Mattheus on his sword side. He believed he could feel the mood in each excited trooper—a combined anticipation, elation, and vengeful determination. Weeks of grueling training, dust, and sweat were now coming to a head; the stronghold of the adversary lay within striking distance and retribution would be required of the scoundrels for the kidnapping. Reeves' own nostrils flared with emotion as well, the heat coursing through his veins before battle, banishing fatigue with each heartbeat like leaves before the gusting wind. He knew his king, he fought for his king, and he loved his king. He would gladly wet his blade again to avenge the wrongs wrought upon his king.

Reeves wondered fleetingly what had become of Aldonzo and his expedition down this same stretch of coast. Possibly the dandy prince lay waiting, anchored within sight of the coast, but unless the crew was watching the shore very closely they would have no indication that the King rode headlong in their direction. Suddenly he thought that they might have already freed the princess, but he brushed that thought from his mind. Aldonzo would never want to leave such a place as a proper smoking ruin; what with the charred bodies and all he might get a smudge on his bright woolen tights. The general allowed himself a smirk.

They rode on, none daring to slow the King. An outcropping of rock appeared and the scout raced around it, when suddenly his horse skidded to a halt and reared, nearly throwing him to the ground. Mattheus threw his arm into the air to signal a halt before the others rounded the rugged obstacle. He narrowed his eyes and, a moment later, waved a cautious advance.

The men loosed their weapons in their scabbards and urged their mounts forward at a walk, the relieved horses blowing steamy froth from their lips. When they rounded the outcrop, a stench filled the air, turning one trooper's stomach inside out.

Over a dozen bodies in various stages of decay were piled in a loose heap against the rock. Some wore the clothing of commoners, while others lay in rusted armor. They were the fruits of a battle, but for some reason they had not been buried, or even given the dignity of a pyre.

"How, in the name of Michael, did you miss this?" Reeves snapped at the scout.

The trooper apologetically pointed to the cliffs bounding the inland side of the sand. "I was . . . riding up there, sir."

"Dismount," Reeves barked. He hopped from his own mount and began turning over the bodies when he noticed the blazon of Mattheus' Home Guard among the dead. "Gods of heaven and hell," he muttered. The soldiers grimly bent their backs to the task of sorting the dead in earnest and under the King's very active eye they identified many of the bodies—Master Kien, Weylin, and others, well known to them all.

"No Aldonzo," Mattheus said, turning his eyes down the beach.

"Aye m'lord, no prince." Reeves looked perplexed and followed the King's gaze. One could only guess at the fate of the Visigoth prince. The beach ahead had long ago been washed trackless by the surging tides. Possibly, the same surf had washed a dead Aldonzo out to sea.

"Bury them quickly," Mattheus demanded, pointing to his soldiers among the dead. Then, sweeping his hand angrily over the other bodies, he added, "Leave the rest for the carrion."

Reeves bowed and ordered his troops to begin gathering stones.

By the time the company once again took up the mad gallop through the sand their reckless anticipation had departed, buried beneath cairns of loose stones. In its place stood a colder, more calculating emotion that could only be satisfied with a retribution payment of death.

Past another spur of rock, they rode along the beach of a wide cove. Midway down its length, a hundred yards from shore, a peak of granite thrust up out of the still waters to support a squared, purposeful structure, in which a few lamps gleamed from scattered windows. A narrow wooden causeway reached out from the beach to a gatehouse on the fortress' shoreward side.

There was motion on the tall battlements.

Mattheus drew himself up in the saddle, recklessly throwing aside all pretenses of secrecy, and rode down the strand until he reined up just out of bowshot of the gate. A solitary torch lit the top of the gatehouse and the two sentries posted there.

The king stood in his stirrups and bellowed, "I demand to see he who is lord of this place!"

Mattheus waited for the reply.

Finally one of the shadowy guards yelled, "By whose order?"

The King turned red in the face. Reeves nudged his horse a few steps forward to his lord's right hand.

"Mattheus ap Jordanes Emrys, High King of Gwent and Unifier of Cymru!" he fired back in a booming voice.

Reeves placed his hand on the hilt of his sword, his better judgment screaming inside his head that he shouldn't have let Mattheus rush into revealing them before they could call reinforcements. The veins in his hands bulged as he drew the weapon, laying the cool steel menacingly across his saddlebow. A figure appeared behind the shadowed portcullis, his boots clacking as he walked to the keep and disappeared within.

Mattheus sat stiffly in his saddle. Behind him, the men grew restless as the minutes dragged on.

"I say we storm the gate and drive them into the bloody sea," growled one trooper. A look from Reeves quickly silenced him.

All the men's attention riveted back to the keep when the door opened again and a small number of figures emerged, shadows against shadows. They approached the gatehouse, vanished within, and moments later reappeared on the battlement. Mattheus drew a deep breath as he prepared to vent his frustration on this insignificant bandit, this so-called Black Knight, for causing him so much anguish, so much soul-sucking grief. But when the keep's master stepped into the torchlight, his anger died in his heart, as did the words in his throat.

Marianna stood silhouetted against the sky.

Chapter Twenty-One

COUNCIL OF THE DEAD

THEY'D COME FOR ME, Erik thought. *Yes, they would come and find me out for what I truly am. Then what?* Drive a spike through his sternum, lop off his head, fill his skull full of herbs, and leave the whole bloody lot skewered on a pike atop Caer Baen's walls, that's what. The children would dance and laugh in the dusty streets below, occasionally pointing up at the gruesome sight; while the old folk, those that had heard something of the tales of the East, would merely mutter and shake their heads, cursing and whispering of the undead.

Of course, they could botch the job, being novices at this sort of mutilation and exorcism. What crueler fate than to shriek in torment while part of his body burned in the sun as the rest was left forgotten in the mad dash to wipe this blot from their lives?

Probably neither would happen, and the bishop would merely drive him from the town, Erik finally concluded—admonishing him by all the sacred relics buried beneath the altar of the church never to return.

That would leave him no better off than when he had first crept into Caer Baen, although he knew Thelwyn would be much relieved to beat a hasty path to Londinium and catch passage on the first ship out of Britain. The magicker did not have to remind Erik of his wishes—he'd made them quite clear to both him and his father. Yet Caius insisted on knowing more about this curse. Erik couldn't blame him for not believing, even though he had seen his son's reaction to an icon of the Lord's pain.

"There are many creatures afoot tonight," Thelwyn said suddenly.

"What do you mean?" Erik asked half-heartedly, knowing that the response would include a suggestion that they flee from Caer Baen and Birkenshire.

The old man shook his head. "I'm already expending too much energy shielding our whereabouts from his probing eyes. I fear that casting about may give away our location. We must leave this place, and we must leave it immediately."

"They will come soon," Erik grumbled. "When they do, this may all be over and you can embark on whatever journey that you see fit. As for me, once this curse is cast off, I will pick up the quest for the princess once more."

Thelwyn's eyes were watery and tired. Erik felt his sadness but wanted desperately to cling to hope. He wanted the devil exorcised from his body—wanted the forces that had engulfed Marianna to leave his family alone. He rose from the keg on which he had been perched and walked over to the basement door, creaking it open and peering out into the growing darkness. A mist had risen, hovering cold and grey above the ground. Voices twittered from all over the village. He could hear them unbidden through their doors and walls. He covered his ears, but could not block them out.

"I cannot help you," Thelwyn said. "Your senses fly about unrestrained, forcing against my own. I can't keep you hidden much longer."

"Can't this be stopped? I don't want to know what's going on in the tanner's shop or the miller's bedchamber."

Thelwyn sighed. "You are a predator now, just like the wolf, the bat, or the snake. These senses keep your ilk of undead fed. They allow you to survive."

Erik looked away and saw his father returning from the church with six men at his back. Their breathing fell heavy and hot, their hearts pounding excitedly in their chests. Erik realized his father must have told them his tale, for they crushed together behind him, afraid of the shadows cast by their own homes.

"Look's like you'll not have to cover my tracks much longer," Erik said. "They come." He leapt up the steps, Thelwyn huffing up behind, and walked out into the middle of the roadway that ran from gate to gate through the center of town, inside the encircling wall.

Caius strode tall ahead of the skittish pack, one hand upon his long straight cavalry blade, the other holding aloft a torch against the descending night. The milky-eyed bishop followed behind, guided through the ruts and mud by a lay deacon. The rest of the group were all faces Erik knew—Gyfon the furrier, Marcus the toll-collector, Simon the money-lender, and Karl the Saxon horse trader. Upon seeing Erik, Gyfon genuflected, Marcus looked quickly away, and Karl shrugged, squinting at him before throwing back his head to let out a hearty laugh.

"This couldn't have happened to our Erik!" His face brightened.

"Ah, here's our boy." He meant to come up to Erik in greeting, but the bishop held a feeble hand in front of his chest.

"Father," Erik said, "you've told them all?"

Caius nodded, motioning his son forward. Erik stepped up and Caius grasped his hand. His fingers clenched the cold flesh, his grip firm. He placed Erik's hand in the Bishop's.

"M'lord, if what you say is truth then do you think that this is wise?" said the deacon, a middle-aged man with no need of a tonsure. "Exposing his eminence to this evil, and at night. He could catch a wicked plague just from the touch."

A look from Caius stilled the man's tongue. "Geoffrey," he said, "this is Erik, or at least something like him. What has happened? What has become of my son?"

The bishop eyed Erik intently, though Erik doubted the ancient man could even make out his features in the flickering torchlight. He pursed his lips and in a quiet voice asked, "Do you realize if he truly is cast back to the earth by death, he must be driven out or destroyed?"

Bishop Geoffrey's eyes searched Caius' face though he would have found nothing there to give away his emotions.

"Yes," Caius forced out.

"Father—" Erik started, but stopped short. Why protest what he had desired when he killed Hadrian?

Simon pulled something out of a belt pouch, muttered, and tossed it over his shoulder. Karl rubbed his beard with a broad hand and shook his head in disbelief, the entire proceedings alien to his Germanic perception of reality.

"T'aint never seen such a thing," he muttered. "Wodin's blood, the lad is a warrior, not some creature of the Hel."

Erik knelt before the prelate and bowed his head. "I submit to your will, holy father. I desired freedom from this curse, but will be satisfied with death."

Geoffrey nodded and pulled his hand free. "Let us have proof then, Caius. Is it not said, out of the mouth of two or three witnesses shall all truth be established? We will test your son to prove if he is human flesh or bedeviled monster. Brother Ethelbert, please begin."

The deacon began reciting a prayer for exorcism.

Suddenly Erik's head reeled. His senses burst out beyond Thelwyn's containing envelope and he sensed all the creatures in the countryside around the city; in the hills, coming through the pastures and plowed fields, tromping up the broken Roman road. Thelwyn fell to one knee, head bent and shoulders heaving. His hand trembled against his chest.

"They—they've found us," Thelwyn gasped.

Brother Ethelbert had pulled out a garland of garlic. Erik could smell the strong aroma of the herb biting his nostrils, threatening to overcome him. He had no time for this uselessness, to prove his status for the bishop, as memories of his dreams flooded his mind. Yes, they'd come, and he was here to stop them.

Erik pushed himself to his feet, unsteady. "They've tracked me here. I fear that—"

Caius clamped a firm soldier's hand on his shoulder. "None of this nonsense," he said. Brother Ethelbert's lips fell silent.

"They have tracked us here and they will tear down Caer Baen's walls to find me." Erik shook off his father's arm and hauled Thelwyn to his feet, pushing through the fog in his mind as the effects of the prayer dissipated. "I am sorry I came. I should have stayed away, but I wanted to warn you. I've no time to waste with this."

Gyfon and Marcus rushed forward and grabbed Erik by the elbows, pulling him back as Simon pulled a flat, round piece of metal from his belt. He held it up in front of Erik's face.

"Look! Look, I say, he does not reflect!" There was a pinch of glee in his voice. "I told you that your prayers and weeds take too long! Look, no reflection or mist on the surface!"

Karl pulled anxiously on the locks of hair that curled down from in front of his ears, his jaw agape. "I've never seen the like!"

"Let me go!" Erik growled. "I've no wish to have anyone hurt. We must go before they attack."

The deacon smiled, "I've heard of this sort of thing in Londinium. There they claim holy water will burn the flesh of the undead." He dropped the garland of garlic and snatched a stoppered vial from his habit.

"Those who would attack the village are at the gates," Erik pleaded, searching Geoffrey's eyes for understanding. "Please let me draw them away from here. They need not—"

Geoffrey nodded to the deacon and traced the corners of the cross before him. "If you be of that great Deceiver, may the Holy Mother of God save your soul."

"No!" Erik yelled, pulling his arms free. "They will not stop at a few drops of blood. They will destroy you!" He pushed past the deacon, the holy water in his hands sloshing and wetting his homespun garments.

Caius' blade scraped from its scabbard. "Hold," he said. Erik froze out of reflex to his father's authority. "I know that my son would not lie. This," his voice quivered, "may or may not be my son, I cannot tell. But I must know if you have told me the truth, Erik."

"I have not lied." He felt Caius' eyes hot on his back, trying to penetrate into his soul. "You've not seen what I have seen, crossed where I have crossed. Look at me!" He turned back to them. He saw them all through a crimson haze, his fingers clenched at his side, his body trembling. His mouth filled with teeth—wild, rabid teeth. The men from the village shrank back.

A tear rolled down Caius' cheek.

"I thought to have time for you to either kill or cure me," Erik continued. "But they are here. Whatever you do now, they will lay waste to the village. I will not allow this."

Caius raised his blade. "If you say that they are here then I believe."

Shouts barked through the night and metal clanged. Someone shrieked.

Thelwyn stumbled to his feet. Erik pulled his own sword from its scabbard and raced for the main gate. Men with torches knotted around it, most of them half-dressed and cursing to be out in the night air. He pushed through them and saw the thick jutting end of a log through a splintered hole in the gate. The marauders on the other side of the portal began to wriggle it loose. A *thwump, thwump, thwump* sounded—the repeated blows of an axe to widen the hole.

Along the inner wall the sentries bent their bows and let loose their shafts. One of the guards cried something to his fellow, threw down his weapon, and leapt from his post to the ground. Others followed. "Damn your hides!" Caius howled over the commotion. "You men heat up the pots! You—you over there—get men up on those walls!" His eyes gleamed as if he were a general marshaling his legion. "Get those new pitchforks from the—yes, you there!"

The log moved and jerked loose. The gate quivered and shards of wood split. Erik snatched up a bow and a handful of scattered arrows, and then scrambled up to the catwalk inside the parapet. He leaned out over the wall.

An army of the dead lay in siege of Caer Baen.

Ghastly naked bodies shambled up to the gate and threw their weight against the straining wood. Others hacked at the timbers with wood axes taken from an unfortunate peasant who even now clawed at the earth under the gate with his head split open. Grey masses of long-dead flesh, ragged bone, and stretched sinews propelled more of the dead from the pastureland and hills surrounding the town. They said not a word, but moved silently.

"If you want me," Erik shouted, "then I will come to you and have done!" Not a single eye turned toward him. They intended to complete their task at Caer Baen's expense, taking Erik's family and home with them to their graves.

Men ran from the smithy, pitch pots dangling from bowed poles. Caius barked orders and the men clambered up the ladders to the catwalks inside the walls. With stolid urging they made their way across the wall to the gate, pouring the pitch and tossing torches, igniting the fluid in a puff of flame and smoke.

But the dead continued their tasks while the fire consumed them.

Thwump, thwump, thwump, and the battering log pounded the gate once again. Erik leaped from the wall and planted himself behind the crumpling portal. He may not have been able to save Merrovaine, but he resolved to fight through this company of dead and keep them from taking Caer Baen.

Caius took a position on his right. He smiled at his son, his steely eyes searching his face for a moment. "What manner of creatures are these?" he asked above the pounding.

"They're dead. That's all I know," Erik answered. He could tell creatures such as Marianna and himself were different than these. He sensed no intelligence, no thought—merely a mass of mindless dead flesh that could easily have been pressed into duty by the Grey Lord once he'd sensed Thelwyn's protective magicks dissolve. And Erik's desire had led them here. As surely as any undead dream, he had doomed Caer Baen. "It's my fault, father. I should have listened to Thelwyn."

Caius clapped him on the shoulder and said, "Then we'd not have this chance to battle together."

Erik embraced his father.

The gate shattered in a groan of twisted hinges and splintering braces. Erik leaped into the breach, swinging his blade with the strength borne of his undead disease. Clawing fingers groped at him as he severed limbs and pressed the first of the dead back into their stumbling comrades.

Flesh and earthy decay splattered all around, but on they came. Gaunt, gray bodies crushed into each other as the shambling dead clambered forward into the breach.

A horn trumpeted a crisp, clear note through the night air. The Huntsman had returned, this time with a pack that could take Erik down.

Someone grunted beside him. Karl the Saxon smashed his broad German axe into a corpse's face. Blood oozed from a wound in his thigh. The Saxon spat and then glared at Erik, his eyes clouded with battle lust. He hooted in his native tongue and plunged deeper into the ranks of the dead. Caius lopped off a creature's head and shouldered the stumbling body out of his way.

Townsfolk took heart at their stand and rallied with pitchforks, hunting spears, and other implements. But the dead continued to surge against the living. Through the broken gates, Erik spied the smoldering lumps that had been ignited by the pitch. They lay quivering, no longer capable of motion.

Fire.

"Torches—get torches!" he cried. He shoved his way forward to sweep the dead clear and push the throng back out the shattered gates. He heard the men to the rear babble about fire and cooking the dead.

The boom of wood on wood rose again above the clamoring clang of arms. A contingent of the dead had made for the opposite gate. Erik hacked the legs from under another corpse and smashed a boot into its chest. Its arms twitched as if to grab at his legs, so he cut off the arms and head.

Confusion broke out and resistance melted as the other gate again reverberated. Men with Caius dropped their pitch pots and ran off with their torches flaming over their heads to man the other gate or to huddle in their homes with their frightened families. Caius shouted oaths to heaven as his forces splintered, but to no use. Caer Baen was doomed.

Karl fell in a gurgle of blood as a corpse caught him from behind and tore open his neck with its fleshless fingers. Erik saw him fall in a spray of crimson and vanish beneath the warring dead.

A crowd of dead tightened their attack on Caius as he stepped forward into Karl's place, swinging his long cavalry blade. Erik rushed to his aid, his blade deftly cleaving through dead flesh and bone. Still they tenaciously continued their attack on him, pulling at his leather jerkin and clawing at his legs. He pulled the corpses from his father and threw them back through the gate.

"Julia," Erik hissed as he pushed Caius back toward the town. "Get to Julia!"

Erik stumbled as two bloodied hands clamped down over his head. The hands were sticky and warm. They were Karl's. The Saxon had succumbed to the foul power of the Huntsman. Erik grabbed Karl's arm with his left hand and slashed over his shoulder. Again and again steel met dead flesh. Other corpses shambled forward through the gate as he mangled the Saxon's body enough to struggle free.

Erik roared his defiance to the silent heavens, launching himself into the midst of the dead. Skulls, arms, jawbones, all became a jumble as he fought to keep the dead from overrunning this gate. If they did, they'd probably drag him to some pit in Hell while the village burned after their spent rampage. He called upon his own dark strength to lend its aid in the battle. Shrieks filtered through his madness—the other gate had been breached.

Pungent smoke filled the air.

Relentlessly, he waded forward into the gate's ruined frame, sweeping the decay from before him. He pushed off Karl's groping embrace one last time and split him from crown to collarbone, and then forced the battle outward, beyond Caer Baen's walls. A vow roared from his lips to take the head of the Huntsman and throw it at the feet of his master. Upon the ashes of Caer Baen, he promised the same fate for the Grey God!

A black-cowled form flitted across his path, moving too quickly to be a corpse. Erik brushed through two rotted creatures and reached to grab the black cloak, focused on catching and bringing it down, believing it one of the Grey Lord's underlings directing the movements of this horde.

Cold metal suddenly bit the sides of his mouth. Links of a chain were pulled tight into his jaw, jerking his head and then his body to a halt. Erik stumbled, dropping his blade to pull off the chain. Cold, strong hands gripped his wrists and pulled his arms back. Erik fought but could not break free. A stout piece of wood slammed against his back and more chains secured him to it. Black figures darted around— wild and ferocious creatures that shredded the attacking corpses with raking claws and rending teeth.

Erik tried to turn his head to loosen the chain, but the more he strained, the more lengths of iron creased his flesh. The dark creatures flopped him on his back, and in the flickering light of burning Caer Baen, he saw a pale face, red eyes, and long dripping teeth, framed by wild locks of dark hair. The face floated before him, breath polluted with the stench of death. Steely fingers clenched his face, twisting Erik's flesh against the chain.

"Blaine may have fought with honor," the creature growled, "but I have none." It turned away and barked orders to others. "The de Dannan, get him—he comes with us."

Screams filled the night, through the smoke and orange flames.

Erik heard many die, but could not break free of the links of metal that held him to the post. For his efforts, the chain in his mouth constricted and bit deeper. Eventually, the dark forms lifted him by the heavy wooden stake and whisked him through the gate.

The sounds and smells of destruction, the Huntsman's horn, and the shambling dead—all vanished as he was carried up the hills outside Caer Baen, across the pastures and into the dark forest. Erik strained against the chains throughout the remaining hours of darkness. He had to break free to save his sister, his father, and his home.

But in the end, he could not.

Before the first rays of dawn broke the eastern horizon, Erik's captors made for a crack in the earth, a cave half-hidden by moss and decayed leaves. They dragged him down, the post jarring and bouncing along the ground. One of them shouldered him to the side, the post turning around like a spit over a cookfire, so Erik could not see any of his captors.

A cover was pulled over the opening, throwing the cave into complete darkness. He wanted to turn his head to scan the surroundings, for his eyes quickly adjusted to the blackness, but the tight chains held him firmly in place. The creatures moved about silently, brushing by him occasionally, but no one moved to loosen his bonds or lower him into a more comfortable position. Not that it mattered, he realized. The chains, other than holding him firmly in place, did not cause much other discomfort. One of the fortunes of the undead, he supposed—blood doesn't need to circulate through the limbs.

Eventually the creatures settled in and one of them approached.

"Doesn't hurt, does it?" it rasped. "Ah, me pretty, it hurts less than the kiss of the morning sun, I'll wager." It slapped his shoulder and sent the pole rolling back and forth once more until it settled with Erik's face pointing down to the rough ground.

The creature moved off after the others into the deeper, darker recesses of the cave. He could hear some faint discussion follow the cool draft from below, but all about, his senses felt walled in and chained as firmly as his body to the timber. Hot moisture welled up around his eyes as the magnitude of his situation became more apparent. He'd been kidnapped during the battle for Caer Baen's survival, before its fate could be secured.

He pulled once more on the chains, but they afforded no slack. He cursed himself for a fool. The quarry had been him and all had fallen to satisfy the lust of the hunter—the Huntsman, the Grey God, it mattered not who pulled back on the bow. All his family was dead; of this he was sure.

The cave became quiet, except for the dripping of moisture further down. Erik rocked the pole until it turned face up and caught into place in the rock and dirt. Above the covering at the entrance of the cave, the day passed, while beneath the dead slept and waited for the following night. He strained against his bonds, twisting the links about, but they held firm. Dirt fell in his face and the pole spun about once more until he again faced downward. There was nothing for him to do but wait for his captors to rouse from their slumber.

They laughed—a wicked, dark sort of noise, punctuated with the groans and gurgling of their victim. Dark forms hovered about the unfortunate villager, ravens about the bled carcass, bickering over the feeding order. One of them stood up straight and looked to where Erik remained bound, now propped against a tree. The creature's face was pale and gaunt, blood smattered about its smiling mouth.

Rending flesh, tongues lapping up streams of blood from the cool ground, splitting bones; all the sounds of their unholy feast filled his senses. He strained against the chains but could not move. He could barely twitch. Another of the creatures stood up and looked about. Its eyes burned red against the fading glow of the sun beyond the horizon. It reached down and grabbed another by the scruff of the neck and said something in muffled tones. The other creature hesitated, wagged its head and then loped off into the forest.

"Alright, you leeches," the creature said aloud. "We best mount up afore that damn horned-demon sniffs out our trail. Won't do us much good to get caught out here, yet."

It shoved heads and shoulders out of its path as it pushed from the knot of dark feeders and stalked toward Erik. Black hair framed its face, its eyes bright against its pale skin. It wiped blood from its mouth with its sleeve then hissed, "What's wrong, boy? Hungry?"

The creature pushed the pole over and Erik toppled to the ground, the impact jarring his teeth and jerking the chain deeper into his cheeks. The creature waved its companions over.

They lifted him upon their shoulders. From his vantage point all he could see was the ground passing beneath him. They spoke not a word, but remained deathly silent throughout the night. Once,

the sound of a horn broke in the distance, but it was barely audible, though it did spur his captors onward at greater speed.

Erik passed the time deep within the recesses of his mind, grieving at the loss and possible damnation of his family and village at the hands of the dead host. Hatred simmered in his chest, for the Grey Lord, for the Huntsman, for his captors, and for himself. He breathed a vow of vengeance most foul to be exacted upon those responsible.

The threatening dawn found the ragged party hunkered down in a musty old cellar beneath a ruined villa. The creatures propped him up once more against a corner. They lay down one by one in the darkest recesses and fell into the sleep of the damned. Bodies stiffened beneath their long black cloaks and the cellar became pungent with the stench of death. Outside, the sun's rays hit the cellar door. Even if the chains could be loosened, Erik was effectively sealed in the cellar until the sun set.

⁂

On the third night they entered the outskirts of what appeared to be a large town. The creatures loaded Erik onto the back of a wagon and pulled an oily tarp over him. Townsfolk talked, laughed, and cursed one another as the wagon creaked down the streets. Someone twanged a stringed instrument, squawking a few lines to a song; someone else gruffly threatened his life if he didn't stop. The distracting babble was almost comforting in a way, quite unlike the experience in Caer Baen.

Eventually, the sounds of carousing gave way to the quiet of a slumbering town, marked by the creak of a few moving wagons and occasional voices. The wagon driver spoke in hushed tones to someone as the wagon stopped. Then the tarp was pulled back and a number of the shrouded creatures hauled Erik up, whisking him into a dark building.

"Release him," said a woman's voice, deep from within the darkness of the chamber.

A few of the cloaked figures mumbled to each other, but they obeyed the command and loosed his bonds. Erik staggered as the pole clattered to the stone floor and the chains fell in coils at his feet. Rubbing his jaw, he raised his eyes to penetrate the darkness, seeking the source of the voice.

It belonged to a woman, coldly beautiful beyond measure, young, in appearance only about eighteen summers old—younger, even, than Marianna. Her body was wrapped in a sheer linen dress of Egyptian style, despite her clearly Latin heritage. She stood near a statue of a man pulling back the head of a bull with one hand, while readying a knife to slit the bull's throat with the other—Mithras, the Eastern god of warriors and resurrection.

She stepped away from the statue and Erik felt his eyes riveted to the graceful movements of her body, heightened senses stirring. He realized with a start that while her hips swayed alluringly, there was no heave to her breasts—she was not breathing. She drew close and held out a white-skinned hand. She smiled at Erik's hesitation to take it. It was, not surprisingly, pale as death.

"What place is this?" he asked. "Why am I here?"

Her black eyes brushed over him casually.

"You're to meet with the Council," she said. Her eyes locked onto his. "Much has happened of late that must be considered."

"What place is this?" Erik repeated, his hand reaching for the hilt of his sword, only to grasp nothing.

Her face became stony. "You should show respect to your elders—and your blood," she said curtly. She noticed his surprise at her response and her face softened. "Yes, you and I are bound twice by the sacred ties of blood." She slid gracefully away a few steps, regarding him over a cold ivory shoulder. The effect was breathtaking.

"I have been watching you, Erik of Birkenshire. You are the center of attention, indeed. Blaine had been mine, you see," she laughed lightly. "When I found him in Thrace, he was nothing more than a petty bandit. I have wished since that I had simply slit his throat and floated him down the Danube. But, Magnus was dead, the empire was a wreck, and I needed companionship."

She paused, sensing Erik's confusion. "You owe me blood respect as my birth posterity and as the throw of my . . . extended family."

His thoughts raced. This woman was an ancestor through blood, predecessor through the curse? "No!" He stepped back from her. "You're Flavia of Aquitaine?"

"Ahh, you've heard of me then. I do believe family traditions should be passed on to our children."

"But you were killed in Gaul when the Magnus marched on Rome to war with Theodosius, the Emperor of the East. That was over a century ago!"

"All those many years," she said. "My, the histories aren't very accurate, are they? And you're descended from Aurelian, our only surviving son. You know, after butchering the fool Magnus, Theodosius tried to hunt me down—as if I were some beast. He feared that the West would rise to Magnus' heir; and rightly so," she snarled. "I warned Magnus that he couldn't control the sword, but he wouldn't listen and it betrayed him. But, you . . ." she stepped forward and placed a slender ivory hand against his chest, "you have the power to fulfill the destiny of your blood."

He grabbed her wrist. "Destiny be damned. What of my family Why did you have me ripped from them? The town was burning!"

"You couldn't bring down the Huntsman. Do you think he came just for you? For whatever petty quest you follow? Do you?" Her eyes narrowed and probed Erik's face. "Think, son! Think! You are the last of your line. He feared you. The Grey God in his fright has unleashed the very forces he thought to suppress. I doubt even his agents knew."

Her voice dropped to a whisper. "I bought you time. Many on the Council would rather hand you over to Annwyn and be done with the whole mess. But they cannot see what I see. They're blind to the dangers of complacency. You see, Blaine opened up a Pandora's box by unleashing a novice. You should have been bled to death, not brought unwillingly into this state." She ran her tongue across her upper lip. "Yes, I can feel your heart beating, though slowed it may be. In his error, Blaine blundered into the secret for ensuring his lord's demise.

"You see, my young son, you are of my womb and also of my blood—a direct descendant of the Magnus by birth and of my undead brood in death. In neither living nor dying, you may be able to bend the blade to your will and be the master that the Spaniard couldn't be." She easily pulled her wrist free of Erik's grip and waved it casually in the air. "Or you might fail and drive us all into the clutches of Annwyn, just as Arawn has planned all along." Her eyes burned. "But fail or succeed, I'll not follow Blaine into His service, and my seed shall bear the sword!"

Eric struggled to process this as the trials, emotional and physical, took their toll even on his enhanced stamina. Flavia thought to thwart the powers of Annwyn by using him as her pawn? She was no better than Blaine or Arawn. She had sacrificed his family, her own flesh and blood, and fulfilled the darkest of Erik's dreams to further her own sense of familial pride?

A sharp tooth bit into her lower lip and her hands pressed firmly against Erik's cheeks. She pulled his face down to meet hers. Again he noted that where he should have expected to feel her hot breath there was only the stillness of the grave. She clearly had been in this state long enough to dispense with the trappings of life.

"They are my family, they are my flesh," she said in response to his thoughts. "I couldn't have anticipated the attack of the Huntsman, though I since have puzzled the reason. Our party barely found you in time as it was. It appears the screen placed around you by your de Dannan magicker failed under the strain of converging forces."

"What of Thelwyn?"

She waved her hand again in the air, her deep eyes narrowed. "Come."

"Where?"

"The Council awaits us, and if I don't bring you before them soon some may lose patience with me, if they haven't already."

Erik looked about the room. The dark cowled creatures had silently left them.

"You'll not refuse this, or they'll hunt you down and either hand you over to Arawn or destroy you," she whispered before he could even form the thoughts.

He took her proffered hand and walked with her through a doorway that led to a long hallway.

The corridor ended at a closed door. Flavia knocked and then pushed it open.

"So this is the scion of the Magnus? An arrogant foreigner he was, though he may have been fit to wear the purple." The dark figure leaned forward, his hawkish features gaunt, eyes dark pools that sucked up the flickering lamplight. He leaned an elbow on his knee and looked at Flavia, who sat to his right. Her spine remained erect, her eyes fixed straight ahead, boring into Erik's. "Do you really believe this child can humble a god? Magnus was knowledgeable and strong, yet he couldn't control the blade. Arawn will spit this boy out and then crush his sponsors—us."

"Master Ganelon," Flavia said, "Magnus didn't understand the power he wielded. I must admit, neither did I, while I lived." She turned to meet Ganelon's cold gaze. "But, the sorcerer Merlin foresaw the birth into my family, into the lineage of the Magnus, of the one who could wield the blade."

"If I may," another spoke up. "This creature, Merlin, could not be trusted while alive. Why should we take stock now in his revelations?"

Flavia rose from her chair, casting an icy glance in the direction of the other. "My colleague forgets himself. By questioning Merlin at this point, you also question my judgment."

The other creature, dressed from head to heel in a black that matched his raven hair and dark shadowed features, chuckled—a vicious sound that rattled in his throat like a choke. When he spoke, Erik recognized him as the leader of his abductors.

"I'd not have questioned your judgment, coven mistress, until the Huntsman left three of our party hung from a tree for Apollo's pleasure." His eyes left Flavia and locked on Erik. "I thought we'd decided to steer clear of the whole affair!" He struck the arm of his chair, his lips trembling with barely masked anger. "Let none doubt, he knows. The Grey Lord knows, and he'll seek retribution for this."

"Has yer spine left ya, man," an older-looking man chimed in. He was more bones than flesh, pulling on his beard and smiling a toothy grin full of wicked, yellowed teeth. "Never thought to see the Kraken shrink from a brawl—any brawl."

The man-beast Kraken's nostrils flared and he snarled, exposing a long ivory tooth. "I'll not have a live child and a bumbling throw of hers bring down my—"

"Your own get?" Flavia finished for him. "We all know where your interests lie, Kraken. Don't use the coven to cover for your own brood. Any one of yours could slink out tonight and enter Annwyn's service."

"No! Not mine!" Kraken's face darkened. "None of mine would leave an unfinished like this walking."

Flavia smiled, "Maybe one already has."

Kraken's face blanched a shade whiter. "Beware your words, Flavia."

Ganelon leaned back in his chair and tapped the side with a finger.

"Hmmm," he mused. "Annwyn does hold this one to be of some importance, else they'd not have contracted the Huntsman so far afield."

"I want none of your games," Erik said finally.

"Silence your tongue, boy," Kraken warned.

"Let him finish," Ganelon said, his voice calm and measured. "Boy, why not play our game? The other choices are few."

"I've faced death, I don't fear it," Erik replied, meeting each deathly face one at a time.

"Ahh, but damnation," the old man interjected. "Have ye thought of that? You're on the outside, lad. Who claims your soul?"

"I don't know all the mysteries of God's kingdom."

"That's it—that's it!" The old man clapped his hands. "Yer not in His kingdom, or anyone else's. Ye shouldn't exist."

"Then let's turn him over and have done with the whole affair," Kraken said. "We've no interest in this."

"But we do," contested Flavia. "We will fall under His dominion if we do nothing. I do not serve Annwyn."

"Now, Flavia—" Ganelon started.

She jumped to her feet and pointed at Erik. "He could end this threat forever! Why should we sit back and allow the Grey Lord to squeeze us out of existence? That is what he will do—press us into submission or destroy us!"

Kraken snorted. "What makes you think this half-breed can stop Annwyn's move on the isle? He couldn't stop the Huntsman."

"You people dragged me off!" Erik shouted. "You doomed everyone in the village to death!"

"Aww," Kraken said. "What's the matter, do we not fight with a knight's honor? I'm no Blaine, to be intimidated by breaches in ethics, boy. Besides, they were all doomed already. You think the Huntsman would've just let you win, like Blaine? Do you, boy?"

"Enough," Ganelon said absently, his eyes wandering. His fingers continued tapping against the side of his chair. "I've heard enough. It's time to end this hearing of the Council. Hold him through the day and when we reconvene on the morrow, I'll ask for a vote."

"Have done," Kraken hissed. "Annwyn may be more powerful than we imagined."

"Annwyn," Flavia retorted, "has not been able to muster enough strength to protect its own. Ask Blaine."

Kraken rose in a flurry of black. He stood before Flavia, poised as if to strike. "There is strength in Annwyn. I've seen it, and I fear it."

With that, he left, brushing past Erik. A whisper of cold stabbed at the knight, a fleeting blade of fierce hatred.

Ganelon rose, his figure tall and straight. His eyes rested on Erik for a moment, cold and harsh, then on Flavia. "Is he the last of his blood?" he asked.

Flavia shrugged and brushed a strand of black hair from her face.

"I could lie to you, Ganelon, but it would not get me what I want."

"Don't toy with me, I'll not tolerate it." Flavia frowned, then waved a hand. "Yes, he is the last of the line of Magnus."

"I see," Ganelon said. "Very interesting, indeed. He's not to leave the chamber. The Council will meet again on the morrow and determine his fate." He pulled a heavy black cloak from his chair and tossed it about his shoulders. "Very little time left to feed, Flavia. I suggest you make good use of what's left, if you hunger." He departed the room, followed by the old man.

When they had gone, Flavia shrugged her shoulders. "Little time is what we need," she said, drawing her tongue across her lips. She took

Erik's hand in her own. "Come, we must go."

Erik remained rooted. "No," he said. "I don't know what you have in mind, but I'm not going anywhere."

Her eyes flashed dangerously. "I'll not have Kraken deal you away, boy," she hissed, her fingers tightening on his arm. "You're the last of the Magnus' bloodline. Your forebears fought under the banners of Julian the Apostate, Valentinian, Arthur the Pendragon, and Constantine of Cornwall. There will be nothing more if you perish, or are enslaved by the Grey Lord." She pressed close, still cold breasts pressing against Erik's tattered shirt. Her tone softened. "You must leave Briton, just as I left for a time. You must leave and find that which our family has lost. Only then will you be able to free us all from the Isle of Annwyn's machinations, and possibly fulfill your oaths to your king."

"And save you and your lair of vipers?" he asked, though his thoughts went to his quest for Marianna and his promise to bring her back to her father. Thelwyn's course of action was also Flavia's.

"Perhaps, perhaps not. It doesn't matter, truly." She shook her head. "If you stay, they will barter you off for their thirty pieces and he will still crush us. They just don't realize it yet. If you go, you may not find the item for which you seek. And, if you do, you could end up following the same path as Magnus and leave your head atop a pike."

A chill crept up his spine as he realized the import of her words.

"What of this sword Ganelon spoke of?"

She pressed a slender marble finger to his lips and leaned in close to whisper in his ear. He was surprised at the venom and urgency in her tone. "Do not ask of it while yet within these walls! If you accept my offer there will be time enough to tell later!" She stepped back then; and Erik was relieved that her body, at once sensual and repelling, was no longer so close.

"I've a ship waiting at the docks to take you to the continent. And money, enough to purchase berth wherever you must go," she said hurriedly, pulling Erik toward the door. "Come, we must be out of this place."

"What of Thelwyn?" Erik asked again.

Flavia seemed to shrink from the question this time. "He is being held. Kraken's creatures have him."

"Then we must go to him," Erik demanded. "I'll go on your ship, but not without him." He planted his feet, pulling her up short.

She glared at him for a moment.

"Damn you," she whispered. "They'll butcher you and send you off to Annwyn in bloody pieces."

"Then I'll not go alone."

The dark corridor was lined with pitted, damp stonework, water dripping from the ceiling and walls into pools on the floor. Two of

Flavia's brood moved ahead, their black figures flowing in and out of the gloom, cloaked in a shroud of invisibility that Flavia wove with expert skill.

Probes from Kraken's brood roved through the area, searching for intruders. Erik could feel them push in against his own senses, but he pressed ahead, trusting Flavia's mastery of her supernatural abilities.

A scuffle broke out before them in the darkness, and something let out a muffled gasp. They froze and waited a long moment. A white face appeared, a deep gash extending from its ear to the middle of its throat. It smiled wanly and waved to Flavia.

"The way has been cleared, but we must hurry. Kraken knows of our movements." Erik followed Flavia down the corridor to a stout door. One of her brood crouched outside it, leaning over a still, broken body on the floor. The creature stood and tried the door. It bent to its shoulder, but did not give. Erik leaned into it as well; the hinge jerked free and the door opened with a whoosh.

The place smelled like a crypt, thick with dust and decay. What appeared to be a funeral bier lay at the far end of the chamber—he assumed that this was Kraken's resting place. A form lay crumpled in a heap nearby.

"Thelwyn?" Erik rushed forward and knelt by the bedraggled magicker.

"Rest," Thelwyn muttered. "Just need—"

Erik picked him up in his arms like a babe and turned to Flavia.

"I'll go now, by St. Michael. Lead the way."

Flavia nodded and hurried her creatures from the chamber. He noticed the one standing over the still form pull a silver-tipped spike from the motionless figure on the floor.

"Hurry!" Flavia hissed. "No time!"

They raced through the corridors to the surface. Now Erik sensed the movements of others, others that wanted revenge—their emotions threatening to crash through Flavia's skillfully crafted defenses.

The group emerged from the corridor into the center of a large, ruined Roman building. As they climbed through the crumbling mass, one of Flavia's brood turned to grapple with a shadow that solidified near them, locking its hands about the neck. Flavia pulled on Erik's arm, pointing toward the muddy street beyond. One of her brood slipped a long, slender shape into her other hand.

"There," she hissed. "Straight down the street to the docks. Board the Pagan Dancer and have the captain cast off at once." She handed him the object in her hands. It was his spatha. She looked up at the sky, at the moon shining through the gaping beams. "The tide, he must make the tide. They'll not follow you to sea. They've no stomach for the water. Go now. You must make for Rome. It was Rome where Theodosius sent what you seek."

With that she turned to face the oncoming rush of undead. Not the shambling, possessed bodies that had taken Caer Baen, but the lethal creatures of the covenant breed.

"But you—" Erik started, the words dying at the look she cast back at him. He snatched up his charge and stumbled toward the street. Behind him, Londinium's dead fought in eerie silence.

Beneath Thelwyn's robes a small form wiggled. Erik knew it for the fox.

He ran between huts and ruined buildings toward the river. He could hear the ships swaying at their docks and the wooden creak of their hulls against their moorings. The odor of rotting fish and muck grew stronger, as did the presence of another—a hunter. He redoubled his effort to reach the ship ahead of his pursuer, but stopped short when a lithe form dropped from a rooftop to land like a cat in the lane before him. Behind the creature, a multitude of masts bobbed in the harbor.

Kraken smiled. His teeth flashed dangerously as he stepped forward.

"So, boy, you thought that Flavia—dear, sweet Grandmother Flavia—could get you away from the Council? From me? You forget, I'm not Blaine; I do not fight with honor."

"I've no quarrel with you," Erik said, his hand tightening around the scabbard of his sword.

"Ahh, but I have with you, you see," Kraken's eyes narrowed to red slits. "I've lost some of my own children to bring you here. Her creatures now shed more of my blood to free you. You owe me, boy."

Anger bubbled from deep inside Erik. "I owe you nothing! Not one thing, cur. Step aside." He eased Thelwyn down against a building. His blade scraped free of its scabbard.

"We've no need of such toys," Kraken sneered. He lunged, springing into the air like a carrion bird taking flight. His outstretched hands curled and gleamed like vicious talons. Those terrible claws buried themselves into Erik's shoulders, his momentum driving them both away from Thelwyn, into a wall. Kraken's teeth, long and sharp, pressed close to his face. "I'll finish what that fool Blaine started."

Erik hammered his body into Kraken's, but could not dislodge the beast. Kraken wriggled one claw loose and grabbed at Erik's throat. Erik swatted at the lethal hand and grasped his opponent's wrist, and

Kraken shoved a shoulder into the knight's chest. Erik could not free himself.

A bloodcurdling shriek suddenly let loose nearby. A black figure sprang from the shadows, enveloping Kraken and raking his exposed flesh with razor claws. Kraken's grip on Erik slipped. The knight staggered free as the two combatants locked in a vicious struggle. The newcomer's claws tore at Kraken's throat again and again. Tangled hair fell over its face as it buried its teeth into Kraken's back. Its blood red eyes averted from its target for a moment to linger on Erik.

It was Flavia.

Words rushed into Erik's head: To the ship!

Her eyes shot back to Kraken without missing a beat of the heated contest. Erik stooped and snatched up his blade. Supporting Thelwyn, he shambled down the alley toward the docks. Another shriek rose into the misty night air from behind them, but Erik fought the urge to pause and look back, instead dragging Thelwyn forward at a faster pace.

The Pagan Dancer pulled against her moorings as the tide tugged the ship. Erik hesitated at the edge of the wooden gangplank. Water. A long voyage lay before him, and the hackles of fear rose in his breast. He placed a foot onto the plank and drove down the emotion. All around, his senses felt the crush of more pursuers from the rear. A man's face peered down from the deck.

"You must hurry, lord, if we are to make the tide," he said.

They came, hot with the anticipation of battle. Erik glanced over his shoulder and. though he could not yet see them in the alleys, he knew that ere long they'd swarm the docks.

"Sweet Jesu," he muttered, "protect the foolish." The gangplank bounced under his step. He leaped over the rail and hauled Thelwyn over behind.

The skipper called to his crew and they appeared out of the cover of darkness to cast off. The ship slipped loose of the riverbank and rocked quickly into the current of the Thames, leaving Erik's erstwhile pursuers milling about the dock, shaking fists but cowering fearfully at the water's edge. Men scrambled through the rigging and oars clacked in their locks. Erik fought the fear long enough to stand at the rail and watch Londinium fade in the mist.

Before long not only the city, but also the coast of his beloved Albion would fade from sight. He knew not when, or how—or even if—he'd ever return.

About The Authors

Mike has wanted to write since he was very young. His earliest memories are of carrying a battered old notebook around full of illustrations and stories that he would often transpose those ideas on his grandmother's old typewriter.

While in college at BYU he was inspired by professors and visiting writers. Literary classics such as *La Chanson de Roland* and *Inferno* were often in his backpack. Chapter 3 of *Annwyn's Blood* was written during this time as a short story.

He now lives in Northern Virginia with his wife, Lori and his wonderful children, and dreams of one day driving in his old Defender to Alaska with his family.

Steve grew up on a farm in Northeast Ohio where he spent his free time reading Burroughs, Lovecraft, Zelazny and Tolkien, and his earliest writing efforts were creating adventures for his Dungeons & Dragons group. A veteran of the Army and the Navy, he currently lives near his childhood hometown with his family, two dogs and two cats. He has won awards for his writing in collaboration with Michael Eging on *The Silver Horn Echoes: A Song of Roland.*